# Pledge

PALM SOUTH UNIVERSITY 3

# KANDI STEINER

Published by Kandi Steiner
Edited by Elaine York, Allusion Graphics, LLC/
Publishing & Book Formatting
www.allusiongraphics.com
Cover Design by Kandi Steiner and Staci Hart
Formatting by Elaine York,
Allusion Graphics, LLC/Publishing &
Book Formatting, www.allusiongraphics.com

# Episode 1

# THANKSGIVING

*Jess*

WORST.

Friendsgiving.

Ever.

I thought it was my best idea since I'd decided to change my major, to get the gang together to overdose on mashed potatoes and red wine, especially since my original plans for the holiday had fallen as flat as my hair in the Florida humidity. I couldn't be with Jarrett, so I'd be with everyone else I cared about. It seemed genius at the time.

But here I am, sitting in the proof that I was very, very wrong.

We're all gathered around a long, folding table usually used for beer pong, though now it's covered in a deep red table cloth with gold accents and several plates of food. I say *all* lightly, because Ashlei is halfway across the country due her stupid internship and Erin is MIA.

Her…and the turkey she was supposed to bring.

"Maybe we should just start," Skyler suggests, smiling softly, though her blue eyes are strained. The bags under them tell me she hasn't been sleeping. "I'm sure she'll be here soon. We can at least eat the sides while they're hot."

Clinton scoffs, crossing his hard, dark arms over his chest as he rolls his eyes. "Oh, right, because you always know what's best, don't you, Sky?"

Skyler's face crumples. "Bear, please. I apologized. Can we just... can't we have a nice meal?"

All eyes are on Clinton, mine shooting daggers as we wait for his answer. He's been a prick since he walked in the door, and though I have no idea what happened, I'm almost positive he's being a little bitch about whatever is going on.

Then again, that could just be because right now every man in the entire world is the enemy to me. I hate them. I hate how they make us feel things, how they make promises they can't keep, how they have a gift for building us up with hope only to let us down in the end.

And I'm not even on my period. God help the poor suckers who hit on me the next time I am.

Clinton picks up his fork like he's ready to play nice, at least for a while, but then he grits his teeth and drops it back to the table again. The legs of his chair scrape against the hardwood floor of the chapter room as he pushes back and stands.

"How the fuck are we supposed to have Thanksgiving without a goddamn turkey," he growls, and without another look at any of us, he steamrolls out the back door, letting in the tiniest sliver of the setting sun before the door closes behind him.

Skyler sighs. "He's not mad about the turkey," she explains, standing up for him even when he's being a giant dick to her. "He's just worried about his little brother and…"

"It's fine, Big," Cassie says, offering a soft smile. "I agree, we should just eat."

"Yeah, who says you can't make a meal out of green bean casserole?" Adam chimes in, and for some reason Grayson is giving him a death glare from across the table. I know they had some tension between them after the dodgeball tournament, but was it really so much that he's still not over it? "Challenge accepted."

Skyler nods, but she's chewing her lip between her teeth, eyes on the door Clinton just blew out of. Adam starts, piling mashed potatoes and gravy on his plate first before passing the serving dish to Skyler. She glances at it briefly, then pushes back from the table with another sigh.

"I'm sorry, I just need to check on him. I'll be back."

So, she skips out the door, too, which leaves me alone with the peanut gallery: Cassie, Adam, and Grayson.

*Joy.*

Adam swallows, offering the dish across the table to Cassie, instead. I'm kneading my temple now, eyes closed until I hear my phone buzz on the table. My hands fly, unlocking the screen quickly and expecting to see Jarrett's name, only to find a sorry ass excuse from Erin.

**- Sorry, got caught up with some Panhellenic stuff. I'll be there soon! -**

I grumble, but before I can even text back, another chair scrapes against the floor.

"Oh, for Christ's sake, what now?!"

It's Grayson who's standing now, jaw all tense and chest puffed out. I'll admit, he's still a sexy motherfucker with that man bun and those steel eyes, but even he's not immune to my man-hating today.

"I can't do this anymore, Cassie," he says, eyes hard on Adam across the table. "You have to choose. Him," he snarls, thrusting a hand toward Adam. "Or me."

"Andddd, that's my cue." This time it's me who stands, tossing my napkin on my still-empty plate. "You guys can have your pissing match. I'm going to get a cheeseburger."

Tossing my long, freshly highlighted hair over my shoulder, I snag a dinner roll and take a large bite before saluting them and walking out the opposite door the other two had exited. I roll my eyes as soon as the door closes behind me, crossing through the sorority house and taking the stairs two at a time up to my room.

I hit the speed dial for Jarrett, switching my phone to speaker before dropping it to my bed and filtering through the clothing options in my closet. By the second ring, I'm stripped free of the tea-length dress I'd had on. By the fourth, my favorite pair of skin-tight jeans are hugging my hips. And by the time his voicemail picks up, my boobs are pushed up to the heavens and barely covered with a black crop top that criss-crosses over my cleavage.

Huffing, I end the call before the beep, stepping into a high pair of candy red pumps and checking my reflection in the mirror. I run my fingers through my hair, swiping my purse from where it hangs off my closet door and fishing through it for the lipstick that matches the shoes.

Rubbing my lips together with approval, I give myself one last look before adding my last accessory — a smile that screams trouble.

Jarrett is busy. I get it, really, I do. But he could at least call. He could at least *text*, especially considering we were supposed to be together today.

But if he wants to play hard to get with his attention and affection, I'm not afraid to step up to the table and play the game. I have tricks up my sleeve, ones he isn't exactly oblivious to. Still, maybe he's forgotten. Maybe he needs a reminder.

If he's going to sleep on me, then I don't really have much of a choice anymore.

Time to wake that motherfucker up.

# THREE MONTHS EARLIER

# Cassie

I'M OFFICIALLY A SOPHOMORE.

It seems impossible that an entire year has gone by since I first stepped foot on the Palm South University campus, and even more impossible that I'm now on the other side of recruitment. If I thought it was hard rushing as a freshman — choosing a sorority to call my home — I clearly had no idea what it was like to stay up late every night for two full weeks practicing and preparing for rush as a *sister*.

Erin wants the best pledge class Kappa Kappa Beta has ever seen, and she's stopping at nothing to get the most premier girls. Top GPAs, athletes, dancers, pre-med, pre-law, previous class officers, and yearbook editors — she wants them all. We've been studying bios for weeks, and with only two days left before the girls make a decision, Erin is pushing us even harder to lock in the new members.

With all the chaos, it's a miracle I was even able to sneak out. I'm exhausted, I barely have a voice left, and all I want to do is sip a cup of coffee in a quiet coffee shop and kiss my boyfriend whom I haven't seen all summer.

But apparently, quiet is out of the question.

Pushing through the crowded coffee shop, I keep checking the time on my phone, knowing I won't have long before Erin will be blowing it up wondering where I went. I've never seen Cup O' Joe's so packed before. There are girls in every bit of free space, some sitting at tables while others line the walls. None of it makes sense until Grayson comes into view, and when he croons out a smooth note from the Maroon 5 song he's currently playing, I have a feeling this is going to be the new normal.

The longest sigh leaves my lips as I take him in, noting how his eyes look brighter with the tan still bronzing his skin from the summer. His hair is pulled back, bun messy, beard clean and trimmed, guitar strapped over one shoulder like it's an actual limb and not an object he can take off.

"Can I help you?" I hear the barista at the counter ask when it's finally my turn to step up and order, but I can't tear my gaze from Grayson.

I wait for his blue eyes to connect with mine, but they keep wandering the crowd as he sings to every single girl like they're the only ones in the room. I can't deny there's a sting in my chest every time he winks or gives them that same sexy smile he hooked me with last semester, but I try to remind myself it's all now part of the show.

As if he senses my discomfort, Grayson furrows his eyebrows, and he searches the crowd until he finds me.

Then, he smiles.

A radiant, too-hot-for-a-coffee-shop, drop-your-panties-now smile.

"Get that girl a caramel latte," he says, nodding to the barista behind the counter. "And don't let her leave before I kiss her breathless."

He keeps that smile on his face and his eyes on me as he finishes the song, but he's not the only one watching me now. Every girl in the room is staring, eyes flicking from me to Grayson and back again, likely wondering how in the hell I landed him.

I'm still trying to figure it out, too.

When he plays the last note, the whole shop cheers, whistles ringing out, but I barely register them. All I can see is Grayson jumping down from the stage, his stride confident, eyes on my mouth. All I can hear is the beat of my heart in my ears matching each step he takes. All I can smell is his cologne, and I remember sleeping in it, in his sheets, in his arms. And when he finally reaches me, hands framing my face as I taste him for the first time in months, all I can feel is everything.

Longing, excitement, fear, relief, passion — all wrapped into one kiss in a crowded coffee shop where only the two of us exist.

When he pulls back, forehead still pressed against mine and hands on my cheeks, I smile.

"Well, mission accomplished. Officially breathless."

He smiles, pecking my nose and pulling me into his chest for a hug. "God, I've missed you."

"I've missed you, too, rock star. Speaking of which," I add, eyeing the girls around us as they throw knives at me with their eyes. "I think you're going to start a riot in here if you don't let me go."

He laughs, shifting to pull me under one arm and leading me through the crowd to a blessedly empty table in the back corner. It's marked with a *reserved* sign, and Grayson slides it aside when we sit down in the two chairs behind it.

"They'll live. It's crazy, though, isn't it? That video, Cassie… it changed everything."

"You had the magic formula," I remind him. "You, shirtless, lights turned down low, acoustic guitar, and an original song better than anything on the radio right now. All it took was that one YouTube fangirl to share it on Facebook and all her groupies attacked."

He chuckles as the barista from behind the counter sets down two matching coffee cups, smiling at both of us before leaving us alone again.

"I guess. But seven-hundred thousand views in less than two months?" He shakes his head, reaching for his coffee to take a sip. "It's crazy. I maxed out on Facebook friends, Cassie. Like… I can't add anymore. It's insanity."

My heart skips as I watch him, eyes all glowy and smile wider than I've ever seen it. He's like a puppy in a blanket — too damn adorable not to kiss.

So, I lean in, taking his coffee from his hands to set it back on the table as I thread my hands behind his neck. His lips are sweet, sticky with caramel, and I lick them clean before letting him slide his tongue between my teeth.

Grayson moans into my mouth, arms wrapping around me and sliding down to palm my ass. His knee is right between mine, and when he pulls me closer, I catch just the slightest bit of friction that makes me whimper.

"Come over tonight," he whispers, slowing our kiss enough to say the words.

I groan. "I can't. Recruitment, remember? I actually snuck out to be here…" I check the time on my phone. One missed text from Erin, soon to be five, I imagine. "I should probably get back."

Grayson pouts, but he doesn't get to throw much of a fit before they're announcing him back up on the stage.

"What about Sunday, then? I'm playing at this swanky new restaurant downtown and I want you there as my date."

I bite my lip, debating my options. Bid Day is Saturday, but there are usually Sunday Funday celebrations at all the houses the day after, too.

"Please?" Grayson adds, pulling me closer. "I need you there."

Smiling, I run my fingers through the hair at the back of his neck with a nod. I'm sure Erin will have something to say about me not being present, but she'll get over it. I've been in her captivity for over two weeks now.

"I wouldn't miss it."

He smiles, leaning in to kiss me once more before pulling me up to stand with him. "Have fun pillow fighting or making necklaces or whatever it is they have you doing over there."

I smack his arm and he sneaks in another peck on my nose, adjusting his hair in the messy tie he has it in as he jogs toward the stage. Allowing myself one last minute of gawking at him as he straps on his guitar, I debate staying a little longer. That is, until a string of three texts come in from Erin all at once.

Sighing, I give Grayson one last longing look before taking my coffee to go for the walk back to the house.

"There you are," Erin says as soon as I walk through the door, her voice tight with annoyance.

Sisters are running all over the place, some of them balancing protein bars in one hand and bios in the other. Just because the potential new members are done for the day doesn't mean we're even close, and that fact is cemented when Erin thrusts a thick packet into my chest.

"I need you to run this down to the Alpha Sig house and get it to Adam. Then come right back because we're doing dress check for tomorrow and I'll need you to help me fix the sisters who apparently don't understand what *cerulean blue* means."

She rolls her eyes, tucking a misplaced blonde strand of hair behind her ear before checking two items off the list on her clipboard.

All I can do is stand there and gape at her.

"Why are you still standing here?" she snaps, then she closes her eyes and forces a breath. "God, sorry. I didn't mean that to sound as bitchy as it did. I'm just stressed. You okay?"

I nod, forcing the swallow I couldn't seem to get a grip on before. "Yeah, I just… is there anyone else who could maybe run this down to Alpha Sig?

I was actually hoping to take a shower before—"

I don't even get the rest of my pathetic excuse out before Erin cuts me off.

"I need you to do this, G-Little. Please. I've already got Jess, Lei, and your Big off doing other pertinent things and honestly I'm too exhausted to even try to find someone else I trust enough to deliver that packet without somehow getting lost at one of the campus bars." She sighs, pinching the bridge of her nose and closing her eyes again. "Please?"

I clear my throat, holding the packet up with a forced smile. "Of course, it's no problem. Be right back."

"Thank you," she says, squeezing my arm before jetting off toward the kitchen, yelling out demands at every sister she passes along the way.

The walk to the Alpha Sigma house is short, but I feel every step like an agonizing hour at the gym. I haven't seen Adam since the dance last semester, the dance where I walked out on him, where I chose Grayson. Just thinking about that night, about the look on his face right before he walked out that door — it sucker-punches me right square in the gut.

*"Just because the timing isn't right for us now doesn't mean it never will be."*

I shake the memory from my head as I turn,

walking up the drive to the large, wooden door with his letters proudly displayed on the front. Taking one last shaky breath, I walk through the door.

Had this been last year, I likely would have knocked. But I'm not a freshman anymore, and I know well enough now that you don't knock when you go to a fraternity house. I don't even stop to say hi to the guys playing foosball in the living room, just walk straight toward the back hall. Adam will be in the president's suite now, and I'm going to drop this stupid packet on his bed and leave. That's it. The end.

Except as soon as I round the corner leading to the hall, my plan goes up in flames.

Adam is walking toward me, head down as he uses a small towel to dry his hair, wearing only a slightly larger towel tied low around his hips. I freeze, breath catching as I watch the water droplets fall from his shoulders to his chest to his abdomen, all the way down to the hem of the towel. When he's less than ten feet in front of me he looks up, eyes widening at the sight of me.

And then he freezes, too.

"Cassie?" he asks, tossing the small towel over his shoulder. "What are you doing here?"

My eyes are still glued to his chest, to the new

muscles stretching over his ribs and abdomen. He's filled out over the summer. His hair is a little longer, his arms a little bulkier, and his skin just as dark as the day we came back from spring break.

I have no clue how long I stare, but it's long enough for him to follow my gaze down to his chest, which immediately makes me flush and squeeze my eyes closed tight. I thrust the packet out toward his chest that I can't stop looking at and turn, practically sprinting for the door.

"Hey, wait," Adam calls out behind me, but I just throw an awkward wave over my shoulder and plow through the front door and out into the humid August air.

I inhale a deep breath, shaking my head and burying my face in my hands.

*God, what was that?*

I've seen Adam shirtless before — plenty of times, actually. So then why did I just act like a sixteen-year-old virgin seeing her first boy sans clothing? All summer I'd been hoping Adam and I could be friends again this semester, get rid of all the tension between us and go back to how we were before. Zero awkwardness, that's what I was aiming for.

My arrow didn't even hit the target, let alone the bullseye.

# Bear

WEIGHTLIFTING, PARTYING, and fucking.

Three things I do better than anyone else.

I finished the first one early this morning, I'll be doing the second one later tonight, and the last? Well, it's like they always say — there's no time like the present.

"Oh, fuck, Bear. Don't stop. Don't… stop…"

Lacy bites her lip hard as she rides me, hands wrapped up in her hair and thighs tense as she tightens around me. I grip her hips harder, pulling her down as I thrust my hips, hitting her deeper, deep enough to make her scream my name as she comes.

She may not be the brightest color in the crayon box, but one thing I can always depend on with Lacy? She's down to fuck. Down to *just* fuck. She'd had a moment last year where she wanted more, but it was brief, and now I know I can count on her when I need a distraction or a release.

And she can count on me.

"God," she sighs, rolling off me, chest still heaving. "You've ruined me for other guys, you know that, right? Your cock is a fucking treasure."

"Yeah?" I ask, standing and pulling her small wrist until she's standing, too. "Why don't you show me just how valuable it is to you."

She smirks, tongue running the length of her bottom lip before she drops to her knees. She keeps her dark brown eyes locked on mine as she swirls her tongue over the head and I moan, flexing my hips. Lacy takes the cue, swallowing me whole, gagging a little as I groan again.

It's so fucking hot staring down at her, brown skin smooth and shining with a thin sheen of sweat as she works my cock with her hands and mouth. Every time she flicks her eyes up to look at me and takes me in her throat I surge closer to climax, and when one hand cups my balls and squeezes, I curse, pulling out of her mouth.

"Open," I command and she does, closing her eyes and stretching her mouth open wide, tongue out, breasts perky and waiting. I pump myself twice more and then I bust, coming on her mouth, her neck, her nipples. Lacy trails her fingers along the pearly white lines as I finish, tucking one finger in her mouth and sucking it clean before opening her eyes and grinning up at me.

"Fuck." I breathe the word, falling back onto my bed as she giggles and scampers to my bathroom. A few minutes later she returns with a towel, wiping herself clean before handing it to me.

And this is my favorite part.

Because Lacy doesn't ask to cuddle, or talk, or for me to text her later. She just pulls her dress on, tucks her bra into her purse, and slips on her sandals.

"See you around, Bear."

She winks, and then she's gone.

*Perfect.*

It's been a hell of a summer. Getting my little brother, Clayton, set up at his best friend's house and making sure he had everything he needed for the school year was challenging. I hated that I wasn't there for him, even if Mac's family was. Still, he made it clear last year that the last thing he wanted was for me to give up PSU and move back to Pittsburgh. So, I'm trying to let it go, to give him the respect and trust he's asking for, and do everything I can from Florida for now.

Then there's the fact that I'm a junior now. Classes aren't going to be a breeze anymore, and studying is *not* among my list of things I'm good at. I'm excited for the advanced art classes and harnessing my skills in the Adobe Creative Suite, but I've also heard horror stories about my professors this semester.

Sighing, I try to drop the stress and float on the high from getting my rocks off with one of the hottest chicks on campus as I make my way to the shower. But as soon as the hot water hits my bare back, another girl floods my mind.

Erin.

I wash my body quickly, trying not to think about her too much until I'm out of the space we shared after formal last semester. I won't ever be able to shower without that memory sparking to life, and now that I'm back in the exact shower it happened in, it's even harder to push the thought away.

When I'm dressed, I realize I still have plenty of time before the party starts, so I swipe my wallet off my desk and make my way down to the Kappa Kappa Beta house. It's after nine now, which means the girls rushing are halfway across campus making their final selections before bid day. It's likely a mad house over at KKB, but I don't care.

I need to see her.

"You're joking, right?"

Ashlei laughs, arms crossed as she rests her weight on one hip. The house is bustling behind her, all her sisters still dressed in all black cocktail dresses from Pref Night.

"I just need five minutes."

"You *do* realize how impossible that is, right? To see the recruitment chair on Pref Night? Even for five minutes?"

She wasn't being rude, just simply stating facts, and the truth is I knew it before even walking down.

"Humor me. Just ask her."

Ashlei opens her mouth, likely to shut me down again, but then I spot Erin behind her as she zooms by, clipboard in hand.

"Better yet, I'll ask. Excuse me."

I slide past Ashlei before she has the chance to stop me and fall in step with Erin.

"Hey, Dictator Xander."

Erin's face screws up in confusion as she whips around to face me. When she realizes who it is, she pauses, but only for a second. If I would have blinked, I'd have missed it.

"I don't have time to talk, Bear."

"I see that," I muse, walking with her as she continues barking orders at every girl we pass. "How was your summer?"

"I just said I don't have time to talk."

"Come on, just five minutes."

She huffs, propping her clipboard on her hip and coming to a halt. "My summer was fine.

Recruitment has been busy, but fantastic. We're going to have the best pledge class this campus has ever seen. I'm all signed up for classes, my immune system is being pushed to its limits but I'm overdosing on vitamin C, and yes, I cut my hair. I think that just about covers it, right?"

Erin starts walking again and I chuckle, jogging to catch up with her. "My summer was great, too. Thanks for asking."

"Can we do this another time?" she asks, distracted by the long list on her clipboard. She turns to head for the chapter room but I reach for her, gently catching her elbow.

But gentle or not, the touch triggers Erin in the absolute worst way.

She jerks back, eyes wide and fists clenching together as she drops her board. It clatters to the floor and I hold my hands up, palms open, and take three steps back.

Erin watches me, swallowing hard, and the fear in her eyes is like a nail gun to my chest.

"Sorry," I say softly, bending to retrieve her clipboard.

She takes it with shaky hands, tucking her hair behind her ear.

"I just wanted to make sure you were okay."

"I'm fine."

I give her a pointed look. We both know she's not fine, but she's clearly not ready to talk about what happened last semester, so I opt for distraction, instead.

"You should come to the O Chi house tonight, let loose a little."

This time it's her who deadpans. "It's the night before Bid Day, Bear. I'm not going to a fucking party."

"Come on, you know half your sisters are going to sneak out and be there, too. You guys need a break. The hard part is over."

"I'm not going," she says, her answer final. "And five minutes is up. I'll see you around."

With that, she slips right back into her role as Recruitment Chair, and further from the girl I was afraid she'd never be again.

*Jess*

"GODDAMN IT!"

I throw my phone across the room with a roar, watching as it bounces off Skyler's bed and plops down to the floor anticlimactically. Having a shatter-proof phone case is not helping in this moment of rage.

Skyler pokes her head out of the bathroom, curling wand still wrapped around one strand of hair as she eyes the phone and then cocks one eyebrow at me. "Bad horoscope again?"

"No," I huff. "Jarrett got a job."

"And that made you hurl your phone at my pillows?"

"Not a job here. They offered him a job at the nonprofit agency he's been interning at all summer. And that fucker took it!" I punch my pillow, crossing my arms over my chest like a child. I'm whining like a little bitch, but I can't help it.

Skyler drops her curling wand on the counter and pads over to me, hopping up onto the bed as Ashlei leans a hip on the doorframe. She's still brushing her teeth, all of us getting ready to go to the first Omega Chi party of the year.

"This is a good thing, Jess. He's worked hard and it's paying off now."

"Yeah, but this was supposed to be temporary — this whole long-distance thing. Now he's there for, what? A year? Two? Forever?" I flop back against my pillows and pull one to cover my face, muffling my next selfish whine. "I don't want to be in a long-distance relationship."

It's silent a moment before the pillow is pulled from my face and I find myself staring up at Ashlei, her blonde hair straight as a pin and falling all around her face as she points her toothbrush down at me. "You love him, remember? You'll make it work. It's going to be hard," she concedes, glancing at Skyler who nods with a sympathetic smile. "But he's crazy about you, Jess. And you're crazy about him. Don't make him feel guilty for following his dreams."

I sigh. "I know. You're right. But I'm not ready to admit that to him, yet. Right now I just want to be mad and whiney and drunk. I've got the first two down so can we work on that third?"

Skyler grins and Ashlei pops her toothbrush back in her mouth, speaking around the bristles. "Now *that* we can do."

We finish getting ready just before eleven, and without even trying to convince Erin to come with us, we sneak down the stairs and out the back kitchen door, waiting to pull on our high heels until we're safely outside.

Skyler and Ashlei chat as we make the short walk to Omega Chi, Skyler telling us about the national poker tournament she's thinking of entering while Ashlei talks about how nervous she is to start her internship next week. It reminds me that since I changed my major so late, I won't even be able to intern until next summer, at the earliest. My boyfriend is off kicking ass and taking names, already working in the government sector for a top nonprofit, and I can't even apply to be someone's intern bitch yet.

It's not that I'm not happy for him, because I am — I know he deserves this and I know it will make him happy. It's just that *I* want to make him happy, too. And I'm not sure how long I can do that from more than a thousand miles away. Still, I try to remind myself that a plane ride to New York City is short, and it doesn't have to be hard. If we both put in the effort, it won't be. It's fine. It'll all be fine.

*I need to seal that mindset with a shot.*

"SKYLER FUCKING THORNE!"

We don't even make it up the sidewalk and into the house before Clinton comes barreling out, throwing Skyler over his shoulder and spinning her around as she squeals and kicks. I laugh, and instantly I feel back at home. I can always count on Palm South University for drunken shenanigans and distractions from girly feelings.

"Alright," Clinton says, dropping Skyler's feet back to the sidewalk. "Let's get you three to the kegs. Time for the KKB girls to get this party started."

We throw our fists into the air with a shout and follow him through the house, the three of us lining up on the backside of the kegs, hands braced on the cool metal handles. Clinton grabs Skyler's ankles just as two of his brothers slide up behind me and Ashlei, and the next thing I know, our feet are in the air, taps are in our mouths, and every thought of Jarrett is erased.

At least for now.

"I love you two," I slur with a smile.

"Aww, we love you, too, babe," Ashlei says, but when she turns and finds me staring down at my two beautiful boobs, she snorts. "Oh, my God, you are not talking to your rack right now."

"What? I *do* love them. I mean, seriously, have you seen them?" I shimmy my top down a little more and push my chest toward her. "What's not to love?"

"They are always there for you."

"*Always*," I agree, hugging them again. "Through thick and thin. I can't even stay mad at them for the boob sweat terror of the summer."

Skyler giggles, handing us another Jell-O shot just as a loud chant begins to break out in the backyard.

We follow the noise, arms slung around each other and still giggling as we take our shots. When we reach the back, there's a large crowd gathered around the trampoline that surfaced at the Omega Chi house sometime over the summer. Everyone is staring up, and when we follow their gaze, we find a freshman perched on the roof.

Well, I assume he's a freshman, anyway, judging by the fact that he's in nothing but his tighty whities and is wearing a pirate hat.

"Do it, do it, do it!" the crowd chants. I glance at Skyler, whose face is twisted up in concern as she stares up at the naked pirate.

"This isn't a good idea," Ashlei says, her voice soft, but neither of us have time to respond before Clinton pushes through the crowd to join the three of us.

"What's going on?"

I nod up to the freshman. "I think he's going to jump from the roof down to the trampoline."

"What?" Clinton turns, and then his eyes widen as he screams out, "No!"

But it's too late.

The pirate jumps to the roar of at least a hundred people, all of them throwing their red plastic cups full of beer into the air with approval. He hits the trampoline, body flailing as he tries to gain control, but the bounce is too high. He flies forward as the cheers turn to gasps, and then he hits the concrete with a sickening crack.

"Oh, my God." Ashlei covers her mouth with her hands as Clinton curses and pushes through the screaming crowd, rushing to the side of the freshman and hollering for someone to call an ambulance.

Skyler pulls out her phone. "You guys gather up any KKBs you see and get out of here. There's too much underage drinking going on and Erin will flip her shit if any of our sisters get caught here."

"What about you?" I ask.

"I'm going to stay back with Bear. Don't worry," she says when Ashlei and I both start to protest. "I'll be out of here by the time the cops show. I just need to calm Bear down."

We both nod, jogging off in the opposite direction as she runs toward Clinton and the now lifeless pirate. We gather all the sisters we see, ditching drinks and shoving them toward the door until we're all stumbling back up Greek Row. When we get to the house, we all take our shoes off and tiptoe inside, retreating to our rooms or to the chapter room where sisters are camped out in sleeping bags for recruitment week.

"You going to be okay?" Ashlei whispers when we make it upstairs. "I'm going to wake Erin and tell her what happened. She needs to know before the morning and I can tell her we got all our sisters home safe."

"Yeah, I'm going to wait up for Skyler. I'll see you in the morning."

We hug, both of us sobered up from the chaos, and then I retreat to my room, chucking my heels into my closet and falling onto my bed with a sigh.

The silence is deafening, my ears ringing from the music blasting all night as my thoughts race to the sound. I hope the freshman is okay, I hope Skyler gets out of there, I hope the Omega Chi brothers don't get suspended. That last one is a futile hope, because after the shit they pulled during Spring Break last year, the ice they're skating on is thin enough to crack with a finger flick.

My phone lights up with a text from Skyler that she's safe in Clinton's room but that she can't leave yet. I sigh with relief, firing a text back and telling her I'll wait up, then I find Jarrett's number and request a video chat.

"Jess?" he croaks out, voice thick with sleep as his dark screen comes into focus. He flicks on a low lamp beside him and sits up in bed. Shirtless. "Everything okay?"

"Oh, shit, I'm sorry," I whisper. "It's late, I can call you in the morning."

He leans up more, a sleepy smirk on his beautiful face. I trace every feature — the stubble on his jaw, his lazy, sexy brown eyes. I've missed him, and seeing him sends an ache through my chest at the realization that this may be the *only* way I see him for a long time.

"I'm up, beautiful." His face falls a little. "Are you okay? Are... are *we* okay?"

I sigh, propping my head on one palm as I balance my phone in the other. "We're okay. I'm sorry I even made you think otherwise. I was being a selfish, whiney bitch and I'm sorry."

"Don't be sorry," he says, rubbing a hand over his smooth head. "It's a lot to think about. For both of us. I know I should have talked to you about it sooner, but it was a decision I needed to make on my own."

"I know," I assured him. "And you made the right choice. I support you, Jarrett. One-hundred percent."

Jarrett smiles, his eyes soft on mine until he trails them down to where my cleavage is in full view of the camera. "You went out tonight."

"I did."

"You look amazing," he says, shaking his head. "God, I miss you."

"Hold that thought." I pause our video chat long enough to text Skyler, asking for an ETA. When she says she'll be there for at least another hour, I smirk, pulling the video chat back up as I slide one strap of my dress down off my shoulder. I bite my lip, eyes on Jarrett's as I slide the other strap down and shimmy the fabric down to rest just below the hem of my bra. Jarrett swallows, running a hand down his chest and abs before it disappears out of camera view and he moans, flexing his hips.

"Show me just how much you miss me."

Jarrett moves his phone down, the new angle showing me his hard-on through his boxer briefs as he strokes it under the fabric with one hand. I groan, eyes on his tattoos as I flip until I'm on my back and slip one hand under the lacy fabric of my panties.

We tease each other with our words and touches, sending chills through the airwaves with our moans, all the while fucking ourselves and imagining we're fucking each other.

And maybe this is all I have for a while, but I'm okay with it. Because Jarrett is mine, and I'm his, and that's all that really matters.

# Cassie

IT'S A LITTLE SURREAL, standing in the backyard and watching our new Kappa Kappa Beta sisters. Well, they're not quite sisters yet, but they've accepted their bids, and I still remember what that feels like. They've all changed into swim suits and cover ups, and now they're taking pictures, throwing up the KKB hand sign and starting friendships that will last long after we leave Palm South.

I can't believe it's already been a year since I was in their shoes, and thinking back on everything that's happened in the last year, I can't help but smile. It's been a wild ride, and I know there's still so much left to come.

"You sure you don't want to take a Little Sister this semester?" Skyler asks, sidling up next to me and offering me a sip from her Tervis tumbler. We're not supposed to drink at the KKB house, but the rules are always broken on Bid Day, and I take a long pull before handing it back to her.

"Yeah, I'm sure. My classes are going to be really tough this year and I just want to get my footing before I try to be a mentor for anyone else."

"That's fair," she says, smiling.

She looks tired, eyes outlined by dark circles. I didn't go to the Omega Chi party last night, but news about what happened made its way across campus by the time I woke up. Skyler was at the O Chi house all night, trying to make sure Clinton was okay, which I'm sure isn't the case.

"I think it's smart of you to focus on yourself for a while. Better than ending up like me."

"What does that mean?" I ask, nudging her. "You're the most bad-ass person I know."

She chuckles, running a hand roughly through her hair and twisting it over her shoulder. "A bad ass without a major. I have no idea what I'm doing, Little."

I frown, rubbing her arm gently. "You'll figure it out. You've got plenty of time."

She nods, smiling softly, but then a yawn overtakes her. "I can't believe I'm being this lame, but I'm going to sneak upstairs for a nap. If Erin asks, can you just tell her I'm not feeling well?"

"Don't worry about her, she's got plenty to keep her busy," I say, nodding to where Erin is coordinating a group photo of the new recruits. She wanted the best of the best, and she got them. I'm proud of her, and I know I'm not the only one.

Skyler yawns again, offering me a half wave before ducking inside.

And then someone bumps into me from behind, knocking me off balance.

"Whoa!" A deep voice says, and I know the voice, know it too well, which is probably why my entire body reacts at the feel of two strong hands steadying me. "Sorry about that."

I spin, his hands still on my waist as I peer up at him. "You're kidding, right?"

Adam grins, and my stomach twists into a tight sailor's knot. "Couldn't help myself. Had to reenact the first time we met."

"You're so stupid," I say with a laugh, pushing two hands into his chest to put distance between us.

He removes his hands from my hips, tucking them into the pockets of his navy blue and white swim trunks, instead. I trace the muscles of his arms, remembering what they looked like without a t-shirt covering them. How has he changed so much over just one summer? It's like he left Palm South University a boy and came back a man.

I have no idea how to act around him now, not after how last semester ended. We crossed over the feather-light line drawn between friendship and something more, and now I don't know what to do without its boundaries.

"How are your classes this semester? Full schedule?" he finally asks, pushing his sunglasses up onto his head.

"Yeah, I'm sure you'll find me in the library most of the year. I have more lab hours than a white rat."

He chuckles. "Well, before classes take over your life, can I ask you for a favor?"

"Uh-oh."

Adam takes a step toward me, pulling his hands from his pockets to place them together over his chest in a *please* gesture. "Just do this one thing for me and I'll owe you."

"Spit it out already," I tease.

"We're gearing up for the concert, since the one I hosted last year ended up being such a success. But now, it's year two, and whereas last year no one had any idea of what to expect, this year, they're going to want bigger and better. I'm working on the lineups and I've got the bar covered, but one of the biggest complaints last year was the guys-to-girls ratio. If you haven't noticed, a lot of the fraternities aren't exactly a fan of little Alpha Sigma excelling at something."

I sigh. "That's so stupid. We're all a part of the Greek community, why is it always some big competition?"

"I don't know," he answers. "But I need your help. I have a reservation in front of the Student Union three days this week to campaign for the concert. I can get the girls," he says with a cocky smirk. I roll my eyes as he continues. "But I could really use your help with the guys."

"You realize I'm like the literal last person in the world to depend on for good flirting, right?"

Adam throws his head back with a deep laugh before settling his eyes on mine again. "I beg to differ. You know you've got that sweet, innocent, naturally pretty thing down pat. And after that stunt you pulled last year? I know you can rock the hell out of a pair of leather leggings, too."

I blush, completely unable to swallow as one hand reaches up to twirl a piece of my red hair. "I don't know... Why don't you ask Skyler?"

"I don't want to ask Skyler," Adam answers easily. I wait for more, but he just stands there, watching me, waiting.

It feels dangerous, accepting his proposal, but I have no idea why. Everything with Adam somehow feels forbidden, even when it's as innocent as handing out fliers for a concert. Still, the way he's looking at me, I know this isn't about the concert. It's about our friendship — the one we used to have, the one we both thought we'd lost, the one we both can't live without.

"You owe me, Adam."

"Yes!" He fist pumps the air, pulling me in for a hug and spinning me around as I continue yelling at him.

"I mean it! You owe me *big* time. And I'm not wearing leather leggings. Or high heels. And I'm not missing class, either."

"Just be there as your schedule allows, Red." Adam sticks out his tongue, dodging my little fists as I attempt to punish him for using the nickname I hate the most.

"Don't push your luck!"

"Fine, fine," he says, grabbing my wrists gently to stop the punches. He looks down at me, our chests close together, laughs subsiding as he releases my wrists again. "Thank you."

"You're welcome."

He flicks his shades over his eyes after a moment, backing away slowly.

"Oh, and Cassie?" he asks, grin growing wider as he grabs the hem of his t-shirt with both hands.

I follow the motion, eyes stuck for a second before I rip them away. "Don't you dare."

"Welcome *back* to PSU!" He smirks, stripping his shirt over his head and tossing it back at me before sprinting toward the blow-up waterslide, just like he did the first time we met. He rushes down it to a roar of screams from my sisters and I bite back a laugh, watching him all the way to the end. When he shakes the water off his hair at the end and grins back at me, my stomach dips.

I've missed him.

I think I already knew it before, but I finally allow myself to admit it. Maybe it doesn't have to be him or Grayson, maybe we *can* still be friends. He doesn't seem fazed by what happened last semester, so why am I overthinking it?

So, I drop the thought, along with Adam's shirt, and then I peel my own sundress off and take off running. When my stomach hits the slide and I fly down to the end, water spraying and sisters cheering, I decide not to take anything too seriously this semester.

Time to make my second year at PSU even better than the first.

"I don't like it," Grayson says the next night after his show. It's a little past midnight and we both have our first classes in the morning, but neither of us could say goodbye after the show ended, so we popped in a movie at his place. A movie we watched all of two minutes before talking over it, instead.

I lean up on one elbow, looking down at Grayson sprawled out next to me in his sheets that smell like him — coffee and cinnamon. His brows are pinched together, forming a deep line between them that I smooth one thumb over before running it across his bottom lip and kissing him there.

"It's just handing out fliers," I assure him.

"Yeah, handing out fliers with a guy who has the hots for you."

"He does not have the hots for me," I say with a laugh, though I'm not sure if that's the absolute truth or not. I know he had feelings last semester, but the way he acted with me yesterday? It felt like old times. "We're friends, Grayson. We have been since my very first day in KKB. And he's asking me for a favor. He wouldn't do that if he didn't need me."

Grayson grumbles, but then rolls me until he's the one on top, sliding his knee between my legs to part them. "Fine," he says, kissing me with the word. "But enough about him. Let's talk about this sexy little dress you wore to my show tonight."

He trails one hand down the side of the sleek fabric where a diamond-shaped cut out lets him feel the skin of my waist. I giggle at the touch, wrapping my arms around his neck as he maneuvers himself until he's settled between my legs.

"You were amazing, by the way. That crowd was huge for a fancy schmancy restaurant."

"You know what else is huge," he says, smirking against my lips as he thrusts his jeans against me. The movement pushes my dress up my thighs, exposing my pink cotton thong.

I swallow hard, heart picking up speed with every kiss Grayson sweeps across my collarbone before sucking my lip between his teeth again. When he grinds into me, the friction catching, I moan into his lips without a single ounce of control.

He groans, rolling into me again and pulling my dress up higher until it rests above my hips. And though I want him so bad it physically hurts, that broken shard Clay shoved deep into my heart last year is still there, and it rubs a sharp pain against my ribs as my breathing grows shallow.

"Wait," I whisper, pressing my hands into his chest to give us a little space.

Grayson drops his forehead to mine, our breaths mixing in a sweet scent between us as he does exactly what I asked. I don't know what to say now, or what to do — only that I'm not ready for what he's ready for. The one and only guy I've ever had sex with betrayed me, and I still don't know how to let that go.

"It's okay," he whispers back after a moment, running his thumb along my jawline before cupping my chin up toward him. "We can take it slow. I just want to make you feel good."

The way he says the words, the way his eyes glow like a rare turquoise in the soft lighting of his bedroom, the way a single strand of his hair hangs down over his forehead — it's too much. Chills race from where his thumb grazes my skin all the way to my toes, and he notices, smirking at the reaction I can't help but have to him.

"I want to make you feel good, too."

"You do," he answers quickly. "Every time we're together I feel good, Cassie. And I can wait. Right now, tonight, I want to show you how much it meant to me that you came to my show tonight."

I smile, leaning up to press my lips to his. Grayson kisses me softly at first, but then one hand trails down my ribs, my hip, down to where my dress is bunched, and when one of his fingers grazes the hem of my panties, I gasp into his mouth.

He kisses me harder, tongue sweeping into my mouth as that same finger slips under the cotton fabric, running the slick line of me.

"Fuck," he groans, dipping the finger between my lips. "I love this, I love how wet I make you."

And with that, he pushes not one, but two fingers, all the way inside.

I arch my back, hands flying from where I was grasping his neck to grip the covers instead. Just his fingers alone stretch me, and thoughts of what it would feel like if it was actually him inside me spark another wave of chills.

Grayson works his fingers as he kisses down my neck, biting at the small swell of my breast before nestling between my legs. He pulls his fingers out long enough to strip my panties off and brace my thighs on his shoulders, and then he looks up at me with a wicked grin, and disappears beneath the fabric of my dress.

His hot breath is all I feel at first, and then the rough pad of his tongue as he runs it from my opening to my clit. He sucks when he reaches it, and I arch up off the bed, moaning loud, reaching for a pillow to mute the noise. I pull one over my mouth but Grayson reaches up and throws it across the room.

"I want to hear you when I make you come."

"Oh, God," is all I manage before his tongue is on me again, this time aided by the help of his fingers. He slides two of them deep inside me again, working them in a rhythm, his tongue drawing circles and teeth biting with just the right tender pressure to make me squirm beneath the touch.

I lean up on my elbows and look down at him, his auburn hair between my pale white thighs, his hungry eyes gazing back up at me as he brings me closer to ecstasy with his mouth. It's too much to watch him, so I fall back again, this time reaching down to pull his hair and guide him to the sweet spot.

The first and last guy to go down on me was Clay, and he was a drunken mess after the Halloween party at Ralph's. I'd faked an orgasm just to get it to end, but I know I won't have to fake it with Grayson. Not with his tongue moving like that, or his hands touching me like that, or his moans vibrating through me to my very core.

When my breathing is scarce, hands twisted in the sheets, Grayson pushes his fingers in even deeper and wiggles them quickly, hitting my G-spot in rapid fire as his tongue flicks my clit in sync. And that's the magic combination.

I feel myself pulse around his fingers as the moans leave my lips, his name riding them like waves as they crash into the four walls around us. I can't see, can't feel —everything is like a numb, icy, burning fire. He wanted to hear me, and I'm pretty sure his roommates are hearing me, too, but

I don't care — I want him to know exactly what he's doing to me.

He slows his movements as my breaths even out, kissing my clit softly before climbing up my body to kiss my mouth, instead. I taste myself on him and moan, arching into him.

"Remind me to never miss a show of yours," I pant into his lips. "Ever."

He laughs, and then we kiss and talk until my eyelids are too heavy to hold. And when I fall asleep on his chest, his arms wrapped around me tight, I know I'm the luckiest girl at Palm South University.

# *Bear*

I HATE HIM.

I fucking *hate* him.

The literal last person I want to see, ever, is standing behind the podium at our first Omega Chi Beta chapter of the semester. Alec Carriker is a highly respected alumni of O Chi, but he's still a Class A douchebucket. He only shows up when there's a threat to be made or a wrist-slap to be given.

Unfortunately for us, I think it's past that this time.

"I want you all to know that I don't want to be here tonight," he starts once the room is quiet, his brows bent low as he surveys my brothers. "Least of all to deliver the news I have. But I have tried for a year now to warn you about what would happen if you didn't get your shit together, and not a single one of you listened to me."

Someone makes a snarky comment in the back of the room which garners a few stifled laughs, and Alec fumes, shaking his head before raising his voice.

"The Palm South University chapter of Omega Chi Beta has been suspended."

That shuts up the brothers in the back.

That shuts up everyone.

Even me.

Because though I was pissed the last time Alec told us we were on a probation period, I can't even be mad this time. We fucked up. *Bad.* And I knew this was coming before I even saw Alec stroll in.

"Riley Butler just turned eighteen a month ago. He has been away from home for all of one-hundred hours. And now? Now he's in the hospital with two broken ribs, a fractured wrist, and a severe concussion."

The heaviness of the reality settles over the room like a thick fog, weighing us down into our seats.

"And you can try to say it's not your fault, that you just threw a party, that you're not responsible for what a dumb freshman does after drinking his first beer, but the truth is, you are. You *are* responsible — for anything that happens at that house or to any of your brothers or anyone trying to *become* a brother."

At that, a few of us look around with questioning eyes.

"That's right. Riley was going to pledge in the spring, and a few of you knew that, because he told the police officers at the hospital that two guys told him this was a pre-pledge test."

"Jesus fucking Christ," I mumble, sinking down into my chair as I shake my head in disbelief.

I don't even register the rest of Alec's news. Everything is muted by the fact that the fraternity I love is on suspension. I hear Alec say that it will be a year minimum, and that's all it takes for me to tune out every other sentence that comes after. Because none of it matters, not anymore.

Chapter is called early, without a single ounce of good news, and I'm the first to bolt out of the room and down the hall to my bedroom. I throw on a pair of gym shorts and a PSU t-shirt quickly before tugging on my sneakers and blowing back out the front door.

I need a release. I need to zone out. I need to make every inch of my fucking body burn.

But when I round the Student Union and veer off toward the gym, I get that burn in the worst way possible.

Because Shawna is walking toward me.

"You've got to be fucking kidding me."

Shawna managed to crack through my exterior last semester, and I fell for her. Hard. But when her parents came for family weekend, she showed me her true colors — and they were the ugliest shades.

I see her before she sees me, which gives me just enough time to trace the edges of her new, shorter purple hair before I zero in on her glasses. The glasses that always drove me crazy in the best way. The glasses framing her big brown eyes as they stare back at me.

I stop, and she does, too — watching me as she waits for me to make the first move.

But I can't deal with her, not right now. Maybe not ever. So, I turn the volume on my iPod up higher and jog to the right, taking the longer way to the gym, not even giving her a second look before the decision was made.

I feel marginally better after a two-hour session at the gym, and my body is on fire just like I wanted. The last few steps into the O Chi house are brutal, and all I want is a shower and my bed.

When I walk inside and find a dozen brothers lugging in a keg, the fire coursing through my muscles boils my blood, instead.

"What the fuck is this?" I ask, pointing to the metal as two sophomores carry it past me and toward the back door. I shove one of them until he loses his balance and drops his half, forcing the other to do the same.

"Calm down, Bear," Patrick says from behind me. He's in my pledge class and we're both given credit for the best of the O Chi parties, but right now I just want to murder him. "It's just one keg and we told a few sorority chicks to come over tonight. Nothing big."

"Are you guys really that stupid? Are my *brothers* really *this fucking dumb?!*"

"Bear, it's fine. It's—"

"IT'S NOT FINE!" I snap, ripping my earphones out of my ears and heaving my iPod across the room. It hits the wall and shatters, making my brothers jump as I try but fail to calm down. "Don't you get it? We're suspended. There is only one punishment past this and it's losing our letters forever. Losing. Our. *Letters*, you fucking dickwads."

More of my brothers have filtered in from the back hallways and chapter room, and since I have their attention, I decide to say everything I need to.

"You can be mad at Alec and the other alums and nationals all you want, but the truth is we did this to ourselves. And now we need to suck it up and deal with the consequences for a year so we can get this chapter back to being the greatest one on campus like it once was."

"That's easy for you to say," I hear from the back. When a few brothers step aside, our new president, Richard, steps forward. "Some of us are seniors. Some of us don't get another year."

His words sober me. I was supposed to be a senior this year, too, but due to fucking up in classes when I was too busy partying, I'll be a fifth year senior. Still, I stand even straighter before firing back.

"Then I suggest you step up as the fucking president, *Dick*, and figure out a way to make the most of this fraternity and what time you have left here before you're gone. But don't drag an entire chapter with more than a hundred years of history down just because you can't snuff your ego and go party somewhere else. This isn't about you, or about me," I say, sweeping a hand over the entire room. "Or about any of us. It's about those letters." I point to the ΩΧΒ letters that hang on our door. "And this chapter. And this university. It's about all the brothers who came before us, the ones who stand with us, and the ones who will only come after us if we can turn this sinking ship around and put life back into its sails.

"Now to some of you, none of that may mean a single damn thing. But to me?" I shake my head, letting my hands fall at my side. "It means everything. So, as long as I'm in this house, as long as I have anything to say about it, I'm not going to let any of you throw a brotherhood away out of pure stupidity."

The room is silent, most of my brothers staring at the laces on their shoes as I push past them toward my room.

"Get that fucking keg out of this house or I'll knock all of you out with it."

Flying down the hall, I slam my bedroom door closed behind me and rip my shirt up and over my head, kicking my shorts off next and taking the hottest, fastest shower I can manage. When I'm dressed again, I collapse into bed, staring up at the dark ceiling with a million thoughts racing through my head.

I don't try to digest any of them — not the ones of Erin, or Shawna, or Omega Chi or Riley, the kid I never got to meet who probably hates our fraternity now. I just let them all fly at me, taking turns for my attention, none of them getting it for long before another shoves it out of the way.

I'm not sure how long I lie there before there's a hard knock at my door and it creaks open, a stream of light leaking in.

"What."

"Hey, it's Richard."

I sigh, letting my head drop to the right so I can see him as I repeat myself. "What."

"I'm sorry," he says, voice low. "We all are. You're right. We were being stupid, and we care about these letters just as much as you do. The keg is gone, and we're going to come up with some kick-ass philanthropy ideas for this semester and next to make the most of our situation. And we'll party at the other houses or at Ralph's or off campus, and even then, we'll behave." He pauses. "Thanks for helping us see straight."

I nod, looking back up at the ceiling. "Let me know how I can help with the philanthropy."

"We will. Oh, and," he says with a chuckle. "Lacy is here. Should I send her back?"

"Not tonight."

He chuckles again. "Alright. Night, Bear." And then the small stream of light is gone.

I roll over toward the wall, shifting until I'm under the sheets. I'm just about to doze off when my door opens again and a shadow slips through, closing it behind them.

"Lacy, I'm really not in the mood. Not even for a blow job as good as yours."

"How about a best friend cuddle buddy, instead?"

Skyler hops over me, sliding between me and the wall and wiggles her way under the covers. She watches me for a moment, only the light from the streetlights outside my window helping me see her face at all. After a moment I sigh, holding my arms out for her to come closer.

She nuzzles into my side and I wrap her in my famous Bear Hug, setting my chin on the top of her head as she hugs me back.

"You okay?" she asks.

"Not even a little bit."

She hugs me tighter. "You will be."

I sigh, feeling the smallest bit of relief wash over me. Because Skyler Thorne is the only one I actually believe when she says that.

It's not going to be easy, and I have no idea where to even start, but I'm going to help my brothers turn this chapter around. Palm South University only knows us as the party boys, but they're about to see us in a brand new light.

And with that final thought, I tug Skyler closer, and finally fall asleep.

# Episode 2

# Ashlei

THIS SEMESTER IS GOING to be different.

That's all I can repeat in my head as I heave the large glass door open to enter one of the tallest buildings downtown, the building where my new internship is, the building where my new life begins.

My dainty, nude heels clack against the marble floor as I pass by the reception desk, smiling at the young man sitting behind it. His name is Christopher and he was the one who gave me my parking garage pass when I'd accepted the internship. He eyes my first-day outfit, throwing me a subtle thumbs-up with a wink as I strut past him with a wide smile toward the elevators.

On the outside, I look completely put together — pairing my favorite strappy Steve Maddens with the brand-new, navy blue Imporio Armani trench coat dress I begged Mom and Dad to buy me for this internship specifically. The sleeves of it are cuffed up to right under my elbow, and I love the way I feel with one hand in the pocket of it as my heels click across the floor.

I cinched the waist of it this morning with a thick, gold-plated belt, the deep V neckline of the dress dipping down to end only a few inches above it. My jewelry is simple, long blonde hair softly curled, and makeup natural. I don't look nervous, not even a little bit. I look like I belong here, striding right beside the other young professionals, coffee in hand, ready to take on the world.

But inside, I'm completely freaking out.

I toss my half-empty iced coffee into a trashcan on my way to the elevators, casually hooking my damp palm around the base of my small purse as I unclasp it and dig for a mint. I'm not sure why I'm so nervous. I *never* got nervous when I pole danced, not even at regionals, so why does the first day of an internship have my knees unsteady?

Maybe it's because I feel like I have something to prove this semester. There is no Hayden, no drugs, no Xavier, and — though this one actually hurts more than I admit — no Bo. It'd taken me most of the summer to realize that Bo leaving PSU wasn't the end of the world, though it felt like it. In fact, in a way, I'm kind of grateful. Because for the first time in my college career, I have no distractions. I'm single, I don't owe anyone a single thing, and I've landed an internship at one of the most reputable event agencies in South Florida.

The nervous energy flowing through me is almost palpable as I step into one of the six elevators, so I let out a long exhale as the doors start to close.

But then a dark hand reaches in to stop them.

The doors slowly slide back open, and when they reveal the man attached to the hand, I'm glad I got in one last calming breath because there's absolutely no way I'm breathing now.

There's only one word to accurately describe him: Pristine.

Everything about him is sharp — the edge of his short fade, the line of his nose, the angle of his cleanly shaven jaw. My eyes skate over every inch of him, focus shifting from his broad shoulders to the button of his charcoal suit jacket as he uses one hand to fasten it before stepping inside the elevator with me. He reminds me of Clinton, the same smooth skin and full lips, but Mr. Pristine is a little taller and leaner. I chance another glance at him as the doors begin to close, and he tugs his shades off, tucking them into the front pocket of his jacket before acknowledging me with a smirk and dark, intense eyes.

I swallow, eyes shifting to focus on the white light illuminating floor thirty-two as we start to ascend. I'm absolutely not looking at his reflection in the doors of the elevator. Totally not noticing that his eyes are still on me, roaming my skin the way mine just did his. And when his tongue sweeps his bottom lip subtly, almost so imperceptibly I'm not even sure I really saw it, my thighs *definitely* don't clench together under my dress.

I'm one-hundred percent cool.

Until he speaks, that is.

"So, you're on an elevator with a complete stranger for approximately twenty-five seconds," he says, the deep baritone of his voice filling the small space between us. I'm still staring at the way his suit tapers at his waist in the elevator door reflection. "Do you A, ride up in awkward silence, or B, tell this stranger why your hands are shaking."

My eyes snap to his, and he smiles a little wider, knowing he got my attention. I watch him for a moment, his demeanor so cool and calm, and then I clear my throat, facing forward again. I have no idea what to say to that. And if I ignore him much longer, he'll assume I picked option A. Which is probably the option I *should* choose, but after a few long seconds, I figure *what the hell?* Might as well get it out to someone, and why not a stranger?

And so, my nervous energy flows out like word vomit.

"Today is the first day of my internship for what I consider to be the best corporate event agency in Florida and I'm just… I'm nervous, which is weird for me because I'm *never* nervous, like when I used to pole dance I never once got nervous before I went on stage." I pause, eyes widening at what I'd said just as one of Mr. Pristine's eyebrows shoots up to his hairline. "It was competitive pole dancing," I clarify. "Like fitness."

He's still smirking.

Floor seventeen.

"Anyway, I've just had a shit year and this semester I'm determined to turn things around. I want to walk into this internship and impress every single person I talk to — boss, colleague, client, and everyone in-between. So, I guess I'm okay with the fact that my hands are trembling now, so long as they're steady as stone when I start shaking *other* peoples' hands."

He nods, tongue pressing against the inside of his cheek as he eyes me with what feels like respect as the elevator comes to a halt with a soft ding. The doors swing open, and I offer him one last shrug and a smile.

"Wow, that actually helped. Thanks for being the smokin' hot stranger in the elevator," I say, stepping off as he holds the doors open.

His eyes spark with even more intensity when I pass him, my arm grazing his jacket. "My pleasure. Thanks for choosing option B."

I chuckle, giving him an awkward, small wave goodbye.

But then he steps off the elevator, too.

"Oh, and welcome to the best agency in South Florida," he says, still smirking as he uses his badge to enter through the sleek metal doors under the *Okay, Cool Event Agency* sign. I catch the door before it can close, mouth gaping wide, eyes glued to his back as he walks down the row of cubes.

"Hi!" a chipper voice says, snapping me back to reality. The voice belongs to a short, curvy girl around my age with dark blonde hair and freckles lining her cheeks. "You must be one of the interns. I'm Mykayla, the receptionist for *Okay, Cool*. I see you already met our CEO, so we can skip his office on the tour."

"CEO?" I ask, voice a little squeaky as my eyes jet to Mr. Pristine's back again. He turns his head just as his hand finds the handle to an office all the way at the other end, and damn it if he doesn't smirk again as he pushes the door open and disappears inside.

"Yeah, that's Brandon Church — Mr. Church to us," she adds with a wink. "Come on, let's grab some coffee and I'll take you around and introduce you to everyone. Your manager won't be in for another hour or so."

"Fantastic," I murmur. Then I follow her to the break room, all the while wondering why the universe hates me.

# Adam

I FLOP DOWN ON my bed with a sigh, closing my eyes and reveling in the silence.

Being president of Alpha Sigma is amazing, but damn is it busy. We've only been back at PSU for a little over a week and we're already in full swing, working on preparing for our second annual concert, signing up for philanthropy event after philanthropy event, and now with the suspension of Omega Chi, planning a full calendar of socials and parties. I told the guys when they elected me that we were going to make a name for Alpha Sigma this year, and already I can feel that promise coming to life.

It's rewarding, but it's also exhausting, so I cherish the feel of my cool comforter against my back and close my eyes, letting out a long breath.

As much as I enjoy the quiet, it doesn't take long for the flurry of thoughts in my head to dissipate, leaving only one left. The one I can never escape, not even in my sleep.

Cassie.

It was a long summer without her, with only the last conversation between us to keep me company while I wondered what she was doing. I didn't know what to expect this semester, and after she basically sprinted out of here the first time we saw each other, I figured there was no way in hell we'd have a chance at friendship again.

But she'd showed up when I asked her to, helping me spread the word about the concert by handing out fliers in front of the Student Union. It's been fun hanging out with her, and every day we spend together I feel more and more of the awkwardness disappear.

Still, it doesn't change the fact that she's still Grayson's, and I have no idea how to handle that.

I inhale another deep breath, wondering if I have enough time to catch a nap, but of course, the silence doesn't last long enough for me to find out.

Two loud knocks hit my door before it swings open and Jeremy flies in. "We have a problem."

"Shhh," I tell him as he kicks the door closed behind him and flops down in my desk chair, ripping his laptop from his backpack in the process.

"Wha—"

"Sixty seconds," I say, cutting him off. "Just… let me have sixty seconds of silence and then you can tell me about the problem."

Jeremy huffs, sitting back in my chair and crossing his arms over his chest. I give him a slight nod and close my eyes again, but he's too fidgety for me to enjoy the rest. He can't stop huffing, and his knee is bouncing, foot tapping against the hardwood floor. I get it, he's under a lot of stress, too, being my right-hand man and second-in-command. It's pretty awesome running the fraternity with one of my best friends, but at the same time, I'm learning a lot about our leadership styles.

For instance, Jeremy has about as much grip on handling stress as bald tires have on a rainy road.

I laugh, sitting up and moving to the edge of my bed to face him well before the full minute has passed. "Okay, Jeremy. What's the problem?"

He blows out a breath and grabs his laptop, flipping the top open. "Futile Destiny pulled out of the show."

"What?! They're our headliner!"

"*Were*," Jeremy says, shaking his head and typing away on his laptop. "They were our headliner. And now we don't have one."

I sigh, scrubbing a hand over my face. "The concert is in three days. What the hell are we going to do."

Jeremy watches me for a minute, and he doesn't even have to open his mouth for me to know what's coming next.

"Ugh, don't even say it."

"I don't think we have a choice now, Adam." Jeremy sets his laptop aside and leans forward, elbows resting on his knees. "Look, I know he's not your favorite person, but… if we don't book another headliner, we're going to have to cancel the concert. Tickets won't sell without one, and those who already bought them will want a refund if we don't find a replacement."

I want to argue with him, convince him we have other options, but I know I can't — not without putting the concert in jeopardy and failing at my first big challenge as president.

"I know," I admit dejectedly.

"Do you want me to ask him?"

"No," I answer, standing and swiping my wallet off my desk. *So much for a break.* "I'll go. Cassie said he's playing at the coffee shop today. Maybe if she's there, she can help me convince him."

"Probably not a bad idea to have her giving him a nudge, all things considered."

I grunt in answer, clapping him on the shoulder as I pass. "Don't worry, I'll handle it."

Cup O' Joe's is packed when I walk in, and I squeeze between groups of people — mostly girls

— standing around with their eyes on the stage. Grayson is belting out *Butterfly* by Jason Mraz and I can practically see the panties dropping to the floor with every note he sings.

I roll my eyes, the taste of disdain for having to be here at all growing more sour than a rotten lemon in my mouth. One thing I've learned about being president is that you have to make sacrifices, and you have to do shit you don't want to. Still, even though I know I'm out of choices and this is my only chance to save the concert, I don't want to be here. I don't want to ask Grayson for anything, least of all to headline my show, but here I am.

Swallowing down the last bit of pride I have, I keep pushing through the crowd until I spot Cassie.

Her unruly red hair is braided to the side, the ends of it frayed out in all directions. She aimlessly plays with the ends of it with one hand while the other holds her coffee cup on the table, thumb tapping along to the beat of Grayson's guitar. She's seated at a table in the back right corner, eyes on the stage, though they seem distant, as if she's somewhere else entirely.

My stomach drops at the sight of her, just like it always has. Every step takes me closer to her and further from any semblance of calm I had managed to have when I walked in the door.

"You're pretty good at that," I say when I reach her, shaking her from her thoughts as I nod toward her tapping thumb. "Ever ask Grayson if he needs a drummer?"

Cassie's eyes brighten, as if seeing me is a relief, and my pulse kicks up a notch as I take the empty seat next to her.

"Yeah, right. A girl on stage with him would ruin all of this," she says, sweeping a hand over the crowd.

I nod, brows pinching together as I look around. Girls are huddled together in packs of three or more in every space of the shop, eyes locked on Grayson, camera phones at the ready as they giggle and will him to look at them with their longing gazes.

"Yeah, this is a little intense. Is it hard for you at all?"

She shrugs. "Nah, it's all just for show. I know he's still mine at the end of the night."

The words leave her lips easily enough, slicing my skin with the precision of them, but something in her eyes tells me she doesn't believe them as much as I do.

I clear my throat. "Hey, thanks for all your help with the concert. I really appreciate it. I know you have plenty of other things you'd rather be doing than hanging out with me and sweating your ass off handing out fliers."

Cassie smiles, wrinkling her nose at me. "Ah, it wasn't that bad. Mild torture, at most."

Our eyes connect and I hold her stare, silently thanking her again, wondering if she sees the other words laying just beneath the surface. Words I've never said, words she's never heard. Silence always seems to be the way Cassie and I say what we need to say most.

The song ends to a roar from the coffee shop crowd, and Cassie's attention snaps back to the stage as she claps along with them. When I turn, Grayson is staring directly at us, eyes narrowed as he hangs his guitar on the stand. He forces a smile and waves at the crowd, which makes them go even crazier, and then he jumps down into the masses, making a beeline for our table.

Hands reach for him as he passes, and he politely dismisses each one, focus undeterred until he's swooping Cassie up from her chair and into his arms.

He kisses her hard, which earns him a few groans from the girls standing nearby and a hard eye roll from me. I stand to join them and wait for his power play of possession to end.

Cassie is flushed bright red when he finally pulls back, tucking her under his arm before finally turning to me with a wry grin. "Oh, hey, Adam.

Surprised to see you here. Let me guess, more *fliers* to hand out?"

It's clear he's not happy about the fact that I asked Cassie for help with the show, which kills my optimism that he'll be willing to help me out himself. Still, I'm not leaving the shop until I do everything I can to save the concert.

"Came to see you, actually."

His brows shoot up right along with Cassie's.

"You came to see me play," he deadpans. "Really."

I crack my neck, standing a little straighter and biting back the smart ass comments I want to send flying back at him. "Really. We've had a lot of requests for you for the concert, and after hearing you myself, I can see why," I lie, forcing what I'm sure is the fakest smile I've ever had on my face. "How do you feel about headlining the show?"

Cassie's eyes light up. "Oh, my God, that's amazing!" She turns to look up at Grayson, but his eyes are still narrowed, jaw set. "Did you hear that?"

"I thought Futile Destiny was your headliner," he says, ignoring Cassie's enthusiasm.

"They were," I confirm. "Past tense."

"They're okay with stepping down to opener so I can headline?"

I clear my throat again, shoving my hands into my pockets. "They had some other opportunities, so they were cool with it."

At that, Grayson barks out a laugh, his arm still dangling over Cassie's shoulder. "So, what you mean to say is they pulled out and now you're fucked."

I grit my teeth, ready to say *fuck it* and find someone else when Cassie steps out from under his arm and turns to face him.

"Grayson, this is a great opportunity. They've already sold three thousand tickets. That's twice what they sold last year, and that's more people you can potentially turn into fans."

Grayson is still smirking, eyes narrowed at me like he has me all figured out. And right now, as much as I hate it, he holds the power.

Cassie tugs his sleeve and he looks down at her with a sigh. "You want me to do it?"

She nods. "I do. I always feel like my Greek life stuff is so separate from you, but this is a great way for you to be a part of it. And you'd be the headliner!"

He eyes me again before smiling down at her and pulling her in for a kiss. "Okay, I'll do it for you, then."

She lights up, this time pulling *him* down for a kiss, and I nearly double over from the pain of watching it. I've seen them dance together, seen them kiss, but this is the first time I've seen what I've been trying to ignore all along.

She's falling for him, and there's nothing I can do about it.

"Cool," I finally say, clearing my throat. "I'll have Jeremy call you tonight with details."

"Wait," Grayson says as I turn to leave. "I want five bucks a head minimum. And I want a booth set up for merchandise sales."

"It's for charity," Cassie says to him softly, her hand squeezing where it holds his hip.

"Oh, well… fine. No charge per head. But I need a merch table. My agent won't agree to it without one."

I scoff, trying my best to hide it. One viral video and the guy's douche level skyrockets to ten. "Whatever you need. Just let Jeremy know and he'll make it happen. Thanks for agreeing, Grayson. Glad to have you."

I offer him a hand, determined not to let him see how much it pains me to work with him. And the truth is, I really am thankful he agreed to help. The show would have tanked without him, so if I have to bite down my pride and play nice for the next week, I'll do it.

Besides, he clearly makes Cassie happy, and as much as that kills me, it's all I want. Her happiness. Even if I can't be the one responsible for it.

Grayson shakes my hand firmly. "Happy to help."

He wraps Cassie up for one last, ridiculously long kiss before making his way back to the stage. And then I'm alone with her again, alone as we can be in a crowded coffee shop, and suddenly it's too hard to breathe.

"Thanks for the help with that," I say. "See you around."

"Hey, wait!"

I pause, forcing a swallow and facing her again. One deep red strand has fallen loose from her braid, hanging diagonally across her forehead, begging for me to sweep it aside. I shove my hands back in my pockets to avoid it.

"Do you… can I help at all? Want me to print up more fliers or take tickets at the door?"

And though we could use the help with taking tickets, I know without a doubt I can't take it from her. Not after seeing her with Grayson, not after knowing how deep she's in it with him. I thought I could handle it, wait on the sidelines, but it turns out I have absolutely zero chill when it comes to Cassie.

"We're good, but thanks. Enjoy your coffee."

I bolt for the door before she can respond, weaving through the crowd until I'm finally able to breathe in the hot summer air outside. The first breath I take is sticky and painful, and I wipe the sweat from my brow, storming back to the house with a new determination.

Cassie isn't mine.

That fact hasn't been more clear than it is right now, and though it's like filleting my heart slice by painful slice, I know I have to let her go. I have to let the idea of *us* go.

So, with every step, I do just that — dropping every memory, every fantasy, every shred of hope I have. I take the long way back to the house. I replay her kissing him until I'm almost too nauseous to keep walking. And even after all of it, when I reach the house and jet straight back to my bedroom, flopping down into the cool sheets, I know I've failed.

I still can't shake the very last piece.

And I know I never will.

# Erin

YOU KNOW THAT SHINY, pink skin that makes up a scar? The kind that is a little bit thinner, yet somehow a little more resilient? The kind that marks you forever with a warning sign, with a memory, with a reminder? Well, I am covered in that skin, from head to toe, and I've never felt more beautiful.

The summer made me stronger.

I left Palm South University last semester broken. Shattered. Completely and utterly destroyed. I didn't know if I'd come back — hell, I didn't know if I'd *survive*. But here I am, stronger than ever, and it's all thanks to my mom.

She helped me take the pain and the fear and transform them into drive and determination. It took months of tough love and reality checks that hurt almost worse than what had happened with Landon, but I was finally standing on my own.

And this semester, I was standing even taller.

I realize this is the best part about my new scarred skin as I apply the last bit of my foundation, working it into my skin with a makeup sponge and a soft smile on my face. The best part about my scars is that no one else can see them but me.

And *that* is power.

"I just don't understand why she won't take a Little," I say to Skyler again as I dig through my makeup bag for my eyebrow pencil. "I mean, I get that she's got a tough schedule this semester, but so does everyone else. This is prime time to add to the family. And if she ends up taking a Little next year, that's one less year they'll have together and she'll be so young when she takes president like the rest of our family. It'll make everything more difficult for her. It just doesn't make sense. You *always* take a Little after your first year. You just do."

"Ex," Skyler sighs my nickname, sitting up on the edge of my bed. "Please, can we just let it go? Cassie wants to wait and we need to support her. It's fine, our line will be fine, the presidency legacy will be fine, it'll all be *fine*. Just chill."

I would roll my eyes if I wasn't currently lining them. "Fine. I'll let it go. But I think it's a mistake, especially since this is the best pledge class we've ever had."

"All thanks to you," Skyler reminds me with a wink.

It's a transparent attempt to change the subject and drive me back to Happy Town, but I let it happen. Mostly because the first goal I wanted to accomplish with my newfound determination was to land us the most amazing girls KKB had ever seen, and I'd succeeded.

"I still can't believe it," I say, grabbing my mascara next. Skyler is still in her pajamas, but I have the first Panhellenic all-chapter meeting in thirty minutes, and I plan to make a statement when I walk in. "Highest average GPA, highest percentage of athletes, highest percentage of on-campus involvement. We're going to be unstoppable this semester."

"You killed it. I've never seen a recruitment run so smoothly, Big." Skyler beams as I brush the last of my lashes. "You definitely don't have to worry about getting president now. It's a definite."

I smile. "You think?"

"I *know*."

Suddenly my bedroom door flies open and Jess tumbles into the room, jumping onto Ashlei's bed across from where Skyler is sitting.

"HE'S COMING!"

She bounces on the bed, the floppy mess of hair piled in a bun on her head jumping right along with her as she claps her hands.

"Jesus?" Skyler asks.

"Close. Jarrett!"

This time we all squeal with her, and she falls back on the bed, legs kicking in the air.

"He's coming to visit and he'll be here a whole week! Andddd, I'm going to introduce him to everyone! No more secrets. I want every single person to know I'm his and he's mine."

"You could always get t-shirts made," I offer.

Jess tosses a pillow in my direction, but it thumps against my closet door and slides down pathetically. "Whatever, Ex. Not even the best of sarcasm can get me down today. My *boyfriend* is coming to town!"

Skyler and I both laugh and then I turn to rummage through my closet while Jess goes on and on about what they'll do while he's here. I know it's a big step for them, since most of their relationship has been kept a secret due to his job on campus. Now that he's working up north, there's nothing to hide, and I'm happy for Jess.

A small part of me wonders if I'll ever know that happiness. The thought of letting another guy in, letting him close, seems so impossible it's like imagining winning the lottery. Fun to think about, but depressing all the same.

My phone buzzes on my desk just as I pull on my favorite Lilly Pulitzer dress and I check reflection before swiping it off the desk. Clinton's name is framed by a small box, and I swallow, heart kicking against my chest as I slide my thumb across the screen.

**- Hey, you, what are you doing for your birthday next week? Big 2-1 deserves a bad-ass party. -**

I stare at his text, a mixture of emotions swirling inside me. Clinton was the one who saved me the night of formal, the one who held me together when the last thread snapped. I'm forever thankful for him holding me, for him taking care of me, and most of all, for him not telling anyone else what happened. I knew when I asked him for that, it would be hard for him to do, but he did it because he cared about me.

Still, I don't need any man — not even him — and what's more, I know the minute we're alone, he'll want me to talk. He'll want me to tell him I'm okay, to tell him what I've done to work through what happened.

But I can't reopen that wound.

I won't.

So I ignore the text, dropping my phone into my purse and slinging it over my shoulder before turning back to the girls. "Okay, first Panhellenic meeting. Wish me luck!"

"Good luck!" they both say in unison, and I slip back into business mode without a second thought.

# Ashlei

I AM EXHAUSTED.

It's only Tuesday but I feel like I've worked an entire week. Between classes, the sorority, and my internship, I have exactly twenty minutes of downtime each day, and I usually use it peeing.

And it's only been a week since my internship started.

I guess most people would be complaining, wishing they had more time to sleep or party, but honestly? I'm thriving. It reminds me of when I had pole dancing taking up my time, giving me purpose — a goal to work toward. I'm working alongside three other interns this semester, and I'm determined to be the best. Blame it on always being in competition with my sisters growing up or maybe just on the fact that I have something to prove this semester, but I'm all in.

Which is part of the reason I'm the last to leave the office.

We had a meeting first thing this morning to discuss the event all the interns would be working on, a product launch for a local, high-end skincare line. The only information we'd really been given was the date of the event and a packet with information on the new line they're launching, so I spent the rest of the day researching the company, founders, mission statement, and current marketing struggles. It might have been a little excessive since we'd only be involved in the launch event, but in my opinion, they booked *Okay, Cool* because they want the best, and I'm determined to give it to them.

To meet their needs, I need to understand them.

And then, I can find a way to exceed them.

Balancing my binder now stuffed full with the research I've done all day, I dig through my purse for my phone to call Cassie. We're supposed to meet at Ralph's to talk about Erin's surprise party at seven and I'm already ten minutes late. But when I finally fish it out, I lose the grip on my binder, and it tumbles to the floor, hitting the toe of my high heel in the process before spewing paper all around me.

"Oh, for fuck's sake," I yell, eyes rolling up to the ceiling before I let out an exasperated sigh and kneel down to start retrieving the pages. I hadn't taken the time to hole punch them and actually put them *inside* the three-pronged binder, and now I'm paying the price for it.

My phone lights up with a text from Cassie and I angrily thumb out a response before tossing my phone back in my purse, gathering the paper and trying to keep at least some of the organization I'd worked all day on. I'm so grumbly I don't even register the cherry-brown Ermenegildo Zegna shoes until I'm trying to swipe up a page trapped underneath them.

I pause, fingers still on the paper as my eyes trail up the beige suit pants, skipping the open jacket altogether to land on Mr. Church's face. His hands are resting easily in his pockets, Carolina blue dress shirt exposed and navy tie loosened around his neck as he smirks down at me.

Me.

The intern.

Who is currently on her hands and knees in a pencil skirt.

"I didn't realize we were keeping the interns so late," he booms, bending to my level as he helps gather the last of the pages.

I just gape at him for a moment before clearing my throat and shoving the papers in my binder, not taking the time to keep them in order anymore. My fingers brush his when he hands me the stack he's gathered and I keep my eyes on the binder, cheeks flush with heat.

"*Bare•ly?*" he asks, nodding to my binder as he stands. "Didn't you just get assigned to their event this morning?"

I nod, attempting to stand without flashing him my underwear or breaking my neck. He reaches down for me, one hand grabbing the binder from my grasp as the other stabilizes my elbow.

"Yeah, I just wanted to get a head start on the event. I don't know much about them yet."

"Looks like you will soon," he says, handing the binder back to me when I'm fully standing. "You know, most interns just wait to be told what to do when we assign them their event clients." He checks his watch before lifting a brow back at me. "And most of them leave well before five."

"Guess I'm not like most interns," I offer with a shy smile and a shrug.

"I'm starting to realize that."

He takes a moment to really look at me then, and the heat I feel from his gaze is unlike anything I've ever experienced. It's not a look just reserved for me, either. I've seen him give it to plenty of other people just in my first week. It's not him coming onto me or checking me out, it's just how he is naturally — intense, ablaze, striking.

"Mr. Church, I'm really sorry about that first day in the elevator. I... well, clearly I was nervous, and I didn't know who you were, and—"

"That was the best part," he says, hand finding the small of my back as he leads us to the elevators. "You didn't know who I was, so I got to see you unfiltered. It's rare for me to see anyone that way. I liked it."

"You liked watching me make a fool of myself?"

He chuckles as the doors slide open and we both step inside.

"You didn't make a fool of yourself. You made an impression. There's a difference."

I nod, biting my lips between my teeth for the rest of the ride down. When the doors open again, we both walk in silence until we're out of the lobby and standing in the warm evening air.

"Thanks for your help," I say, sheepishly holding my binder up. "I'll see you in the morning."

"Have a good night, Miss Daniels."

And where I need to turn left for the garage, he turns right, unlocking a pearl white Acura NSX parked in the reserved section with a soft beep before sliding inside. I can't even move another inch toward the garage until I hear him rev it to life, the engine roaring and purring under his touch. It idles for a minute, my eyes on the blacked-out windows, wondering if the ones inside it are focused on me, too.

When I finally turn, the engine hums again as he throws it in reverse, and it takes every ounce of self-control I have to not watch him drive away.

"Okay, now that Erin's party details are hammered out, I have a favor to ask you," Cassie says, ordering us another round of margaritas. Ralph's ended up being packed so we moved to the Mexican restaurant just off campus, and after two margaritas I was thankful for the switch. Nothing makes a long day better quite like tequila.

"Ah, so that's why you've been buttering me up with chips and queso."

"*And* Patrón," she adds with a wave of her finger.

"Fine, I'm as buttered as toast. What's the favor?"

"Okay, so ever since Grayson agreed to headline the Alpha Sigma concert, I've been trying to think of ways to make it even better than last year. Not that Adam doesn't already have that covered, but I just…" She pauses, tucking her wild hair behind her ear. "I know it was hard for him to ask Grayson to help, since they don't exactly get along, and I want to try to take some of the stress off him."

"That's really sweet, Cass. Why don't they get along, anyway?"

She shrugs, but something in her eyes gives me the impression there's something she's not saying. "Who knows. Boys are dumb."

"Indeed. So what's the favor?"

"Okay, so I pitched this idea to him and he's in, but he doesn't have time to do anything else. I told him I'd handle it, but… well, I need your help."

"Just spit it out already."

"I need you to auction a date." She throws her hands up when I start to object. "Just hear me out. It's almost exactly like the KKB auction we have every spring except instead of auctioning just the girl, we auction the whole package. So, basically they bet on the 'date' but the catch is that the girl auctioning it off has to go on the date with them. So, it takes the pressure off them for deciding what to do and it's a little bonus, like paying for the activity itself instead of just the girl."

"It sounds great, but I seriously can't, Cassie. I barely have time to breathe, as it is, this semester."

"*Please,*" she begs, sliding my new margarita to me when the waitress drops it off. "All I'm asking for is two nights — this Friday for the concert, and then whatever night the guy picks for the date. I already have the date items to auction so you don't even have to worry about that."

"What is the date?"

"It's a four-car experience at *Palm South Exotic Auto Racing*. You'll basically just have to sit shot gun while the guy gets wet over driving fast sports cars."

I blow out a sigh, taking another, longer drink from my glass. "Fine. I stayed late tonight so I should be able to head out on time Friday as long as my manager is okay with it."

Cassie squeals. "Thank you, thank you, *thank you*. I owe you."

"Yeah, you do, and as you can see, I happily take queso as payment," I say, popping another chip in my mouth with a grin. "How are you and Grayson, anyway? I know you're excited about the show, but it can't be easy having all those girls drooling over him all the time."

Cassie's face falls. "It's not really the girls who bother me. I just don't see him much anymore, and anytime we are together, it's always me watching him from the crowd at the coffee shop or a local show. We haven't had a single date all semester."

I frown. "That's kind of shitty."

"Yeah," she agrees, but shakes it off. "But I get it, and I'm sure we'll spend more time together once the semester settles down a little."

"Have you guys had sex yet?"

Cassie blushes, and I can't help but laugh. She gets so nervous talking about anything sexual.

"Not yet…"

"But?" I probe, sensing more to her statement.

"Well, he did go down on me."

I clink my oversized glass to hers. "Atta girl! How was it?"

She flushes even harder. "Magical. His tongue is just… wow."

"Ugh," I groan. "I haven't had attention down there in way too long."

"Not since Bo?" Cassie asks, and we both fall silent at the mention of her name.

I stir the ice in my margarita, the same part of my heart aching at the loss of her. "Not since Bo."

"Any new girls or guys catching your eye this semester?"

For some reason, Mr. Church's smoldering smirk flashes into my mind at her question, but I shake it off. "Nope. Just focusing on my internship and getting myself stable for once."

"I like that," Cassie says with a smile, lifting her glass this time. "To getting our shit together."

I laugh, tilting my glass toward her.

"I'll drink to that."

# Adam

WHERE THE CROWD IS, everything is perfect.

We more than doubled our ticket sales once Grayson was announced as the headliner, which called for a last-minute relocation to the park near the Student Union. The stage is set up right in front of the large fountain, lights bright enough and speakers loud enough to make it feel like a summertime festival. And in front of the stage are more than seven-thousand students, alumni, and local residents with their hands in the air, screaming as Titanium Rush starts their set.

But backstage, everything is a mess.

"Where the fuck is Grayson?!" I scream into my headset, flipping through the documents on my tablet until I find the one that confirms we asked him to be here before the openers went on. His contact information isn't listed, only a number for his "agent."

*Tool.*

"No one's seen him," Jeremy's voice crackles through the headphone piece as two brothers zip past me with the banner backdrop for Grayson. "We tried calling the number for his agent but it's going straight to voicemail."

"How many songs does Titanium Rush have in their set list?"

"Six."

I curse, jogging down the stairs backstage and veering toward the auction booth. "I'll work on getting ahold of him, you guys come up with a plan to stall. We still have a few auctions to go up for bidding but after that we're screwed."

"We're on it."

My feet are quick as I make my way to where Cassie is working the auction table, taking the money from the bidders and explaining how to claim the prizes. It was her idea, and though I didn't want her help or to be around her more than what was absolutely necessary, I couldn't turn down an opportunity to rack up a larger donation for our philanthropy.

The sky is clear, still casting a soft blue and purple haze as dusk settles in, but it's hotter than hell. I use the small towel around my shoulder to wipe my face just as I reach Cassie's table.

"We're up to four-thousand dollars with that last set of bidding!" she says excitedly, the red mess of curls on top of her head bouncing a little. Her cheeks are bright red, too, freckles more pronounced in the heat as she blots at her own face with a spare event t-shirt. "I think we'll crack at least five-thousand with the last set."

"Awesome. Now if only we knew where your diva of a boyfriend was, we'd be cruising on Easy Street," I spit back.

Cassie's face falls, her big green eyes softening under bent brows.

I sigh, pinching the bridge of my nose and holding out a hand toward her. "I'm sorry. I think the auction is amazing, Cassie. I do. I'm just a little worried because Grayson still isn't here and Titanium Rush has five songs left after this first one. Is there any way you can try to get ahold of him?"

"It's okay," she says, voice timid. She places a hand on my wrist and squeezes it, not knowing that squeeze is still tied to my heart, too. "I know you're stressed out. Let me try calling him, okay? Can you watch the table for a second?"

I nod and she offers a soft smile before pulling out her phone and walking away from the table.

Leave it to Cassie McBee to still be sweet as sugar when I'm being a complete dick. I don't think that girl has a mean bone in her body, and if she does, I hope I never get to see it. It's one of the things I love most about her, that wide-eyed innocence and kindness.

She's gone longer than I expect, and Titanium Rush finishes their set to a roar from the crowd before half of it disperses to get more booze and the final auction girls take the stage. Skyler is emceeing, which is a perfect job for her since she's quite possibly the most charismatic girl on campus, not to mention one of the hottest. She's wearing tiny, ripped-up jean shorts and one of Grayson's t-shirts tied just under her ribs. I hate seeing her in his shirt, but damn if she doesn't look incredible in it.

"Give it up one more time for Titanium Rush!" she screams into the mic and the crowd goes crazy, cheering and waving their drinks in the air. She continues talking, explaining how the last set of auction items will work, as Jeremy freaks out in my ear.

"WHERE THE FUCK IS HE?!"

"Calm down," I answer, trying to appear unfazed. Someone has to appear calm and collected, even if I feel like throwing up. "Cassie is trying to get ahold of him now. Just gather up how much we've raised so far and be prepared to go on stage with some facts about our philanthropy and the donation they're all helping make tonight if he's not here by the time the auction is over, okay?"

"And if he doesn't show at all?"

My stomach turns. "He'll show."

The last three auctions take a while, since they're the most expensive prizes, but when we finally have winners for all three and Jeremy takes the stage with clipboard in shaking hands, I panic.

*This motherfucker really isn't going to show.*

I know we don't exactly get along — AKA, he's the lucky bastard who managed to land the girl neither one of us deserves — but even for him, this is low. To wreck an entire concert and put the reputation of Alpha Sigma at stake like this? It's a completely different level of disrespect, one I won't let him forget.

Blowing out a long, hot breath, I push the button on my headset. "Just keep talking. I'm on my way up there to break the bad news."

Jeremy pauses mid-sentence on stage, his eyes jetting to mine through the crowd, and I shrug. Nothing to do now but apologize and hope there isn't a riot.

He swallows, forcing a smile as he continues talking about where the money from tonight will go and what it will fund.

"He's here," Cassie says, sniffling a little as she tosses her phone on the table. "He and Cal, his agent, just pulled up. They're parking back behind the stage now, I told him not to worry about a parking ticket, that we'd handle it."

"Oh, thank fucking Christ." I turn back toward the stage and push the button for my headset. "He's here. Stall a little longer, Jeremy, then you can announce him. Carter, you copy?"

"Here," Carter's staticky voice answers.

"Grayson is parking backstage. Get him set up as fast as you can and have the other brothers take care of his car."

"On it."

I let out a long breath of relief, scrubbing a hand over my face and turning back to Cassie. "God, thank you so much." But when I see her, *really* see her, my heart stops. "Wait, are you crying?"

"I'm fine," she whispers, holding her head high as she gently wipes a tear from her cheek. Her smile is as weak as her lie. "He's here, all is good. The show goes on and all that, right?"

Her face crumples, and I reach for her on instinct, pulling her into me and wrapping my arms around her. Her shoulders shake just slightly, her cries nearly silent as I hold her.

"Shhh," I whisper, kissing her forehead before pulling her in tighter and resting my chin on her head. "It's okay. Want me to kick his ass? Put auto-tune on his mic?"

She laughs into my chest. "He was just kind of snappy with me and said some things he didn't mean. He's got a lot going on. I get it, I do. He's just a little… different. That's all. But when we're alone, he's the same Grayson I know and lo—"

She doesn't finish the sentence, stiffening in my arms at the realization of the word that almost slipped out. I just hold her tighter and pretend like I didn't notice, like it wasn't a shotgun shell to the gut.

"Who the hell was that who bid on me?!"

Ashlei rushes the table in a flurry, eyes searching the crowd as Cassie sniffs and pulls away from me, crossing her arms over her chest. "Oh, the guy who bid ten-thousand out the gate? Yeah, we're all dying to know who he was, too."

"That's just insane," Ashlei says, hands flying. She pauses when she looks at Cassie again, no doubt noticing the red blotchy skin under her eyes, but she doesn't push for answers — not in front of me. Instead, she shakes her head and crosses her arms to mimic Cassie. "I mean, honestly, what college kid has that kind of money to throw around? And for an auto racing date that's worth *maybe* fifteen-hundred, if even."

"Maybe it was you who made it worth more to them?" I offer, trying to stick up for the poor sap.

She scoffs. "That's even more ridiculous."

A young girl with the biggest tits I've ever seen stuffed into a small tank top skips over to the table, handing us a check with a wide grin. "This is for the auto racing date with Ashlei Daniels," she says with a high-pitched voice.

"Mykayla?!"

She blinks, turning to Ashlei. "Oh! Hey, you. Good job up there. This event is really cool! I never really did any of this when I was in school. I lived at home and really only came to campus for class. Are you sticking around for Grayson Anderson? He is *so* swoon-worthy."

Cassie chews the inside of her cheek and I reach for her, grabbing her hand behind the table where no one can see. I smooth my thumb over her wrist and she closes her eyes with a sigh before squeezing my hand in return.

"Yeah, he's a hunk," Ashlei deadpans. "Mykayla, why did you bid on me?! And ten-thousand dollars?! Are you insane?!"

"Oh!" Mykayla shakes her head, dark blonde hair framing her rack as she giggles. "No, silly, it wasn't me. I'm here on behalf of Mr. Church."

Ashlei's face goes sheet white as Cassie and I exchange a look and a shrug.

"Mr. Church bid on me?"

"Uh-huh," Mykayla says, dragging out the words and bouncing on her heels. "He heard me talking about the concert and the auction. I just thought it was *so nice* of you to donate your time like that. And to risk going on a date with some random guy you don't know? That takes guts. He agreed, and he wanted to help the cause, so he sent me with a check. Isn't he the best boss ever?"

This time, Ashlei's face flushes red, and she slowly closes her mouth that has been hanging open since Mykayla started talking. "He's something."

Cassie gives Ashlei a look that says they'll be talking later just as Jeremy calls me backstage through my headpiece.

"I have to run," I say, nodding to Ashlei and Mykayla before turning to Cassie. The lights on the stage go black and the crowd roars, more than seven-thousand people on their feet for the asshole who made my favorite girl cry. I keep my eyes on her, ignoring the first note from Grayson's guitar. "You going to be okay?"

Cassie nods. "I'll be fine." She watches me, questions dancing in her eyes as the stage lights up again and the crowd goes even crazier. "Thank you, Adam."

"I'm always here," I remind her. Then, I lean forward, kissing her cheek with the same promise before jogging toward the stage.

# Erin

A FEW DAYS AFTER the Alpha Sigma concert, I turn twenty-one almost silently and without fuss — exactly how I want it. My sorority sisters bake me an adorable pink cake with white, polka-dot frosting, and my parents call me to let me know they've wired some birthday money into my account, but other than that, it's a normal Monday.

It's perfect.

Around nine, I'm just about to take off my makeup and pull out my planner to see what Tuesday has in store when my phone lights up with a text from Skyler.

**- SOS. I know it's your birthday but I need you. Can you throw on something cute and come to Ralph's? -**

I groan, thumbing out a polite "no" as fast as I can, but before I can send it, another one from her comes through.

**- Please. It's important. You know I wouldn't ask you to come if it wasn't. -**

This time I groan louder, but I know I can't leave my Little hanging. She's pretty self-sufficient, even when she has boy or family drama going on, so the fact that she's asking for me tells me she really does need someone.

I send a text back telling her to give me twenty minutes, rummaging through my clothes hamper to pull out the same dress I'd worn all day. It's a little too pink for Ralph's, but I don't feel like putting together another outfit, so it'll do.

When my makeup is touched up and my hair is re-straightened, I grab my phone and purse and head downstairs. The house is surprisingly quiet, only a few sisters studying silently in our small house library, and I wave at them on my way out the door.

There are usually cabs waiting all along Greek Row on the weekends to shuttle students to Ralph's and other off-campus bars, but since it's a Monday, I have to call one, and I wait patiently at the pickup point at the end of the road, going through social media on my phone as I wait.

I glance up when a cab from a different company than the one I ordered pulls up, dropping three tipsy students off before it pulls away again. Two of them stagger toward Greek Row, but the other stands completely frozen, eyes on me.

"Erin?"

I squint through the darkness, and when he takes two steps toward me and the light from the street light catches his face, my entire body goes into fight or flight mode. The hair on my arms sticks straight up, a chill racing from my heart to my toes as my pulse races to catch it. I want to run. I want to knee him in the balls. But more than anything, I don't want to do either of those things.

Because the last thing I want to give him is the satisfaction of knowing he's had any kind of effect on me at all.

"Oh, hi, Landon," I say casually, dropping my gaze back to my phone and pretending like I'm typing out a status update.

"Well, I'll be damned. Can't believe we're running into each other," he offers with a laugh that makes me want to grind my teeth and punch him in the mouth all at once. "How was your summer?"

"Fine."

Every inch of me squirms the closer he moves toward me, and a small part of me dares him to try something. I took self-defense classes all summer long and I'm dying to use them on him if he even so much as puts a pinky finger on me.

"Hey, look, I'm actually glad I ran into you. I wanted to thank you," he says, and I pause, fingers still hovering over my phone. "For being cool about what happened that night of formal. We were all so drunk," he adds with a laugh. A fucking *laugh*. "And it just got a little crazy. I appreciate you not being dramatic about it and causing more trouble than there needed to be."

Nausea rolls through me like a bad shot of alcohol, burning its way down my throat and back up again as I fight against it. My blood is cold, hands shaking as I grip my phone harder.

How fucking *dare* he.

The urge to send my knee flying into his groin and break his nose is almost too strong to contain now, but I use everything my mother taught me and do just that, settling for a sinister laugh of my own before tucking my phone away inside my purse just as my cab pulls up.

I step toward him, looking straight into his eyes, which makes him take a full step back.

"No worries. Your dick is so small, I barely felt anything, anyway."

His smile drops, and I blow him a kiss and wave my fingers in his face before dipping inside the back of the cab.

"Ralph's," I say to the driver, and then I nearly pass out, black and white spots invading my vision as I press one clammy hand hard against my forehead. I focus on my breathing, inhaling for eight seconds before holding the breath and letting it go even slower. I knew I would eventually run into Landon, but the way he just acted — so casual, like what happened didn't matter — it hurt worse than if he were cruel about it.

The farther we drive away, the harder it gets to breathe. I just want to go home, to my bed, but then I hear my mom's voice telling me to be strong, to not let that fucker get even one ounce of power from my emotions.

He hurt me, and now I want revenge.

In the back of this cab, I vow that I'll get it this semester. I don't know how, or when, but I will. And until then, I'll remind him every chance I get that what he did to me doesn't change who I am.

But even lies with intentions to heal are still lies.

My heart's still racing when the cab drops me off, and I walk as best I can with my ankles still shaking as I make my way to the entrance. Before I can tug the door open, Clinton flies out it, ushering me to the side of the building while casting a look over his shoulder to make sure he wasn't seen.

"Uh, hi to you, too, Bear. Care to tell me why you're blocking my entrance to Ralph's and sneaking around like a 007 agent?"

"Skyler doesn't need you," he says. "There's a surprise party inside. For your birthday."

My racing heart stops altogether at his words, deflating like a balloon as I cover my face with one hand and groan. "No. No, no, no, I don't *want* a party."

"I know. I know, that's why I stopped you before you went in. I didn't want you to get overwhelmed."

He's dressed in a bright orange polo and dark jeans, his sneakers matching his shirt, and a flat-billed hat finishing off the look. His cologne is strong and sweet, making me want to curl into him, my body reacting to the way his large arms nearly burst out of his sleeves before I can remind myself why that's a stupid reaction to have.

"Look," he says, bending down a little to catch my eyes with his. His hands find my arms and he steadies me, squeezing them gently. "Just pop in, act surprised, stay for a drink and then you can fake sick and I'll take you home, okay?"

"No," I say automatically. Ten minutes ago, I could have done what he was asking, but after running into Landon, just standing on my own is taking everything I have. "I can't."

"Come on," he urges. "Your sisters planned this for you. It's your twenty-first birthday, Erin. Just have a drink and—"

"I DON'T WANT A DRINK!" I scream, breaking loose from his hold on me. "That last time I drank

I was fucking *raped*, Bear," I remind him, my voice cracking on the word as tears threaten to break. I hold them back, not wanting to let the pain out. "And the time before that, I…"

My voice trails off, realizing what I was about to say, but Clinton doesn't let it go.

"You what? Slept with me?"

I shake my head, biting back the tears and wishing I could tell him it's so much more than that. If he only knew what happened after, he would understand.

But it would also kill him.

And he doesn't deserve that.

He scoffs, crossing his arms over his chest with his eyes on the parking lot behind me. "Fine. Just leave. I'll tell them you got food poisoning and you were throwing up the minute the cab dropped you off so I sent you back."

I nod, glancing at him with the only thank you I have in my eyes. I can't say another word, and he doesn't ask for one, just sighs and shakes his head as he starts toward the entrance again. I take out my phone to call the cab back, but before I can dial the number, his voice stops me.

"I know what happened that night, Erin. I was there. I saw it," he reminds me, his voice the shaky one now. "That's why I'm here. That's why

I'm pushing. You may have toughened your skin over the summer and shoved all your feelings on it down into some box with a bolted lid, but one day that lid is going to pop off from the pressure, and I just want you to know you have someone to go to when it does."

His words are like numbing cream, drying up my tears as I hold the phone to my ear to order another cab and he disappears inside again without another look from me. He may believe he's right, but I can't — because going through the pain of opening that box again would be more than I could handle. It would kill me, and I'm not ready to die.

So, as I climb into the back of the new cab, I seal the box shut a little tighter, add a few more bolts, and swallow back the tears I never want to let fall again.

Maybe someone can see my scars, after all.

Episode 3

# Skyler

I HAVE NO IDEA what I'm doing.

Not just in the current moment as I pack my books for a day full of classes, but in life, in general. Up until right now, the only thing I've ever known to be certain is that I love to play poker. Period. The end. But that's about all I have.

Sure, I like to flirt with boys and party with my sisters, but unfortunately, there's neither a career path for those kinds of hobbies nor is there anything such as a Professional Paddleboarder or Dynamite Donut Eater that I'm aware of. So, over the summer, I asked myself if poker was really what I wanted to do for the rest of my life, because it was the only sure thing I had that could potentially be a career.

It wasn't an easy question to answer.

I love poker, that much is easy for anyone to see. But can I imagine a life of always traveling, always hustling, always wondering if I'd make the next tournament or be able to perform in it? Can I see myself getting married or raising a family and somehow battling poker tabloids at the same time?

I don't have those answers, and I didn't find them over the summer. So, I filled my schedule with classes in all fields of study, hoping to find something that will stick. My first two years at Palm South University were a breeze, mostly filled with general education courses that were similar to high school in content, just more intense. But this semester, I'll be diving into five different subject areas to see if anything sticks.

God, help me.

"You're a mess," Ashlei says with a laugh as she watches me pack my books for the day.

I have my Nonprofit Organizations class today, inspired by Jarrett's most recent job acquisition, followed by Judicial Process and Politics, just in case I want to go pre-law, and finally, Stagecraft I. My mother was into theatre when she was in high school, so I figured maybe it's in my blood. And this is just for my Monday and Wednesday classes. On Tuesdays and Thursdays, I have Principles of Advertising and Introduction to Elementary Education.

Something is bound to stick.

"It's like being at a delicious buffet," I say defensively, zipping up my blue and green Vera Bradley bag when all my books are in place. "I have to load up my plate and try a little of everything before I can decide what I actually want to eat a substantial amount of. In the end, I'll be stuffed and happy."

"Or you'll vomit."

I glare at her as she hops down from Jess's bed, linking arms with me with a laugh.

"I'm just giving you a hard time. I'm glad you're exploring options, Sky. It'll be fun."

"Not as fun as your bad-ass internship," I counter as we make our way downstairs.

It's a bustling Monday morning in the sorority house, girls flying every which way, hair half-done and protein bars in hand. Some are heading out to the gym, some coming back, the rest of us somewhere between classes, internships, jobs, or on-campus activities. Erin was out the door by six AM, which surprises absolutely no one.

"It really has been such a blast, but the real work is starting now. I thought I was busy before," Ashlei says with a sigh. "I had no idea. I want to knock the socks off of this client when we meet with them in a few weeks to pitch the event launch concepts."

"You'll do amazing," I assure her, squeezing her arm before breaking our link as she heads toward the door and I toward the kitchen. "Still on for a girly movie night?"

"Definitely. I'll smuggle in some wine."

"My girl."

Ashlei throws me a wink and then she's out the door, and I make my way to the kitchen, snagging a banana and to-go cup of coffee for my walk to the Business building.

Even in the sticky September morning air, it feels good to be back on the PSU campus. The classes are challenging, the boys are hotter than Hades, and the parties are just as wild as ever. It's home, but there is one thing missing.

Clinton's smile.

I haven't seen it, the *real* Clinton smile, ever since Omega Chi was put on a one-year suspension. I can't blame him for feeling down, and even though he's been trying his best to put on a happy face at the Alpha Sigma parties and social events, I know inside he's miserable. Between his little brother living with a friend in Pittsburgh and everything going on with his fraternity, it's a wonder he can even force a fake smile.

But that's what he's wearing nowadays, and today is no different as I round the corner of the Student Union and meet him in our usual place. We walk to the Business building together every Monday and Wednesday, me for my first class of the day and him for his second, hence meeting outside of the Union instead of on Greek Row.

Clinton is leaned up against the dark brick at the side of the building, his gaze distant as I make my way toward him. He still looks as fresh as ever, red and black Air Jordans matching the Nike design on his casual t-shirt and Omega Chi hat turned a little to the side. He's grown a little scruff on his chin since the beginning of the semester, and I run a knuckle over it when I reach him.

"So manly with your little beard," I tease.

He shakes his head, ridding himself of whatever thoughts he was focused on before I got there and smiles down at me, though it's still not the real smile I know and love. "The ladies like a little friction, if you know what I mean."

"Gross," I say with a laugh, nudging him. "But also true."

This time he laughs, throwing his arm over my shoulders as we make our way across campus.

There are few people in the world I love as much as Clinton, which is why it breaks my heart that no matter what we talk about, and no matter what he *says* about how he's feeling, I can read the truth in his eyes. He's sad, he's broken, and when I get that way, I know the only thing that makes me feel better is going home for a while.

So, when he drops me off at my classroom, I pull out my phone before class starts and book two flights to Pittsburgh for next weekend, screenshotting the confirmation and texting it to Clinton.

**- Pack your bags. It's time for a bestie trip.**

# *Cassie*

"YOU KNOW," ERIN SAYS, a little out of breath as she wipes the sweat from her forehead. "Guys complain about sweaty balls, but they have no idea the torture of sweaty underboob."

I chuckle, glancing up at her from where I'm seated on the turf that stretches in front of the fountain. Less than two weeks ago it was the setting for the Alpha Sigma concert, and in less than a week it will be home to the Kappa Kappa Beta Dodgeball Tournament.

"At least we have a little cloud cover," I offer optimistically.

"Ugh, it's just so muggy," she counters, squinting up at the sky before watching me hammer in another peg for the fence we're putting up to outline the dodgeball court boundaries. "When you're finished here, can you come help me with the referee stands?"

"Absolutely! Be right over."

"Thanks," she says, still eyeing me. She watches me work for another moment before throwing up her hands in exasperation. "How are you this cheery when we're all sweating like pigs and working like men in this God-awful Florida heat? It's gross. And it's creeping me out. Stop it."

I laugh, shrugging as I stand and dust the grass off the back of my shorts. "I can't help it. Grayson is finally taking me on a date tonight. Nothing can bring me down today, Ex. Not even underboob sweat."

"Ugh, fine. Can you at least fake a frown for me?"

I give her my best scowl, but we both end up breaking into giggles as we maneuver through the field of girls toward the referee stands.

"So, where's Mr. Perfect taking you?"

"There's a really fancy steakhouse on the water that he wants to take me to for dinner, and then we're going to walk the beach and you know… I'm sure we'll end up back at his place."

I blush, biting my lip at the thought of Grayson's hands on me. After the rough few weeks we've had, I'm looking forward to having one-on-one time with him, to having time with *my* Grayson — not the one who lives on stage.

"Okay, now I understand why you're all smiley," Erin says, flipping through a few pages of her clipboard. "Think you guys will finally have sex?"

My cheeks heat even more. "I don't know… maybe. I guess we'll see how the night goes. But if

I were a betting woman like Skyler... well, I'd put my money on yes."

Erin eyes me for a second, her brows bent like she's worried about my decision. But that doesn't make any sense, since she's more pro-Grayson than anyone.

Her eyes are soft as she grabs my elbow and squeezes it gently. "Well, just be careful, okay, Grandlittle? Protection and all that."

"Oh, my God. Stop mothering me and go boss someone around. That'll make you feel better."

She laughs, but it's small and soft. "Can't argue with that logic. Let me know before you head out for your big date, okay?"

"Will do."

Erin watches me for a moment more with a slight smile, then she snaps back into business mode, flipping through the pages on her clipboard once more and barking out orders at every girl she passes as she crosses the field.

My stomach catches flight with butterflies as I get to work on the referee stand, helping two of our newer sisters build it from the ground up. It's actually a nice distraction to work with my hands for a while, especially considering my mind is completely in the clouds. I can't stop imagining what the night will be like, what he'll wear, how the food will taste, what conversation we'll have, how amazing it will feel to have my hand in his as we walk the beach at night.

Grayson has been so busy, and after our little fight at the Alpha Sigma concert, we really need the alone time. He was stressed that night, running from his solo performance at a coffee shop in an upscale neighborhood back to campus for the concert. He didn't answer my calls the first few times I tried to reach him, and when he finally called me back, he went off on me for blowing up his phone when I knew he was at another performance. The truth was I hadn't remembered it was supposed to go that late, and I was just trying to help Adam.

I can still hear the bite in his voice, the snap of it, a sound so unfamiliar to me. He'd blamed me for putting the pressure on him by making him agree to do the Alpha Sigma concert, and said some things about Greek life that I always knew he felt, but never thought he would say. It hurt, and made me feel about two inches tall.

Grayson apologized, of course, and he held me that night after the concert, kissing away any last tears I had to shed over our fight. Then he promised me more dates and more time spent together, and I promised to be more understanding of his new lifestyle.

I'm beginning to realize that relationships take work. Sure, the passion and butterflies are amazing, but to really survive as a couple, you have to compromise. You have to work together. And I'm happy to do that with Grayson, because I believe in us. And the more I learn about him, the more I fall for him.

I think I might be falling in love.

The admission makes me giddy again, and I bite back the stupid smile spreading on my face as I try to keep up with the conversation my sisters are having about what outfits they want to wear for our next social. But when the last stand is finished and I'm free to go back to the house and get ready for my date, I let the butterflies take me over, wings tickling my ribs as I practically skip home.

I scan through my outfit options the entire way back, wondering what he will wear, wondering how he will look when he sees me all dressed up. I imagine his fingers sliding the straps of my favorite emerald green dress down over my shoulders, my eyes fluttering shut at the thought of his hands moving to the long zipper on the side. It's impossible to know how everything will happen, but one thing I know for sure.

Tonight will be amazing.

Tonight is the worst night of my life.

Okay, that might be a little dramatic, but it's definitely in the top five. Here I am, dressed in my favorite green dress just like I imagined, except there won't be any hands sliding it off me tonight. My hair is pulled into an elegant up-do, a few tendrils hanging to frame my face, which is absolutely flawless after an hour of makeup application, and I borrowed Erin's beautiful nude heels that wrap at the ankle with a ribbon. But none of it matters.

Because Grayson bailed.

He was sweet about it, of course, and regretful. His agent booked him a last-minute show and he couldn't turn it down. He promised he'd make it up to me and told me there'd be a ticket at the door with my name on it if I wanted to show up, but I politely declined. I tried to hide my disappointment, but I know he saw right through me.

And the bigger part of me hoped he did.

But now I'm all dressed up with nothing to do, salivating for a delicious steak I won't get to eat, and yearning to be held on the beach by my boyfriend who is across town on a stage singing to a group of swooning girls, instead.

Sighing, I pull my phone from my clutch, thumbing through the contacts to find Skyler's name. I know she'll know exactly what to say to make me feel better, but for some reason I can't get my thumb to drop the last inch to dial her number. I don't even want to talk to anyone, I just want to be miserable.

Pity party, table for one.

So, I let my feet carry me, the adorable heels feeling more and more like medieval torture devices with every step as I meander aimlessly around campus with my mind on Grayson. I wonder if this is really our new normal, if this is how it's going to be now — cancelled plans and IOUs.

My stomach growls as I pass the food court, so I head for my favorite pizza place, the bell above the door announcing my arrival with a sad ding. Pie Heaven sells pizza slices the size of your face, and that's exactly the kind of cure I need right now.

"Two Hawaiians," I say when I reach the counter, knowing full well there's absolutely zero chance of me finishing two slices but ready to give it the college try, anyway. "And a garlic knot. And a large Coke."

The girl behind the counter lifts one eyebrow at

me, looking behind me like I brought a friend.

"Nope, no one else, honey. It's just me and a testy appetite, so stop judging and tell me what I owe you."

A laugh breaks loose at a booth to my right and I snap my head to the source of it, heart stopping when I find Adam staring back at me.

"Easy, killer," he says, lifting himself from the booth and pulling his wallet from his pocket. He slides the cashier his card, eyeing me with amusement as she runs it through the machine. "You and that testy appetite of yours want some company?"

I try to glare at him, but a smile breaks loose and I flop into the booth dramatically. He chuckles, bringing the tray with my pizza and drink over to the table before sliding in on the other side.

"Wanna talk about it?" he asks, pushing the parmesan cheese and red pepper flakes toward me.

I shake fresh parmesan on my first slice and shrug, keeping my eyes on the pizza. "Grayson and I were supposed to go on a date tonight but he bailed last minute. It's fine," I say quickly, feeling a little bad talking about Grayson to Adam. Even if I am upset, I already know how Adam feels about Grayson. "He apologized and he's going to make it up to me, but I'm just a little bummed."

"That's understandable," he says, the weight of his eyes still on me as I take my first bite. "But sometimes things come up. I'm sure he's just as sad as you are that he had to cancel."

I pause mid-bite, glancing up at Adam. *There has to be a hint of sarcasm there somewhere*, I think, but find no traces when I search his eyes. He seems genuine, and for some reason that brings the dead butterflies in the pit of my stomach back to life.

"You look beautiful, by the way," he says, his voice softer.

I swallow, cheeks flushing as I reach for my drink.

"Thank you, Adam."

He smiles, finishing off his own pizza before changing the subject. He asks me how my classes are going and tells me all about the concert aftermath and his time as president so far. I fill him in on the dodgeball tournament prep and he tells me about the summer spent with his aunt, the one whom he lived with after his grandpa passed away. After an hour passes, the sadness I felt from Grayson cancelling is like a dull ache in the back of my mind. After two, it's gone completely, and I'm laughing and eating too much instead of feeling sorry for myself.

"I was thinking about going back to the A Sig

house and putting on a movie," Adam says when the same cashier who rang us up starts wiping down tables and putting the chairs on top. It's almost eleven. "You're more than welcome to join, if you want to."

His eyes are hopeful as he waits for my response, and a wave rushes through me at the thought of spending more time with him. We always have so much fun, but a bigger part of me knows it's the feeling I have when I'm with him that I want to hold onto. I should feel guilty for wanting it at all, but I don't.

Still, I have a head on my shoulders, and I know when to walk away from trouble.

"I think I should probably get back to the house," I say, gathering our empty plates onto one tray. "I have class pretty early."

Adam smiles, shrugging it off. "No biggie. Maybe another time."

We clean up our table and Adam waves to a guy back in the kitchen before holding the door open for me, the bell sounding a little less sad this time as I step into the warm summer night.

Adam walks me to the Kappa Kappa Beta house, carrying the conversation easily until we reach the front steps. I turn to face him, folding my arms over my chest as he slides his hands easily into his pockets with his eyes on mine. It's quiet on campus now, only a few other students still out, the soft rush of water from the fountain filling most of the silence.

"Thank you for tonight," I say softly.

He watches me for a moment longer, and instead of responding, he untucks his hands from his pockets and reaches for me, pulling me into his chest.

I hate this feeling.

It's the feeling reserved for Adam, the one only he can elicit from me. He owns it. No one else has ever made my body react the way it does when we're in situations like this, his arms around me, my head on his chest, boundaries between us that feel invisible and like barbed wire all at once. He looks at me, my stomach tightens. He holds me, my chest aches. He lets me go, whispering a goodnight before turning to walk away, and everything I've ever known about how to breathe disappears.

I hate this feeling.

I hope it never goes away.

# Jess

THE AIRPORT IS SURPRISINGLY busy for a Wednesday evening, men in business suits and families dressed in Mickey Mouse gear speeding by me in both directions as I wait at the bottom of the escalator.

Jarrett's plane landed ten minutes ago, which means he should be coming down the escalator toward baggage claim any second now. I can't stop bouncing, my hands a little shaky as I wring them together and watch the top of the moving stairs, waiting to see that glorious bald head.

Boys never make me nervous — ever. But I haven't seen Jarrett since he left for his internship at the very beginning of the summer, and that was right after I admitted out loud that I loved him. Sure, video chatting has been a nice distraction, but it's no substitute for the real thing. Just imagining his hands on me, his lips on mine, his body — so hard, covered with tattoos… it's enough to make me come in a crowded airport before even setting eyes on him.

I pull out my phone, checking the time once more before shoving it in my back pocket again. A few more minutes pass and I debate calling him, but just as I go to grab my phone again, he appears at the top of the escalator.

And time stops.

Seconds stretch and tick as I take him in — his tan, smooth head, the scruff lining his jaw, the way his simple, navy t-shirt hugs the muscles on his arms and chest, tapering off at his narrow waist. And when my eyes find his, when the corner of his mouth quirks up in a small smirk, I can't take it anymore.

I run to him.

"Excuse me, sorry, excuse me." I push through the other travelers on the stairs, working against gravity as they move down and I try to move up… up to him.

Jarrett cracks a wider smile watching me struggle, nearly laughing by the time I reach him and throw my arms around his neck, pressing my lips to his with a sigh of relief. His strong arm holds me close and lifts me from the ground, my feet dangling just a few inches above the escalator stairs as he kisses me with everyone watching. His other hand dips into my hair as one arm holds me steady against him, and I tug him closer by his shirt, wanting more, needing him closer.

"I've missed you so much," I whisper against his lips, kissing him before he can answer.

He wraps both arms around me when we reach the bottom of the escalator, making sure we're on solid ground before he drops my feet down. I'm still holding his shirt, feeling the fabric between my fingers, rolling it around to make sure it's real.

*He's here.*

"I've missed you, too," he says, pulling back to look into my eyes. His are still the same deep mocha, gold spiraling out from each pupil as he scans my body the way I did his. "Let's grab my bag and get out of here."

We can't keep our hands off each other, not the entire time we wait in baggage claim or on the walk to the taxi lane as I run over everything I have planned for the long weekend. We only have five days together, and I plan to make the most of it.

"I can't believe you're going to introduce me to your sisters," he says when we slide into the backseat of a black sedan. I tell the driver the address of Jarrett's hotel and she smiles politely with a nod.

"It's about damn time."

"Well, we couldn't exactly broadcast our relationship before."

"No," I agree. "But now, I'm going to show you off like a pack of gel pens at show and tell. Everyone on campus is going to know you're mine by the time you leave."

Jarrett chuckles, eyeing the driver's rearview mirror before leaning in to nuzzle my neck. "You wanna show me off, huh?" His voice is low and gravelly, one hand sliding up the inside of my thigh and up to the hem of my jean shorts.

My eyes flutter closed at the contact of his skin on mine, chills racing up to my core. "Mm-hmm," I manage in answer.

"What if I don't want to leave the hotel room?"

He slips two fingers up under the denim fabric of my shorts, brushing the tips against my panties. I bite my lip hard, squirming under his touch, eyes opening just enough to make sure the driver isn't looking at us in her mirror.

I can't even respond, especially when his lips find my neck again. He kisses me softly, fingers running along the edge of my panties before he dips them inside. My lips are pinned between my teeth to hold back my moans, but when Jarrett circles my clit twice and then slides both fingers inside me at once, I nearly combust, letting out a loud pant as my eyes snap open.

The driver glances back at us and Jarrett rests his head on my shoulder. I offer her a smile and she narrows her eyes, but focuses them back on the road again, and as soon as she does, Jarrett withdraws his fingers and slides them in again, wiggling his fingertips to curl against my G-spot.

He continues his slow, quiet assault the entire drive, and by the time we reach the hotel, I'm two feather-light touches away from orgasming in the back of a fucking taxi cab.

Jarrett pays the driver as I sprint inside to the front desk, checking in with weak knees and an unbearable ache between my thighs. I swipe the keys from the counter as soon as the girl tells me our room number and barrel back outside, grabbing Jarrett's hand and leading him inside through the lobby to the elevators.

"Room 813," I pant as the elevator doors close, pushing him against the wall. I cover his mouth with mine as he fumbles to push the button for the eighth floor. He runs his hands down my ribs and to my ass, cupping it firmly and pulling me flush against him as we ride up. The seam of my jean shorts rubs me in the spot I'm aching most and I gasp into his mouth, my orgasm already within reach. One more touch and I'll fall apart.

Jarrett's lips don't leave mine as we stumble down the hall to our room, him pulling his suitcase behind him as my hands get to work on his belt. He taps the plastic card to the scanner on our door and shoves us through, dropping his suitcase right behind the door before picking me up and carrying me to one of the beds.

"Two beds?" he asks, breaking our kiss long enough to appraise the room.

"I asked for a king, probably a mistake. Want me to run downstairs and have them fix it?"

"Are you kidding?" he asks, looking back down at me with a wicked grin. "I'm going to fuck you on both of them." He drops down on top of me, sucking the skin on my neck between his teeth and letting it go with a pop as I cry out at the sensation. "And then the floor. And the shower." He kisses me again. "And that chair over there." Another kiss. "And that desk. *Definitely* that fucking desk."

I giggle against his mouth as he unzips my shorts and tugs them down my thighs. I've missed him, mind and soul, but it's his body that calls to mine first, begging to be touched, to be fucked. My eyes can't devour him long enough, can't get their fill of him before he touches me in a way that has them fluttering closed again.

I wiggle my legs back and forth to help him with my shorts, making quick work of my tank top and bra in the process. When he hooks his thumbs under the lace of my panties and slides them down my legs, slowly pulling them one by one from each ankle at the end, he runs his tongue across his bottom lip and pulls me up until I'm on my knees in front of him.

"I want that perfect fucking pussy on my face," he growls, tugging my hair back with both hands and running his tongue along my jaw. "Now."

And this is why I want everyone to know this man is mine.

Jarrett moves quickly until he's on his back on the bed and I rip his shirt up and over his head, tossing it to the side before crawling up his body. I take my time, reveling in the feel of him underneath me. The man I was never supposed to have, now the only one I ever want.

What has he done to me?

I kiss every tattoo on the way up, tracing the ones I know with my tongue, eyeing the new ones with appreciation until both of my knees are braced on either side of his face.

And then, his mouth is on me.

I gasp at the feel of him, my orgasm already so close I can feel the first tingles climbing. His tongue circles my clit before he sucks it gently between his teeth, hands smacking my ass and pulling me closer to him. I arch my back, crying out with loud moans as I ride his face. Each swirl of his tongue sends me closer to the edge, and when he slides two fingers deep inside me, working them like I'm riding his dick, I go flying.

His name is on my lips as I cry out, nails digging into the headboard, orgasm rocking me from the inside out. A numbing fire consumes every inch of me until I shake and shudder around him, and I barely have time to recover before he flips us.

Jarrett kisses me hard, the taste of me fresh on his tongue, his hands hard on my thighs as he drags me to the edge of the bed. He breaks contact long enough to strip out of his jeans and boxer briefs and then my ankles are on his shoulders and he slides inside me mercilessly, filling me with a moan, his head dropping back.

"Oh, my God," I moan with him, fists twisting in the sheets as he wraps his hands around my thighs and pounds into me again. Every thrust hits deeper, and Jarrett lets my ankles fall to the side, leaning down to suck one nipple between his teeth as he curls his back, pushing in again and again, each time with more purpose than the last.

And it's this I'll never get enough of. The touching, the kissing, the fucking. It's this that reminds me that no matter the distance or the time, what we have is real. It sparks to life as soon as we're together again, like no time has passed, like nothing can ever come between us.

Unstoppable. That's what we are.

Pressing a hand hard into Jarrett's chest, I push him back until he slips out of me, the backs of his legs hitting the edge of the opposite bed. I follow, dropping to my knees in front of him, running my hands along the hard length of him in appreciation.

"I've missed this fucking dick so much," I say, glancing up at Jarrett. He smirks, but as soon as I wrap my mouth around the tip of him, any trace of a smile fades and his eyes roll back as he groans.

I work him into my mouth slowly, sliding down farther each time until he's coated and wet. When I slide my lips all the way down to the base of him, fighting against the gag, he curses, flexing his hips forward. I pull back, circling my tongue over his crown before dipping down again, this time holding my breath so he can fuck my throat.

When I palm his tight balls, I know he's close, but he grabs me by the arms and yanks me up, kissing me hard once before spinning me around until my hands are braced on the other bed we've yet to fuck on.

I climb up, braced on my hands and knees, and Jarrett slides his wet cock down the line of my ass before slipping inside my pussy again. He feels bigger in this position, every inch of him stretching me open as I arch my back and flip my hair back for him to grab.

"I want you to come again," he pants, hips rolling and pushing him in deeper.

"Fuck, I don't know if I can."

"Do you trust me?" he asks, tugging my hair and leaning down to suck the skin of my neck.

I gasp, his cock so deep inside me now I'm seeing stars. "Yes," I breathe, and Jarrett runs his thumb along my bottom lip before dipping it inside my mouth. I suck it gently, rolling my tongue all the way down to the knuckle and back.

Jarrett groans, pulling his thumb from my mouth and sliding his hand down my back, over my ass. Then, before I have time to register it, I feel a pinch, and that same thumb slides inside my ass.

"Oh, fuck," I cry out, the new sensation rocking through me. He pounds in deeper, thumb working in the same rhythm, and it only takes seconds for me to fall apart again. I come hard, fire scorching me from the inside, and my moans are all it takes for Jarrett to come with me.

We ride out our orgasms until the very last tingle, Jarrett slowly removing his thumb, both of us panting for air when he drops to the bed beside me and pulls me into his chest.

I'm completely sated, thighs and hip flexors already sore as I trace my fingers over his abdomen and up to his chest, outlining the fresh ink there. It's a brightly colored hourglass piece, sharp reds and purples lining the wings that frame the glass, the sand trickling down slowly, top half more full than the bottom.

"I love this," I whisper softly, still running my fingertips over the swollen skin.

Jarrett pulls me closer, pressing his lips to my forehead. "And I love you."

I smile, rolling until I'm on top of him, my hair falling down to frame us under the curtains. "Well, two beds down. But we didn't make it to the floor… or the shower… or the chair… or the desk."

"Oh," Jarrett says with a smirk, hand sliding along my jaw before tucking into my hair and pulling my lips to his. "That was just round one. We're not leaving this room until morning, I hope you know that."

And so I smile, order us a pizza, and buckle in for round two.

"I'm really glad I got to do dinner with you before Bear and I leave for Pittsburgh, Jarrett," Skyler says just as another round of margaritas is dropped off at our table. "Seeing your eyes light up when you talk about your job… I need to find something like that."

Jarrett is completely surrounded by girls as we gobble up the last of our burritos and tacos at the best Mexican place off campus. Skyler and Erin sit across the table while Cassie flanks his left side,

Ashlei and I rounding out the right side. And for the last two hours, he's been drilled with questions, and he's handled it like an absolute champ.

"You get like that with poker," Erin points out, tipping her glass toward Skyler.

"Yeah, but can that really be a career? Like, a forever thing?"

"If it's what you really love, why not?" Jarrett asks.

He makes a good point, and Skyler chews her cheek.

"It seems like that's how you feel about your job, Jarrett. Like you really love it and there's nothing else you want or need to be happy," Cassie adds.

Jarrett smirks, casting a glance at me before tucking me under his arm. He presses a kiss into my hair, holding me close. "There is one thing."

The girls sigh in sync, and I can't help but swoon a little myself. After spending all night with him in the hotel last night, I didn't think the trip could get any better. But we spent the day at the beach together, and now he's getting along with all of the people who are important to me.

I thought I couldn't get in any deeper with him, but here I am, sinking without a single care to save myself.

Jarrett tips my chin up and kisses me sweetly

before turning the conversation back to Cassie and her plans to go pre-med. All I can do is watch him, eyes memorizing the sharp edges of his nose, the line of his jaw, the curve of his small smile as he listens to my best friends tell him about themselves. An ache rolls through me at the thought of him leaving again, not knowing when I'll see him, not knowing how long we'll be long distance.

Jarrett is so good at being alone. He was a loner when I met him, perfectly content in his one-bedroom apartment taking care of himself. He's had to his entire life, ever since his mother passed away when he was thirteen. I didn't even know he'd gone through that, not until he was taking care of me when I was sick last semester.

He's self-sufficient. Independent. Completely fine on his own.

But I need him.

Before Jarrett, I didn't need anyone, either. I *wanted* guys, sure — but just to get me off. I was perfectly content doing it myself if the right guy wasn't around, and when they were around, that was all I needed them for.

But Jarrett snuck inside my heart. He opened me up when I was sure the doors were locked forever. I was like a succulent, needing little attention to survive, and now he's transformed me into a weak little rose in the palm of his hand, desperate for his care.

I've never felt so vulnerable, and it scares the ever-loving shit out of me.

"I've got this," Jarrett says when the waitress brings our bill, and all of the girls light up, their eyes catching mine. They know it, too — how deep I'm in — and I wonder if they're happy for me or worried how they'll save me when it all goes up in flames.

Jarrett holds me close to him as we walk the short distance to Ralph's, one hand tucked into the back pocket of my jeans. We fall a little behind the group, and I feel him watching me.

"Stop overthinking," he says. "You've got self-sabotage written all over that beautiful face of yours."

I chuckle, leaning into him. "I'm just going to miss you, that's all."

"I just got here."

"But you'll still leave in three days."

Jarrett frowns, pulling me to a stop when we reach the parking lot of Ralph's. I wave the other girls to go in without us, keeping my eyes on my feet when it's just Jarrett and me.

"Do you remember what you asked me that day I took care of you when you had that nasty sinus infection?" Jarrett asks, knuckle finding my chin and forcing me to look at him. "You asked me how long it would take you to chase me away. And what was my answer?"

"You can't chase someone who's not running."

Jarrett nods, his dark eyes searching mine. "I'm still not running, Jess. Distance hasn't changed the way I feel about you, and it won't change our relationship if we don't let it. I know this is hard." He pauses, Adam's apple bobbing in his throat. "I know I'm asking you to love a man you can't always touch, and I know that's not fair."

"And I know how important this opportunity is to you," I counter, leaning into his touch.

He frames my face with his hand, thumb rubbing the line of my jaw. "You're important to me, too."

"I know."

For a long moment he just holds me, and I watch him, knowing I'm not making it easier for him to stick to his decision when I make him doubt us in any way.

"We're going to make it through this," I whisper. "I won't lie and say I'm not scared, but we'll be okay. I know we will."

Jarrett sighs, relief washing over him as he tugs me into his chest and wraps his arms all the way around me. I inhale the smell of him, wishing I could bottle it up, wishing I could keep us in this moment forever.

"Want to throw me in the back closet for old time's sake?" I ask with a grin, pulling back from his hold and grabbing his hand to lead him inside.

He smacks my ass with a smile of his own. "You've got to find some cowgirl boots first. You know, to keep the memory authentic."

I laugh as we dip inside the glass doors, joining the girls along with Clinton, Adam, and a whole slew of their brothers. And the rest of the night is easy, Jarrett getting along with everyone he talks to, and me letting go of my fears, if even just for the night. We dance and laugh, drink and play, and when last call comes and goes and I'm back in the sheets with Jarrett, I know only one thing really matters.

I'm in love with a man who loves me, too.

Whether it's forever or just for right now, I vow to make the most of every minute I can say that.

# Skyler

IT'S A BEAUTIFUL, SUNNY day in Franklin Park, a borough right outside of Pittsburgh where Mac's family lives. We're all seated at a large picnic table in their backyard, plates of ribs and potato salad and everything in-between piled high around us.

Clinton warned me that the weather was pretty unpredictable in Pittsburgh in September, so I packed everything from shorts to a thick rain jacket, but we were welcomed by a temperature in the mid-seventies and blue skies with puffy white clouds slowly flowing by. After melting in South Florida for the past few months, it's a nice change.

What's even nicer is the change I've seen in Clinton.

It's been a short trip, but even just a few days spent with his baby brother has brightened him back into the Clinton I know and love. We went to a Pirates game, let Mac and Clayton show us around their new school, and even took the cable car up the Duquesne Incline for touristy pictures since this is my first time to the city. But the truth is it wouldn't have mattered what we did while we were here. Just being with Clayton has made Clinton smile again, and that's all I ever wanted.

"Needless to say, she's begging for me to take her to homecoming," Clayton says, finishing his story about a girl in his math class. He scoops a big heap of macaroni and cheese onto his plate before passing the bowl to his big brother. "But I mean, I don't want to rush into anything. I've got decisions to make. So many choices, you know?"

Mac rolls his eyes. "Yeah, so many. Her, your right hand, however will you choose?"

Everyone laughs, except Clayton, who grabs a toothpick from the small holder and pegs Mac in the nose with it.

"Clayton likes to pretend like he's such a little thug," Mac's mom says, her voice sweet and slow like molasses. She's a little shorter than me, with a tiny button nose and dark freckles on the apples of her caramel cheeks. "But he's a good kid. Finished eighth grade with straight A's last year and seems to be on the same path in high school. And he does it all while juggling football, too."

"It's true," Mac's sister, Kia, agrees. "Already making a name for himself and he's only been in high school for a couple of months."

"Yeah, makes me look bad. Thanks a lot, Clayton," Mac chimes in.

It's hard to tell if Clayton is blushing, but he wears a shy smile, forking up a few macaroni noodles before popping them in his mouth.

Clinton is beaming, his chest puffed out with pride like a dad. "That's my baby brother. What position are you playing now that you're in high school?"

"Wide receiver."

"And what are your stats so far this season?"

He shrugs. "Well, we've only had a few games, but so far I've got a little over three-hundred receiving yards and four touchdowns."

"That's really good, Baby Bear," I say, winking with the use of his favorite nickname. "Especially for a freshman."

Clinton's smile takes up his entire face, and he puts his fork down, turning to his little brother in earnest. "I'm really proud of you, Clayton. Keep up this hard work and you'll get to go to any college you want to."

"I want to go to PSU," he says easily, mirroring Clinton's smile. "Just like you."

It's a private moment between big brother and little brother, and Mac's dad feels it, too, turning the conversation to me to give them a moment as Clinton claps Clayton on the shoulder with pride in his eyes.

"So, Skyler," Mr. Harrison says between bites of his ribs, his fingers covered in barbecue sauce. "Bear tells us you're entering a pretty big poker tournament this upcoming summer."

"I haven't officially decided yet, but I'm seriously considering it."

"What's holding you back?" he asks, pushing his glasses up the bridge of his long nose. Such a simple question with such a complicated answer.

"It's just a lot more intense than the tournaments I've been in so far. Don't get me wrong, I think I'm ready, but at the same time it's a lot of money to potentially lose."

"Or potentially win," Clinton counters.

I blush, squeezing a little lemon in my iced tea before taking a drink. "I just want to think about it for a while longer, but I'm leaning toward entering. I'm confident in my skills, so really, what do I have to lose?"

"Ah, worst thing that could happen is you get humbled a little," Mrs. Harrison says. "And from what Bear has told us about you, you're already humble and kind anyway. So, my bet is that you'll end up winning or at least give it hell trying, which is a great experience either way."

"Very true, Mrs. Harrison." I smile, my wheels turning the rest of dinner as the conversation easily floats from person to person.

Could I really win it?

It's been heavy on my mind all summer, especially after I won a pretty large tournament in

Reno at the end of July. But the American Poker Club tournament is a completely different level. All the big players will be there — ones I've defeated and ones I've been defeated by.

The poker blogs are calling me the next big thing in poker, the next big champ. Can I prove them right?

After the ribs are scarfed down and an entire cherry cheesecake is devoured, Clayton and I work on washing the dishes inside while everyone else cleans up the picnic table and grill. I take the job of washing and rinsing while he dries, but after a few minutes of easy conversation, Clayton grows quiet.

"Has it been nice seeing Bear this weekend?" I ask, handing him one of the large casserole dishes.

He smiles, and it's then that I notice how big he is. I just saw him six months ago, but he's already growing more and more into a young man every single day.

"It's always amazing to have him around. I miss him, but I'm glad he trusts me to live with Mac and his family. I was so worried he was going to drop PSU." He turns to me then. "I guess I kind of have you to thank for helping me convince him to stay."

I shrug. "Ah, Bear just wants you to be okay. He still has a level head. Just have to knock some sense into it sometimes," I add with a laugh.

Clayton smiles, but it fades quickly, his eyes on the dish he's drying.

"Are you, Clayton?" I ask after a moment. "Okay, I mean."

He nods. "Yeah. Clinton is doing everything he can to help me while also taking care of his own expenses, but it's rough, you know? Football is expensive. Mac's mom lets me do some chores around the house for a little extra money, but it's not much, and I'm not old enough to get a job anywhere. At least, not at the places I've applied."

"I get that," I say. "Have you talked to Clinton about it?"

He shakes his head quickly, taking the heap of forks I just rinsed from my hand. "No, he's done so much, Skyler. I'll be fine. If I have to sit out a dance or hang back while my friends go to the movies, it won't be the end of the world." He shrugs. "Just four more years and I'll be out of Pittsburgh, anyway."

My heart breaks at his admission, not just because I don't want him to miss out on his high school experience but because he seems in such a rush to grow up.

"Come with me for a sec," I say, drying my hands on the soft gray dish towel before passing it to him.

He does the same, following me back through the house to the front foyer where my purse is hanging on the coat rack. I flip through it for my checkbook, scribbling one out for three-thousand dollars before handing it to him.

His eyes go wide, his head shaking before I can even speak. "I can't, Skyler, I can't take—"

"Yes, you can," I say, pushing it toward him again. "Look, I was a nerd in high school. Like, I had absolutely zero friends, and I couldn't wait to get out of there, just like how you feel right now. But looking back, I wish I would have taken more chances. I wish I would have gone to the dances and the games and been a part of the class instead of just walking across the stage with them as a stranger at the end of it all."

Clayton's eyes soften, and he finally takes the check, folding it once and tucking it in his back pocket.

"I want you to have fun, Clayton. I want you to enjoy high school, and Clinton would want the same thing. We can keep this between us, okay? That way he doesn't stress himself out thinking he's not doing enough and you don't have to worry about missing a dance. Everyone wins."

"What about you?"

"Meh," I say with a wave of my hand. "I'll just enter a local tournament and clean those suckers out one weekend. No big."

Clayton smiles, because he and I both know it *is* a big deal, but I don't care. I'd give anything to Clinton and his family, because they're my family, too.

"Thank you," he whispers.

"Anytime, Baby Bear," I answer, leaning in to give him a hug. He squeezes me tight, a softer version of the Bear Hug I love so much, and I smile into his chest, heart warm and full and happy to help. "Anytime."

Later that night, Clinton and I sneak onto the roof of the hotel we're staying at downtown, one I booked us with hotel credits I got as a prize in a tournament last semester. The bright, full moon is shrouded by low-hanging, gray, wispy clouds, setting an eerie yet beautiful setting as we polish off a twelve-pack.

"Okay," I say, cracking the top off my fifth beer just since we've been on the roof. Add this twelve pack to the drinks we had at Mac's house before we left, and I'm already three beers past drunk and going strong. "Never have I ever had a threesome."

Clinton grins, happily taking a drink from his own beer.

"Are you freaking kidding me?! Who, when?!"

"Freshman year," he answers with a shrug, as if having a threesome is commonplace. "I don't even know the girls' names. They were best friends, seniors, and it was on their bucket list before they graduated. I was happy to help them tick that one off."

I snort. "Oh, I'm sure you were. Your turn."

"Never have I ever done anal."

"*Really?*" I answer in surprise. "I mean, I haven't either, but I'm just shocked to hear those words come out of your mouth."

Clinton smirks again, reaching for his seventh and our last beer in the pack. "Well, girls aren't exactly jumping up and down to have nine inches shoved in their ass."

I choke on a laugh, spitting Bud Light out like a fountain in the process. "Oh, my God."

"You asked!"

We both laugh, and Clinton flicks the aluminum top with a pop and a fizz. "Okay, new game. Truth or Dare?"

I blow out a long breath, resting my back against the brick wall behind me, the only separator from us and a twenty-seven floor dive down to the earth. "Truth."

"Pussy."

"And a mighty pretty one, if I do say so myself."

Clinton laughs. "Okay, fine. Who are your conquests this semester?"

"Honestly?" I ask, taking another long pull from my can. "I don't have any. I mean, if I meet someone out one night and we're having fun, I'm not saying I wouldn't go home with him, but right now I'm just focusing on figuring my own shit out. You're the only guy in my life, Bear." I wink, nudging his knee with mine.

He chuckles, leaning forward to cross his arms over his legs. "Same here. Lacy shows up every now and then, but after Shawna…"

"I know."

I don't even make him finish his sentence, because I know more than maybe anyone how much that girl hurt him. He still loves her, still wants her, but after Family Weekend last semester, there's no going back.

"Why can't we just be sexually attracted to each other?" Clinton jokes. "We'd be set."

"I mean, I'm not *not* sexually attracted to you," I counter, words slurring a bit.

Clinton jerks his head up to look at me, eyes wide before they narrow again. "Are you fucking with me?"

My head is fuzzy, thoughts stumbling over one another as I mull it over. Clinton is hot and always has been. The first time I met him, I remember thinking I would absolutely be taking him home at the end of the night. But from the very beginning, we just fell so easily into our friendship, and became a sort of family.

Still, with his insanely stacked body and sexy-as-hell smile, it's impossible to not feel some sort of attraction to him. Even for me.

I swallow, finishing the last of my beer before crushing the can down and tossing it back into the empty case. "Truth or dare, Bear?"

He watches me, my pulse ticking up a bit as I wait for his answer. Clinton and I have never crossed the line between our friendship, and maybe it's just the beer, or maybe it's the way his dri-fit, black t-shirt hugs his massive arms, or the way he drags his teeth across his bottom lip, his eyes on mine, but the line feels blurry tonight.

"Dare," he finally answers.

My stomach drops, brain screaming at me that I'm completely insane, but I say it anyway.

"I dare you to kiss me."

The words barely leave my mouth before Clinton's hand is around my wrist, tugging me forward, my knees hitting the concrete on either side of his thighs as I straddle him. My breaths are erratic, tipsy mind trying to catch up, but it doesn't have time before his hands are in my hair, and then his mouth is on mine.

His lips are so soft, so big, so warm. They're lips I never thought I'd taste, lips that feel foreign as they trail down my jaw to my neck before he sucks the lobe of my ear between his teeth.

I roll my hips against him with a moan, gasping when his hands slide up my ribs under my shirt. His hands are so big they nearly encompass my entire rib cage, his thumbs touching as they graze their way up my stomach, the rest of his fingers wrapped around me. He could completely crush me if he wanted to, and in a way, I want him to.

With all nine inches.

I can't think straight, thoughts trying to fight their way through as I cross my arms and grab the ends of my shirt, flinging it to the side when it's over my head before kissing Clinton again.

*I can't believe this is happening. I can't believe this is happening. Holy shit, this is happening.*

Clinton flips us, ripping his own shirt off before falling down on top of me again. He traces the edge of my bra with his tongue, biting and sucking the skin of each swell before working his way back up to kiss me. Our breaths are fast and heavy, hands touching, bodies rolling, and when I feel like I'm at the edge of hysteria, he bites my neck hard.

And it's like that bite is tied to reality.

I burst out laughing, Clinton's mouth still on my neck. It's not a cute laugh, either. It's loud and obnoxious, more like a cackle than anything else, but I can't help it. When I realize I'm actually laughing, I flush with embarrassment, which only makes me laugh harder.

Clinton presses up to balance on his palms, eyeing me like I'm crazy before giving in to a fit of laughter, too.

"We are so drunk," I say through the giggles, eyes tearing up.

He laughs even harder, the sound deep and comfortable as he rolls to the side to lie down next to me, his hands grabbing for his stomach. He can't catch air, both of us hysterical.

"That felt so weird, didn't it?" he asks.

"SO weird," I agree, and we both break into another spell of laughter, ribs burning and eyes blurred with tears.

When we finally settle down, I lean into him and he tucks me under his arm, fingers playing with my hair as we watch the clouds float over the moon.

"I love you, Skyler," he says, tone serious.

"I know," I say, giving his middle a slight squeeze. "I love you, too."

"Thank you for this weekend. I finally feel a little like myself again."

"So, my best friend's back?"

He chuckles, kissing my forehead. "Back and better than ever, baby."

I smile with a sigh, closing my eyes and finally letting the booze take me under.

Mission accomplished.

# Cassie

"CATCH UP, SLOW POKE!" I call out behind me, zipping around a couple holding hands on the sidewalk leading to the Student Union. Grayson is trying to longboard for the first time, and I've finally discovered something he's not effortlessly amazing at.

It's oddly satisfying.

"I think my wheels are messed up," he hollers back, running off the sidewalk for the eighth time. He stumbles off the board, picking it up with a huff before jumping on again and pushing toward me.

"You sound like my big sister when I'd beat her at Mario Kart. 'It's the controller! The buttons are broken!'"

Grayson laughs, the loose strands from where his hair is tied back blowing in the breeze as he catches up to me. "You love this, don't you?"

"Just a little."

I stick my tongue out at him, and he launches toward me when we reach the mall where the dodgeball tournament is, tackling me into the grass. We roll a few times before he lands on top of me, brushing my hair from my face, his steel eyes looking right through me.

For a while he just stays here, eyes bouncing from my lips to my hair to my eyes before making another round. It's as if all the answers to every question he's ever asked are written behind the freckles on my cheeks, or weaved into my red hair, or hidden under my smile.

The butterflies that had been sleeping in my stomach slowly flutter to life as I look up at him, the sun rays framing his silhouette above me. Grayson laughs, tracing my jaw with his thumb before leaning down to take my lips with his. I let him kiss me slowly, not even a little concerned about being late to the dodgeball tournament.

"You're lucky you're so cute."

"I think that makes *you* the lucky one," I point out, pecking him on the lips again after he's pulled away.

Grayson grins, helping me stand, and then we both tuck our boards under our arms and make our way toward where the tournament is already beginning.

It's been a tough week for us, especially after Grayson had to bail on our date, which is a big reason why he's here in the first place. He knew he needed to make it up to me, so he entered the dodgeball tournament with a few of his buddies in the music program. It's the first effort he's truly made to be a part of my world, other than the Alpha Sigma concert, which was almost a disaster.

I've changed my schedule around to be at as many of his shows as I can be, whether he's just playing at Cup O' Joe's or at one of the swanky restaurants downtown. But when it comes to Greek events, Grayson usually rolls his eyes or makes jokes. I get it, it's silly to him, and I guess in the long run a dodgeball tournament benefitting our philanthropy probably doesn't seem as important as a show played in front of hundreds of people or a video shoot that goes viral on YouTube.

But it's important to me.

I know he's busy, and I know he has his own priorities, but it means a lot to me that he's moving me up the list. Even if he doesn't fully get it, he's here — and that's a step forward.

"I'm glad you're here," I say as he tucks me under the arm not carrying his board.

He presses a kiss into my hair. "Me, too. Hey," he says, pulling me to a stop at the edge of the first makeshift court. "I'm sorry I haven't been around as much as I should be. This summer just completely changed everything and I'm trying to figure out what it all means."

"I know." I nod, eyes on my feet, but he tilts my chin up.

"I'm going to be around more. I promise. This, us," he says, motioning between us before tapping my nose. "*You* are important to me."

I smile, leaning up on my tiptoes to kiss him before grabbing his hand. "Come on, let's go find your team."

It's a simple promise, one easy to make but hard to keep. In my heart I believe him, but my head screams for me not to touch the hot water that burned last time. But for now, for today, we're together. So, I focus on that as we walk hand-in-hand across the field.

Erin grabs me as soon as we reach the referee tent and latches on to my arm, shooting off a list of things she needs me to do with her eyes scanning her clipboard. Grayson kisses my cheek with a whispered *good luck* before jogging off to his first game, and then the tournament begins.

The rest of the day is a blur.

Erin has me running all over, bouncing back and forth between courts recording scores, filling water jugs, collecting entry money, and whatever else needs to be done. About the only breaks I get are to pee, reapply sunscreen, and chug down a cup of water of my own each time I refill the jugs.

Before I know it, the sun is setting, and we're in the last game of the tournament. But when I walk up to the board where the bracket is displayed and see the last two teams standing, I know the night is far from over.

Because one team is Grayson's. And the other is Adam's.

"You see me killing it out there, baby?" Grayson asks, picking me up in his arms slick with sweat and spinning me around.

I laugh when he drops my feet back to the ground, my eyes still on the scoreboard with a sickening feeling stirring low in my stomach.

But I fake it.

"You're in the final game!"

"Hell yeah, we are!" his friend, Malik, says. He high fives Grayson, running a hand over his short buzz cut. "Those Greek boys don't stand a chance against musicians. We're too good with our hands."

He adds that last line with a wink and a lewd gesture as a group of my sisters walk by, all of them giggling and helping his inflated ego. Suddenly, a bright red dodgeball is thrown directly at Malik and he catches it last second in his stomach with a grunt.

"That's a lot of talk for a future runner-up," Adam says, crossing his arms over his chest with a grin.

Sweat sticks his light-blue team t-shirt to his chest, outlining the ridges of every muscle. With the sleeves ripped off and the sides stretched to hang down low, my eyes can't move from the ebb and flow of his ribs as he catches his breath from the last game. When they finally trace their way back up to his eyes and they're staring back at me, I clear my throat, turning to Grayson.

"So much testosterone. You guys do know the trophy is just plastic, right?" I joke.

The left side of Grayson's mouth quirks up but falls quickly, his glare still pointed at Adam. "I don't care if it's made of paper. It'll be on my bookshelf tonight."

Adam scoffs, still grinning, not looking the least bit intimidated.

Just as Malik puffs his chest out, ready to fire back, Erin strolls up, pointing her glittery pen in all their faces. "Five minutes, boys. Save the shit talking for the game and go get water."

Grayson and Adam are still leering at each other, but Grayson shakes it off, leaning in to kiss my cheek. "Dinner with the winner after this?"

I laugh. "Sounds perfect."

He winks, glaring at Adam once more before jogging off behind Malik.

The tension is still thick once he's gone, and I tuck my hair behind my ears, but luckily Erin isn't the least bit fazed and is already rattling off the last of my duties for the evening. But I can't help but watch Adam as his jaw flexes and without another look in my direction, he heads in the opposite direction of Grayson, and my eyes follow him the entire way.

The last matchup is best three out of five, with the entire crowd of my sisters and other Greek students crowding around court one for the final showdown. The bleachers are full, Kappa Kappa Beta girls lining the boundary edge and cheering for the team they want to win. I just stand in the middle, pretending to help the line judge, not sure which outcome would make me happier. Or if either one will really make me happy at all.

I can feel it. The night isn't going to end well. I just don't know what will spark the bomb.

Each game makes my stomach hurt worse. Grayson's team wins the first and second one, and Adam's team wins the third. Every single guy on both teams is dripping with sweat by the start of the fourth game, and I'm biting my nails down to the beds, watching and overanalyzing the way I feel when things happen.

Grayson gets hit, I cringe. Adam gets hit, I feel like I'm watching a dog get kicked. Grayson's team wins, I smile and clap, all the while watching

Adam with a pit in my stomach. Adam's team wins and I sigh with relief, all the while wondering what that means and why I feel it.

My sister once watched a football game between her two favorite teams — the school where she went to undergrad, and the school where she did her Masters. She said she felt sick watching and had no idea whom to cheer for. She thought she would be happy either way, but when her undergrad team won, she was more sad than happy. That's when she realized she felt more connected to her graduate school.

I didn't get it then, but now I do.

"We couldn't have asked for a better finale," Erin says as Adam's team clinches the fourth game. They're jumping up and down celebrating while Grayson huffs and huddles his team up to strategize. "These two teams are brutal. *And* we made it to game five. Here," she says, thrusting the brightly decorated donations bucket toward me. "Go make another round while the crowd is all amped up."

"On it."

I take the bucket from her hand and try to keep my mind busy as I walk up and down the bleachers collecting donations. The fifth and final game starts with my back turned to the court, and I try to keep it that way, wondering with every cheer and boo which team is winning.

But it doesn't take long before I'm standing back beside Erin, bucket full to the brim with donations, and all that's left to do is watch to see who wins.

I play with my hair as the game continues, twirling it around my fingers and chewing the inside of my cheek. Adam's team is down to only him and Jeremy, with Grayson still holding on to his entire team so far. But Jeremy catches two balls thrown at him at once, one in each hand, and with a roar from the crowd, Grayson's team is down to three.

Adam strikes Malik in the leg, and he curses the entire walk to the sideline, leaving only Grayson and Steven, a drummer from one of his friend's bands.

For a while the four circle each other, throwing balls and dodging them just the same, and it feels like there will never be a winner. But then Steven gets antsy, chucking his ball square at Jeremy who catches it easily. He laughs, holding up the ball in one hand with an oversized pouty lip aimed at Steven walking off the court, which earns him a hard ball to the ribs from Grayson.

And then there are two.

This can't get any worse.

"I feel nauseous," I whisper to Erin, but she just laughs, thinking I'm joking, thinking I'm so excited to see who wins. But I'm not. I'm dreading it. Because either way, I'm screwed.

Grayson and Adam tiptoe around each other for a long while — advancing on the line and then backing off, throwing balls at each other's feet and retreating back with eyes ready for the backfire shot. They're both too coordinated, too powerful, and now I'm convinced there really won't be a winner.

Would that be worse or better?

"They've got two minutes before time is called and we declare a tie," Erin says, eyes on the game clock. "That would be super anti-climactic."

Now we're both stressed, and when the clock ticks down to one minute remaining, Erin jumps into action, calling out to the crowd in the bleachers.

"Cheer for your favorite team! We need a winner! Let's count them down! Fifty-seven, fifty-six…"

She continues the chant, the rest of the crowd joining in, half of them screaming for Adam to throw his ball while the other half cheers Grayson's name. The two of them just watch each other, murderous, waiting for the other to make a move while they plan their own.

When the crowd reaches twenty, everyone is on their feet, counting down the clock and screaming even louder for someone to make a move. Then, almost as if in slow motion, Grayson takes three long, fast strides toward Adam, winding up his arm and launching his last ball straight at Adam's knees.

Adam jumps high into the air with a spiral kick, sending him up and over the ball, and when he lands on one foot his arm follows through like a sling shot, ball flying back toward Grayson before his other foot even hits the ground. It all happens so fast, I'm barely able to register the fact that he jumped over the ball, let alone that he sent his own back straight toward Grayson. Grayson's eyes widen at the rebound, too, and though he tries to dodge it, the ball grazes his hip as he bends away from it.

And with nine seconds left, Adam's team wins.

"FUCK!" Grayson roars, picking up the ball that hit him and launching it over the bleachers. No one notices but me, because everyone else is crowding the field to congratulate Adam's team. Erin announces them the winner over the loudspeaker as music plays, the tournament officially over, and I slowly make my way toward Grayson.

He just stands there with his hands on his head, breaths heavy and lips in a flat line as he watches

Adam's team celebrate on the other side of the foul line. Malik, Steven, and the rest of the team clap him on the shoulder, dispersing after one of my sisters hands them their silver medals.

"Hey," I say softly when I reach him. I leave my arms crossed over my middle, afraid to touch him yet. "You okay?"

"It's bullshit," Grayson spits, thrusting his hands toward the other team. "Adam was out like twice and the refs didn't call it."

I smile, stepping into him and threading my arms around his slick neck. "The controller buttons are broken," I tease, but he pulls my arms off of him, still scowling.

"It's not fair. It's all rigged for the Greek system. No way would they let a bunch of GDIs win."

*GDI* is code for *God Damned Independents*, or non-Greeks. I didn't know what it meant until Skyler explained it to me at Ralph's once, and I'm surprised Grayson knows the term at all.

"I'm sorry, babe. Let's just get out of here, okay?"

But before the words are even out of my mouth, Adam jogs over, hand outstretched toward Grayson.

"Hey, man," he says, wide grin on his face. "Good game. Seriously. Your team was smart and it could have gone either way there at the end."

Grayson eyes Adam's hand, but doesn't reach out to shake it.

Adam waits a moment before shrugging, letting his hand drop and turning to face me. My knees nearly buckle at his bright smile, the widest I've seen it all semester, pointed directly at me like a blinding pair of headlights. "So, where do you want to eat? Dinner with the winner, right?"

I roll my eyes at the tease, but when Grayson shoves Adam hard, stepping between the two of us, my hands fly to my mouth with a gasp.

"Back the fuck off, Brooks, before you get more than just a dodgeball to the face."

Adam shoves him back. "Calm down, it was a fucking joke."

"Yeah, well, I'm not laughing. No one is going to dinner with my girl but me."

"That right?" Adam says, stepping forward until he's chest to chest with Grayson. "Because if I recall correctly it was me who had dinner with her when you were too busy playing guitar for your little groupies to take her on a date."

Grayson growls and shoves Adam again and I step between them, pushing my hands hard into each of their chests.

"STOP IT!"

They both pause, chests heaving against my hands, eyes hard on each other and noses flaring.

"It was just a joke," I say to Grayson, who's eyes widen as Adam snickers from the other end. I turn on him next. "And you already won, so how about you go gloat somewhere else and stop being an asshole."

"I tried to shake his hand!" Adam defends.

"Yeah, and then made a joke about taking my girlfriend to dinner."

"Wasn't joking the other night, but then again you weren't around, were you?"

Tossing my hands up with a sigh, I grab my backpack and longboard from behind the referee stand, strapping on the bag and fighting against the urge to punch them both.

"I give up. If you two want to compare dick sizes all night, be my guest. But I'm going to dinner." They both take a step forward and I hold up a hand. "*Alone.*"

And with that, I drop my board to the sidewalk and kick off, leaving them both standing there as equal losers in my eyes.

I take my time at dinner, calling Skyler and asking her if she can meet me. She had to miss the dodgeball tournament for a local poker tournament downtown, but she's finished when I call her, so we meet at Tizzy's Tacos.

Two tacos, one bag of chips, and an hour of venting later, and I feel marginally better.

I don't really tell her about Adam, mostly because no one on campus knows about what happened between us last semester, but I do tell her about Grayson. She listens, eating her burrito and offering advice around mouthfuls when appropriate. Even still, nothing is solved when we finish.

So, I take the long route home, zigging and zagging my board across campus, pausing to sit and reflect at the pond by the Student Union. When it's nearly midnight I finally give up on trying to feel better and make my way toward the house. With Bo dropping out unexpectedly last semester, I don't even have a roommate to go home to.

Ashlei is sitting on the front porch steps when I roll up to the house, and she lights up when she sees me.

"Hey, you've got a visitor."

I cock one eyebrow. "A visitor? At midnight?"

She nods, biting her lip with a mischievous smile. "Mmm-hmm. I helped them sneak in. Just… be quiet. And have fun."

With that little nugget of vagueness and a giggle, she hops off the steps and skips inside, leaving me standing in the open door behind her.

Tiptoeing up the stairs with my heart thundering under my ribs, my mind races with what—or rather, *whom*—I'll find in my bedroom. If Ashlei had to sneak them in, it's definitely a guy, but the only question is… which one?

The fact that I even have to ask myself that sends a surge of guilt through me.

As pissed as I am at Adam for making an already tense situation worse earlier at the game, part of me wants to thank him. He finally said what I had yet to fully express to Grayson — he wasn't there for me when I needed him. All week I had looked forward to that date, and when it had all went up in flames, Adam had been the one there putting out the fire.

But Adam isn't mine, either.

Even if I had chosen him over Grayson last semester, if I had given him the chance he'd begged for at formal, I would have ended up with the same disappointment. He's drowning in his new responsibilities as president, just like he thought he would be. I knew he wouldn't have time for me, for us, and Grayson had given me every part of himself last semester.

So, was it fair of me to be upset with him now? He's chasing a dream he's had his entire life. Shouldn't I support that? I know he cares about me, and I care about him. So what if it's not always easy?

With my hand on the doorknob to my bedroom, I realize I don't want to see either one of them on the other side. I'm still mad at the way they acted. And I still have absolutely zero grip on how I'm feeling.

But it doesn't matter, because one of them is waiting. So, with a deep breath, I twist the knob and push through.

And then my breath catches.

My entire room is covered in small candles, bathing my bed in a soft golden light. And as the door closes behind me and I gently drop my longboard and backpack to the ground, my eyes find Grayson's.

He's sitting on my desk chair beside my bed, in only his boxer briefs, hair damp like he's freshly showered and guitar strapped across his chest. He plucks a few chords as he watches me, brows bent inward, tail between his legs.

"Cassie," he starts, the chords finding more of a melody as he speaks. "I am so, so sorry. Not just for being a sore loser earlier and causing a scene at your event, but for making you feel like our time together doesn't matter to me. I should have been there for our date."

I shake my head, opening my mouth to tell him I understand and that he couldn't have missed that show, but he cuts me off.

"No. No excuses, no bullshit about a show or my agent or whatever. I should have been there. And this is my promise to you that from here on out, I will be."

He motions for me to sit on the bed and I do, hands folded together and squeezed between my knees as he keeps his eyes on me and strums out a beautiful song.

It's an original, one that feels like he just wrote it — just for me — and I hang on to every word as he sings to me. It's a song about being scared, about falling in love, about finding who he is in a time when he's not even sure which way is up. And, finally, I get it.

It's not about his music, or about me — it's about him. Grayson is growing into himself, and with that comes figuring out how to balance it all. He's finally getting everything he's worked for and now he's not sure how to handle it. But he tells me with his music how much he cares, and how he's sorry, and he promises to do better, though I realize in that moment it doesn't get much better than him.

When he thumbs out the last note of the song, I reach for him, sliding his guitar strap up and over his head and placing it gently beside the chair before straddling him. I thread my hands behind his neck, fingers playing with the soft tendrils of hair there as my eyes search his.

"That was beautiful."

He swallows, framing my face with one large hand, his thumb running the length of my jaw. "Not as beautiful as you."

Grayson's eyes flick to my lips, and slowly, as if he doesn't think he deserves to, he pulls me into him until his lips are pressed against my own. He kisses me patiently at first, soft and hesitantly, but when I roll my hips against him and tug on his hair, he groans, kissing me harder, with more need, more passion.

And for the rest of the night, that's how he apologizes — with a kiss, a lick, a suck, a touch. And I accept with a sigh, a moan, an arch, a *yes*. He promises me more with his hands on my waist, and I remind him he's always enough with my mouth on his skin.

I still want to wait to go all the way, and Grayson respects it, bringing me to ecstasy without taking me past my comfort zone. He shows me how much he wants me with every single movement and I show him, too, touching him in new ways, tasting him for the first time.

When we're both spent, holding each other as our breaths even out and the dawn begins to break, a light feather of realization floats down slowly in my heart.

I'm falling in love with Grayson Anderson.

I only hope he's there to catch me when I do.

# Jess

"BEING A GIRL IS THE ABSOLUTE FUCKING WORST!"

I flail around on my bed, kicking up the covers and swinging my arms like a toddler as Ashlei chuckles from her front row seat to my pity show. She's perched on the edge of Skyler's bed, sitting on her hands, shaking her head as I detail every thought I've had in my pea brain the past two weeks since Jarrett left.

"He's probably just busy with his job, Jess. He treated you like an absolute queen when he was here," she points out. "It's not like he went home and said, 'Fuck that bitch.'"

"I don't know," I counter, sitting up on the bed and tucking my knees up to my chin. "He did go out to Ralph's with all of us, and we are certifiably insane."

"I thought it was a pretty low-key night."

"Skyler kept hiding under tables, grabbing people's legs and shouting, 'SHARK ATTACK!'" I deadpan.

Ashlei snorts.

"And Bear jumped up on stage and started dry-humping the DJ while begging him to play *Party in the U.S.A.*"

"Okay, so maybe we scared him off and he took a hammer to his phone so you couldn't trace him."

I bury my face in my hands, something between a groan and a whine squeaking through my lips.

"I'm kidding," Ashlei says, hopping down from Skyler's bed to come sit next to me. She places a hand on my back and rubs gently. "Seriously, he's crazy about you. Just chill."

"He hasn't called me since he left two weeks ago, Lei." I sniff, leaning my cheek on my knee to look up at her. "His texts have been short, if he even texts back at all. How the hell am I supposed to do this long-distance thing with communication like that?"

She frowns, rubbing my back in response.

"What if he's cheating on me," I whisper, stomach turning and threatening to forfeit the pizza I shoved inside it earlier. "Oh, God, I couldn't handle that. I couldn't."

"He's not cheating on you."

"How do you know?"

"I only had to spend one night with the two of you to see there's not another girl in this world who has his attention, babe. Just try to relax. He'll call, and you'll talk it out, and it'll be fine. Okay?"

I nod, cheek rubbing against my knee pathetically. "Tell me about your internship. I've sucked up enough of the air in the room."

Ashlei smiles. "It's been amazing so far. I feel like I'm really standing out…" Her voice fades off a little, a slight blush hitting her cheeks. "The CEO knows my name, so I guess that's saying something, right?"

"Uh, yeah. That's amazing. I'm so proud of you! What's it like, being an intern?"

"Thank you," she says, and then blows out a short breath. "And it's exhausting. The other interns are pretty slack-ish when it comes to the account we've been assigned, but I don't want to be just another intern, so I'm busting my ass to stand out."

"You always stand out," I say, nudging her. "Why do you think you're my best friend? I don't just let any basic bitch have that title."

Ashlei scrunches her nose with a grin right as my phone vibrates, and I panic, tossing the covers off the bed until I find it hiding underneath.

"Oh, my God, it's him."

"Answer it. I'm going down the hall to Ex's room, just come get me when you're done."

I nod, not even taking my eyes off the screen with his name and a picture of us on the beach filling it. When the door closes behind Ashlei, I take a deep breath and answer.

"Hello?"

"Hey, babe," Jarrett says on a breath. "God, it's good to hear your voice."

I flop back into the sheets, head hitting my pillow with a *poof*. "Jarrett, where have you been? You haven't called in two weeks… and you've barely been texting me."

"I know," he answers with a sigh. I imagine him running a hand over his smooth head, his elbows propped on his knees. "I know. I'm so sorry. Jenny and I got assigned to a project as soon as the wheels on my plane home touched down and we've been drowning in work ever since. I've barely had time to sleep."

I try to swallow but come up dry, my stomach twisting.

"Jess?"

"Yeah," I croak, fighting the tears pooling in my eyes. My emotions are more unstable than an alcoholic at an open bar.

"Talk to me."

"What am I supposed to say right now?" I ask, sitting up in bed. "Two weeks ago you were telling me I'm everything you want, and then you go back to New York and you're so *busy* with *Jenny* that you can't call me or answer a text with more than one word?" I try masking the pain in my voice, but I know it's ringing out loud and clear. "I mean, what is there to even say?"

"Please, try to understand," he begs, exhausted. "This job is important to me, to my career, and yes, I made a choice to throw myself into this project and do it right. Just because I was busy for a couple of weeks doesn't mean I love you any less."

"You've been spending every hour of every day for the past two weeks with another woman," I point out. "How would you feel if the shoe was on the opposite foot? What if I said I'd been too busy *studying* with Bear to call you."

"I'd say, 'Bear studies?'"

"Not funny."

Jarrett sighs. "Jenny is just my co-worker, Jess. I'm going to have to work with females sometimes, and your jealousy doesn't make this distance thing any easier."

"Wow," I say with a click of my tongue.

"What happened to what we talked about when I was there? Where's the trust? Where's the belief that we can make it?"

"Belief is like a flower, Jarrett, and mine hasn't been watered for two weeks."

Jarrett's voice is muffled, as if he's running a hand over his mouth before responding. "I can't do this. I don't have time for it. I'm stressed out, I've barely slept, I don't even have time to *eat* right now, unless you count coffee as a food item."

I pinch the bridge of my nose, shaking my head as we both sit silent on the phone. *He can't do this. It's over. We're done.*

"So… you're breaking up with me?"

*"What?"* Jarrett laughs. "No, God, no. Are you breaking up with me?"

"No!" I cry quickly, letting the tears run.

Jarrett sighs into the other end. "I wish I could hold you right now. I'm sorry, Jess. Look, what about this…" His voice trails off and I hear the clicking of keys in the background. "Come see me for Thanksgiving. We can do the holiday in the city, and you can meet Jenny and everyone else I work with. I want you to be a part of this journey, too. I want you to understand, and to feel comfortable." He pauses. "And more than anything, I want you to see that even when I'm gone, even when you're not with me, I never stop loving you."

I choke on a sob, smiling through it. "I love you, too. I'm sorry."

"Don't be. I promise to call you more. I owe you that. I know this is hard."

"I don't want to be the needy girlfriend," I say with a sniff. "I don't want to stress you out more than you already are. Just… I don't know, send me a text while you're pooping."

He chuckles. "I can do that."

"And book that plane ticket."

"Already done. I'll forward you the itinerary."

I wipe my nose with the back of my wrist, heartbeat settling back to a steady rate as I pull the covers over my legs. "Sorry I'm such a hot mess."

There's a soft laugh on the other end, and I'm comforted by the sound, by the clarity the phone call has brought me.

"As long as you're my hot mess, you'll never hear me complain."

# Episode 4

# Bear

"I JUST HEARD TWO GIRLS reprimanding their drunk friend in the bathroom because she admitted to spitting instead of swallowing," my Little, Josh, says as he stumbles back up to the bar at Ralph's.

"What a time to be alive."

"I poked my head inside and tried to get her number."

"Which one?" I ask, sliding him his beer and shot glass to continue power hour. One shot of beer every sixty seconds, cued by the DJ changing the song playing.

"Honestly? Whichever one answered."

I laugh, cheers-ing my shot glass full of beer toward him as the song changes before throwing it back.

It feels good to be at Ralph's, surrounded by my brothers who are all trying their best to make our probation situation not suck. They seem to have really listened to me when I went off about keeping our letters alive. Ever since then, we've all been focused on doing what we can for our philanthropy, showing support at other Greek functions even if we can't participate, and of course, partying anywhere and everywhere we're allowed to. Ralph's is basically the Omega Chi house now, and on power hour night, anything can happen.

Josh whistles, his eyes on someone over my shoulder. "Damn, Skyler. How are you going to show up looking that fine and not let me take you out?"

I turn, smiling at my best friend as she rolls her eyes and slides onto the barstool next to me. Her long chestnut hair is down and straight, eyes framed by dark shadow and thick mascara, and legs on full display in the tiny ripped-up jean shorts she's wearing. She paired it with a Guns N' Roses t-shirt cropped at her midriff, and I don't blame Josh for wishing she'd give him a chance.

Skyler is a catch. Any man with eyes can see it. Even me, which is probably why I drunkenly made out with her on a roof in Pittsburgh a month ago before we both burst into hysterical laughter. We're just too close to fuck, and I didn't even know that was a thing until her. I've never been genuine friends with a girl, but with Skyler, it's effortless. I love her, I care about her, and I want to be around her all the time. But for the first time, we crossed that line into something more, and we both found out quickly that it just isn't us.

We're best friends — *just* friends — and I love that about us.

I don't have to pretend with Skyler, and she doesn't have to pretend with me. I don't know what I'd do without her.

"You're seventeen minutes behind," I say, sliding a shot glass toward her and pouring a fresh beer from the pitcher. "Time to catch up."

"Is that a challenge?"

I just raise my eyebrows in response, throwing my hands up like the decision is all hers. And of course, because she's Skyler Fucking Thorne, she chugs the full cup before refilling it again, just in time to throw back a shot when the song changes again.

For the first time since the semester started, everything finally feels okay. Sure, it would be better if we weren't on probation, but for what the situation is, everything is pretty great. And when Lacy walks through the door at the end of power hour, I can't help but feel like my lucky stars are all aligned.

Josh is nearly passed out on the bar, talking to a pineapple cup that some freshman girl on her first social left behind, and Skyler is dancing with her sisters near the DJ. Lacy eyes me when she walks in, smirking in my direction, but of course she doesn't come to me first. No, I'll be her stop at the end of the night, which is exactly how I want it.

That is, until another girl catches my eye.

Suddenly, the room is spinning, and it takes every ounce of willpower I have left not to throw up. I wish it was the beer making my stomach turn, but it's the pair of bright green eyes framed by dark glasses staring at me from across the bar.

Shawna's violet hair is twisted into a messy knot on top of her head, the way she used to style it after we'd fucked for hours under the sheets. She's dressed simple in a tight, short black dress — one that hugs her curves, highlighting the barbells of her nipple piercings through the thin fabric. My balls ache at just the slight view I have of them across the dark room, and the fact that she still has an effect on me makes my jaw clench.

With a shake of my head, I down the rest of my beer, slamming the plastic cup on the bar before making a beeline across the dance floor for Lacy. Her friend points over her shoulder at me, and she turns just in time for me to catch her mouth with mine.

She's surprised at first, hands frozen at her side, but when I slide my tongue inside her mouth and pull her body flush against mine, she relaxes, wrapping her arms around my neck. Alcohol swims in my system, mixing with the adrenaline and anger, stirring up a dangerous concoction as Lacy bites my lower lip between her teeth.

I slide my hands down her small back, cupping her ass and pulling until she grinds against my leg. She shudders at the friction, a breathy *fuck* escaping her lips before I silence her again. And when I kiss down her neck, my eyes find Shawna again, satisfaction flooding through when I see she's still watching.

She grabs her purse, saying something to the group of girls she's with before eyeing me like a homeless puppy again. I push Lacy back, standing tall, not taking my eyes off Shawna as she pushes her way through the crowd toward the door.

Lacy watches me confused, but when her gaze follows mine, she shakes her head before facing me again. "Un-fucking-believable."

She slaps me hard across the face, which zaps my attention back to her, but luckily Shawna is already gone and doesn't see the aftermath. I stretch out my jaw, rubbing it with one hand, heavy eyes finding Lacy again. I wish I cared. I wish I was sorry.

"Look, I've been cool with our arrangement. You want to fuck at two in the morning and not have to wake up to me the next day? Fine. But *that*," she says, motioning to where Shawna just disappeared out the door and back to me. "That's not okay. You may like to fuck me like I don't have feelings, Bear, but I'm still a goddamn human."

She eyes me like a rodent, shaking her head before turning on her heel and stomping away, and I'm left watching the door and knowing only two things are true in this moment.

One, I am an asshole.

And two, I'm not over Shawna Ballentine. No matter how much I want to be.

# Erin

OCTOBER IN SOUTH FLORIDA is a funny thing.

Most days it still feels like summer, the sun hot, the air like a wet blanket slapping you in the face when you step out of the blessed air conditioning and onto the sidewalk to walk to class. Coffee shops are selling pumpkin-flavored lattes and football season is in full swing, yet it's still impossible for it to feel like fall in Florida because the weather hasn't changed.

But some days, some years, a miracle happens, and a "cool front" blows in after an afternoon shower, giving Florida residents a few days of weather *just* cool enough to wear jeans and a light scarf or sleeves past the elbow.

Today is one of those days, and Jess and I are taking full advantage, sitting outside at one of our favorite brunch restaurants just off campus, both of us wearing designer boots that hit our knees and drinking warm coffee — without sweating.

"I wish this weather would last," Jess says with a sigh, crossing one leg over the other as our waitress tops off our coffee. "It finally feels a little like fall."

I chuckle. "We don't *get* a fall. We get two to three months between summers where it's slightly less miserable. And usually that's January into March."

"Oh, don't get me wrong," Jess clarifies, dumping two spoonfuls of sugar into her fresh coffee. "I love Florida weather, especially in the spring, but it's nice to break out the cute winter clothes from time to time."

"Well, you get a whole fourteen days combined of that in a year, I'd say. So enjoy."

"At least we don't have to worry about it not being warm enough for the Alpha Sigma Halloween party," Jess says. "I can't believe they stepped up. I guess when Omega Chi is suspended, someone has to."

I nod. "Yeah, and Adam has had something to prove since he rushed as a freshman. Between the concert that's now one of the biggest fall events and all the parties he's been throwing to supplement the O Chi's being out of commission? He's definitely making a name for the fraternity."

"What are we dressing up as? We need to get creative, since it's a boat party."

"Mermaids?" I suggest, taking a sip of my black coffee.

"Nah, everyone will do that. Too obvious."

"Skyler and Bear are doing *Baywatch."*

Jess rolls her eyes. "Of course they are. And those hot fuckers will actually be able to pull it off, too."

"We could do beach Barbies."

She scrunches her nose, holding her cup of coffee to her lips again. I watch the steam rise while she contemplates.

"Oh!" She snaps. "What if we did like the Chiquita banana girl? You know, we could all wear different color swim suits, like I wear orange, you yellow, Ashlei pink, Cassie green, and then we make cute head wraps with fake fruit the same color. We could pick all that up at the craft store."

"I'm pretty sure Cassie is doing a couples' costume with Grayson, but I'm in! And I'm sure Lei would be, too."

"Ugh," Jess groans. "Cassie and Grayson are disgustingly cute."

"Don't you hate them?"

"So much."

I laugh. "But you and Jarrett are pretty gross, too."

At that she smiles, stirring her coffee with her eyes on the spoon. "Yeah, I just wish we could be gross more often."

"How's that going? The long distance?"

Jess sighs. "It's fine. We had a rough patch after he left. He got caught up in a work project and it was like pulling teeth to get him to text back or call me for a couple of weeks. But we talked it out and he promised to be better at communicating, which he has been. And he's flying me up to see him for Thanksgiving."

"Oh, my God! Thanksgiving in the city!"

"I know!" Jess squeals. "I'm so excited. And he's going to introduce me to his whole team, too. I can't wait."

"It'll be here before you know it," I say, my stomach twisting with a strange but familiar longing. It never fails to surprise me when Kip Jackson pops into my head, especially because it's usually at the most peculiar of times. Like now, hearing about Jess and Jarrett, wondering if Kip and I could have made it long distance if I wouldn't have gone completely batshit crazy.

I loved him. I know that now, and I think I knew it then, but it was my first time being in love. I was fresh out of high school, on my way to college, and I was so insecure that thoughts of him cheating on me or leaving me overtook every other rational thought I had. I would go through his phone, scream at him when he didn't come over when he said he would...

We were just kids, and the first two months of our summer affair had been absolute bliss. He was working for my grandparents on harvest in Kansas and I was there visiting. It was almost too perfect, right out of a country song or a rom-com movie.

But then I'd ruined it.

And now, I'll never know if what we had was real, if it could have survived had I nurtured it instead of torched it with a flame thrower.

The loud purr of an engine shakes me from my thoughts and Jess and I both turn in the direction of it, our smiles falling when we see who's responsible for the noise.

Landon pulls into a parking spot at the pizza place next door in a brand new Corvette Stingray, his brothers crowding him with whistles and cheers. I swallow, eyes narrowing as Jess scoffs.

"Looks like *someone's* overcompensating."

"Clearly."

Jess stirs her coffee again, taking a sip before settling her eyes on me. "What ever happened between you two, anyway?"

My stomach lurches again, this time for a completely different reason, but I don't miss a beat. "Meh, he was fun for formal, but I've got too much to focus on this semester. Elections are coming up soon."

"Mmm," Jess says with a nod. "You ready to take your Big's place as president? Continue the family tradition?"

I wink. "Born ready."

"I figured. I swear it's actually in your blood. If you do half of what you did as recruitment chair as president, our sorority is going to be unstoppable."

"That's the plan."

Jess watches me for a minute, smiling. "I'm really proud of you, Ex. Seriously."

My heart warms, and I reach for her hand, squeezing it gently in response.

For a while we just sit and drink our coffee, but my eyes keep wandering to Landon and his brothers, all still crowded around the new car. But I'm not glaring or huffing — no, I'm smiling. Because where I was stumped on how to exact my revenge before, the answer now is crystal clear, thanks to what I would bet money on is a gift from Mommy and Daddy.

Suddenly, I have a plan, one I know will hit him where it hurts.

Now, the only question is — when?

# Adam

"OUCH!" I YELP, HOPPING on one foot as the other throbs from me slamming it against the corner of my dresser. "Fuck. Shit. Fuck."

I hop over to my bed, stripping my clothes off and leaving them on the floor before crawling under the sheets. The slight cold front that blew in last week is definitely gone, evidenced by the sweat glossing my lower back, so I kick the sheets off and lie staring up at my ceiling, watching the tiles turn like the hands of a clock.

I'm drunk.

It's been a while since I could say that, and now that the multiple shots of Fireball are swimming in my stomach as the room spins, I forget why I wanted this in the first place.

I've been stressed since the semester started. Between my new role as president, the concert, and Omega Chi being suspended, I've had my hands full with everything from philanthropy work and nationals relations to keg parties and now, hosting the biggest Halloween bash PSU has ever seen. We've rented out twenty boats with captains to take us out to the sand bar, all drinks included, and every Greek student on campus is stoked.

Except me.

It's not that I'm not excited everyone is buzzing about Alpha Sigma, or that we're going to throw a killer party, but balancing all of it has been more of a struggle than I thought.

So, Jeremy made me take a night off, dragged me to Ralph's, and got me completely shit-faced. *You need a break*, he'd said. But what he couldn't have known is that every time I drink, I *do* forget about the presidency for a while, but I never forget about her.

Being busy helps me keep my mind off Cassie. It's one of the reasons I try not to take a break or slow down, even when the stress is high. It's easier to pretend what I told her last semester about being busy with the presidency is true than to admit to myself that it's not.

I never would have been too busy for her, but now it doesn't matter. I lost my chance.

Sober me knows that.

Drunk me begs to differ.

There isn't even one small part of me that tries to argue or reason with my drunk logic as I blindly reach for my phone on the bedside table. It's just past one in the morning, but that doesn't stop me either. I thumb through my contacts and find hers easily, a picture of us from Spring Break last year filling the screen as I switch to speaker phone.

The rings fill my room, and I close my eyes, trying to stop the room from spinning for just one second. This is stupid. I know that. But all I can do is hope she answers.

When the ringing stops, my eyes flutter open again.

"Hello?" she whispers.

I smile at the sound of her voice, placing the phone on my chest and resting my hands under my head. "What was your favorite game to play as a kid?"

There's a pause on the other end, then the slight sound of papers shuffling.

"Adam, it's one o' clock in the morning."

"And you're awake."

She laughs. "Well, yes. I'm studying. But why are you calling me to ask me about my childhood at one in the morning?"

"I've just been thinking about it. When I was a kid, I used to love to ride my bike. I'd get on it the second I got off the school bus and ride it until the street lights came on. I also used to play this game with my grandpa, before he passed, where he would name a country and I'd have to figure out the capitol, the native language, and the political makeup. Then he'd teach me common phrases in that language. I know how to say *hello, goodbye, thank you, please,* and *do you speak English?* in fourteen different languages."

"You're drunk," Cassie answers simply.

"Maybe. Humor me, anyway."

She sighs, more shuffling noises coming from her end. "Hold on. Let me go outside."

I listen as she packs up her bag, imagining her bright red hair piled on top of her head, her flashcards spread out on the table at the Greek library. After a moment, I hear the soft sound of a door closing, and then the familiar quiet rush from the fountain in the background.

"Operation," she says finally.

"Like the board game with the guy and the big red nose and all the open body parts?"

She laughs. "That's the one. Even back then, I knew I wanted to be a doctor. My mom said I used to write letters to Hasbro telling them their game was broken, because I absolutely did *not* touch the metal sides but I was buzzed. And I went on to tell them how frustrating that is for a steady surgeon hand and that the surgery room should be free of such awful noises. I suggested they use something softer, like a cat meowing or a bird chirp to indicate the sides had been touched."

A laugh barrels out of me. "Why am I not surprised?"

"So, how do you say *hello* in Portuguese?"

"Olá," I answer. "Or oi, or alô."

"At least you got some useful information out of your favorite game. I only learned how to curse at a young age. Stupid Hasbro."

I chuckle, but then silence falls over both of us. I got her to answer, but now that I have her on the phone, the sharp ache in my stomach is rolling strong. Because I don't really have her, but I want her so bad it hurts.

"Here's another one in Portuguese. Desculpe."

"And what does that mean?" she asks.

I swallow, inching up to lean against my headboard and balancing my phone in one hand. "I'm sorry."

She doesn't respond, so I continue.

"I really was just making a joke at the dodgeball tournament, but I also knew what I was doing. I wanted to get under Grayson's skin, and I was gloating off the win. I was an asshole, and you didn't deserve to be stuck in the middle of that."

"Thank you," she whispers, then she sighs. "I'm sorry, too. I shouldn't have had dinner with you the night he bailed on me. We're a couple, we're going to have fights, and I shouldn't have found comfort in you when he let me down. That's not fair to him." She pauses. "Or to you."

The knife in my side twists in a little deeper, and I shift at the pain.

"But I want to be there for you… I always have been. We're friends."

"I know," she answers quickly.

"But he doesn't want us to be, does he?" I finish for her.

"Can you blame him?"

I can't, but I hate it all the same, so I don't answer her question.

"Have you slept with him?"

She scoffs. "Wow. That is none of your business, Adam."

"I'm sorry. Shit, I'm sorry, don't hang up." I pinch the bridge of my nose, trying to shake my way through the drunken fog clouding my head. "I just… I can't stop thinking about you. Not since that night on Spring Break. And I know you're with Grayson, and I know you care about him, but it doesn't change the fact that I want you."

She inhales a stiff breath. "Adam…"

"I want to know everything about you, Cassie. Everything. Your fears, your secrets, your hopes, and your dreams. I want to know how many kids you want or if you even want any at all. Do you want to travel the world or stay in the same small town forever? And who are you when no one is around, when it's just you and your favorite playlist? What's playing, who's singing to you when you're sad, and who do you dance to when you're happy?"

There's a sniff on the other end, but I can't stop.

"I want to know all of that and more. Does he? Does he know the real you? Does he want to?"

I hear her sniff again and my heart clenches. Sitting up straighter in bed, I close my eyes, trying to reach for her across the airwaves. Does she feel me? Is she reaching for me, too?

My answer comes in the form of a soft click, and then the sniffling is gone, and the fountain is muted, and it's just me alone in my bed again. In the morning, I'll be hungover.

In more ways than one.

# Ashlei

MY SISTERS AND I used to play a game with our pencils when we were younger.

We'd grab them by the eraser and wiggle them slightly in the air, pencil held horizontally, and it'd give the illusion that the pencil was made of rubber. We'd watch that pencil for hours, giggling and pretending like we were magicians.

I'm playing that game right now, though not by choice, because Mr. Church just asked me to stay back after an all-staff meeting. As the room clears, everyone casting eyes back in my direction, the pencil in my hand is just as rubbery as my knees taking shaky steps toward where he's seated at the head of the long board table. I tuck it inside my notebook as I take the seat next to him.

It's been six weeks since the Alpha Sigma concert. Six weeks since the CEO of the event agency I intern for "bought" me for a date at a Greek function at a school he's ten years too old to go to. Six weeks with no explanation as to why, with no mention of it at all — with not a single word said to me *period*.

But that six-week silence was just broken.

In front of the entire agency.

I force a steady breath as the last person exits, the door shutting behind them with a soft click as Mr. Church turns to face me. It's hard to keep my eyes trained on his, to not notice the hard edges of his jaw or the perfect slope of his nose as he smiles easily, as if the two of us being alone in the same room doesn't faze him in the least bit.

"I know you probably have some work to wrap up before you get out of here for the weekend, so I'll try to make this quick," he starts, his posture relaxed as he kicks back a little in his chair, unfastening the two buttons on his cobalt blue suit jacket. It falls open, exposing his crisp white dress shirt beneath it as he steeples his fingers, eyes still locked on me. "You did a great job at the event pitch meeting with *Bare•ly* last week."

I swallow, ankles crossed and hands holding tight to the portfolio notebook balanced in my lap. "Thank you, Mr. Church. That means a lot to me."

His eyes spark a little when I say his name. "I wasn't the only one impressed. Mrs. Delure spoke with your manager earlier this week to get more of the details hammered out for the event, including the lead event planner, and she asked specifically for you."

My mouth falls slack. "She... are you serious?"

"I am."

For a second I just stare at him, but then I laugh, covering my wide smile with my hand as I shake my head. "I can't believe that."

Mr. Church chuckles, too. "Neither could your manager, which is why she came to me to ask if it was even possible. We've never had an intern in such an influential role before. She's worried you might not be prepared to do the job effectively."

My smile falters. "Oh…"

"I, however, am not."

My eyes find his then, and they're like lasers piercing straight through me. It's as if every secret I've ever hidden, every dark thought I've ever had is easily accessible to him. But he doesn't look away. He leans in closer.

"You made an impression on me in that elevator, Miss Daniels, and every day since. You can do this. And that's why I told your manager to make you the lead event planner. You'll have a team of three — two associates and one other intern. We've never done this before, and you're going to be met with resistance. I know you can handle it, but before I announce it to the staff, I need to know *you* know it, too."

I tighten my grip around my notebook, knuckles white from the force as my heart thumps like a kick drum under my ribs. I think of the other associates on the project, of how they've already turned their noses up at me when I've excelled. My manager said they're just threatened, but with this news, I know I'd have a new, larger target on my back.

But I didn't come here to make friends. I came here to learn, to prove myself, and to stand out.

I want to be the best, and I won't get there without taking risks.

"I'm ready. I can do this, Mr. Church."

He smiles, kicking back in his chair again. "That's what I hoped you'd say. I'll send the email on Monday. I'm going to have to explain why we're letting an intern take the lead event planner role, but with Mrs. Delure asking for you by name, it should be easy to do. And if anyone gives you a problem over it, just come to me."

I blush, tucking my hair behind one ear. "No offense, Mr. Church, but running to tattle to the CEO probably won't earn me any respect points. I'll be okay. I'm no stranger to gossip or bullying," I add with a laugh. "I've got pretty thick skin."

He watches me, tapping his steepled index fingers together. "I don't doubt that."

I've never been so pinned by a gaze before. I physically *can't* move, can't speak, can't do anything other than stare back at him, wishing I could read his mind.

"Do you have plans tomorrow?"

At that I laugh. "Honestly? Don't judge me, but I plan on staying in bed all day. We finally have a Saturday without a sorority event and I have two months' worth of sleep to catch up on."

Mr. Church smiles. "Would you consider getting out of bed around two if I promised to have you home in time to get a full eight-hour rest?"

Wait.

*Did he just say have me home? As in, he would be taking me somewhere?*

I just stare at him, finally blinking after what I'm sure is a full minute.

He cocks an eyebrow. "The auto racing date? I do believe I was the highest bidder."

I'm still staring. What am I even supposed to say? I want to ask him why he did it, why he hasn't mentioned it until now, and more than anything, I want to know how it's even remotely appropriate for him to spend a Saturday with an intern.

Because I know it's not.

And maybe I should say no. Maybe I should politely decline, thank him for his donation and hand him his tickets to the auto racing place, insisting he ask someone else to accompany him.

But I don't do any of that.

"Okay."

His other eyebrow shoots up to join the first before a grin breaks on his stunning face. "Okay, then. May I pick you up?"

I just nod, the room suddenly too hot, and I stand to end our meeting. But when I do, the pencil I'd tucked into my notebook spills onto the floor. We both bend down at the same time to retrieve it, our noses just inches apart as our fingers brush.

We both pause, his hand on the pencil and mine still over his. When he looks up at me, I meet his gaze, holding it there with unanswered questions until his eyes flick to my lips and back again.

Clearing his throat, he hands me the pencil and stands, helping me up. "Tomorrow at noon. Kappa Kappa Beta house, correct?"

Something between an *uh-huh* and a squeak leaves my lips and I dash out the door, trying to calm my walk as I make my way through the office with multiple pairs of eyes watching the entire way. I can't catch my breath, my heart threatening to sprint right out of my chest and across the office. I just agreed to a date with my CEO. Tomorrow.

In what world is that ever a good idea?

Just as promised, Mr. Church pulls up at twelve on the dot in his Acura NSX. I'm thankful for the mid-seventies, not-a-cloud-in-the-sky weather, because all of my sisters are at the beach getting their tans ready for Halloween. If they were home, they'd all be lined up at the windows as soon as they heard that engine purr.

I'm still questioning my decision the entire walk down the sidewalk to his car, one thumb hooked into the strap of my purse to keep me from playing with my hair. I spent the entire morning figuring out what to wear, curling my hair to perfection, and applying my makeup to look natural but flawless. I tried on more outfits than I care to admit before I landed on my favorite black body suit, slim cut with thin spaghetti straps and a deep v-neck. Paired with a bleach-washed pair of ripped-up shorts and my white Keds, I feel sexy without being obvious. I topped it off with a thin, gold headband and reflective aviator glasses, which I'm thankful for when Mr. Church steps out of the car.

He rounds the car, opening my door and waiting with one hand still on the handle as I take in his casual attire. I'm so used to seeing him in a full-on suit ensemble that I almost don't believe it's him in the fitted light jeans and simple white t-shirt, covered only by an unbuttoned red and blue flannel shirt cuffed at his forearms.

I stop when I reach him, swallowing past the sticky knot in my throat. "Hi."

"Glad to see you were able to get out of your pajamas," he teases, holding his hand for mine to help me inside the car. When I'm safely in, he shuts the door behind me, jogging around to his side.

I marvel at the white and black leather interior, the stitching wide and bold, the entire world muted inside his car that costs more than my entire tuition. I let my eyes wander the dashboard and middle console controls, anything to keep from noticing how ridiculously sexy he looks kicked back in the driver seat with one hand on the wheel and the other resting easy on his thigh as he turns to me.

"Ready?"

I laugh out a shaky breath. "Ready as I'll ever be, Mr. Church."

He shakes his head with a grin. "You can call me Brandon, if you'd like," he adds quickly.

"Brandon," I say, trying it out with a nod. But then I crack out a laugh. "Feels kind of weird."

A shadow passes over his dark eyes. "I'm sure the more you say it, the more comfortable it will feel."

And there it is again. The look. The piercing gaze that strips me of any reply other than an open mouth as he throws the car in drive.

I keep my hand tucked under my thighs the entire drive to the auto racing venue, mostly looking out the window as we breeze through town. Wale's *Ambition* album beats through the speakers, Mr. Church — er, *Brandon* — rapping along, thumbing to the beat of the bass on his steering wheel.

Every now and then, he casts a glance in my direction, but neither of us makes conversation. When we pull into the parking lot, he doesn't find a spot, but drives through the back alley and up to a locked gate instead.

I frown, scanning the empty race track inside. "Are they open today?"

"Sort of," Brandon answers, nodding to a young man inside the gate as he removes the locks and motions for Brandon to drive forward.

We pull in slowly, right onto the massive track, and Brandon puts the car in park just before the white and black checkered painted block on the track. He steps out first, smiling at my dumbfounded expression as he rounds the car to open my door.

"I don't understand," I say as I take his hand and step out. "Why is no one else here?"

"Ah, Mr. Church!" a voice calls from our right. I turn to find an older man with dark hair, peppered with gray, jogging toward us. He's dressed in khaki pants and a navy blue polo, his skin a deep shade of olive and smile bright under his mustache. "So thrilled to have you back. Always a pleasure."

Brandon meets his extended hand with a firm shake. "Pleasure's all mine, Rodalfo. This is Ashlei Daniels," he adds, motioning to me. Rodalfo takes my hand and lifts it to his lips for a kiss. "She'll be riding shotgun today."

"Welcome, Ashlei," he says, squeezing my hand once more before releasing it. "I would say you are a lucky lady to ride beside Mr. Church in such a beautiful car, but perhaps it is Mr. Church who is the lucky one."

Rodalfo winks as a blush sweeps my cheeks, and I'm not sure if it's that blush or Rodalfo's comments responsible for the smile on Brandon's face.

"Well, the track is cleared for the entire day, so she's all yours for as long as you want her. I'll have the boys run out helmets, if you'd like?"

"Please," Brandon answers, and Rodalfo jogs off again, leaving us alone.

"I didn't realize those tickets were so powerful," I say, crossing my arms and waiting for an explanation.

Brandon just shrugs. "Let's just say they know me here."

"So, why pay ten thousand dollars for the tickets, then?" I press.

He smiles, bullet gray Ray Bans lifting on his cheeks with the expression. "I wasn't bidding on the tickets."

I falter, surprised by his boldness. It's the first time he's admitted that he wanted this date with me. After six weeks of silence, I don't know how to even begin to respond.

But with his next comment, I don't have to.

"It was for charity, remember?" He grins even wider, taking two helmets from the same young man who opened the gate for us and handing me the smaller one. "Hope you're ready for a ride, Miss Daniels."

I can't help but smile back, shaking my head before pulling the helmet on. "Show me what you got, *Brandon*."

He bellows out a laugh, leading me back to the car.

As we both strap in, I adjust my helmet tighter, nerves hitting me at the realization that we're about to be speeding around the track. "Is it safe to drive your car? Don't they have like... extra seatbelts and padding in the ones they race here?"

Brandon ignites the engine, raising a brow in my direction. "Don't you trust me?"

"Should I?"

The words shoot out before I can stop them, and Brandon watches me, debating the answer.

"I think that's something you have to decide for yourself."

And with that, he faces forward, revving the engine as the lights change colors in front of us. My breath hitches when they turn green and I don't have time to exhale before I'm flattened against the seat.

For the first five seconds, I completely freak out.

Internally, that is, because I can't manage a breath, let alone a scream as we race from zero to over one-hundred miles per hour in less time than it takes to spell my name. It's almost painful as the laws of physics work against us, crushing my bones into the seat, my body seemingly left on the starting line instead of inside the car.

When we round the first corner of the track, we decelerate just long enough for me to catch my breath.

And then, I laugh.

Not a cute giggle or a soft chuckle, but a full-on, head-thrown-back, tears-in-my-eyes laugh. Adrenaline rushes through me at the speed of light, crashing with my nerves to ignite an uncontrollable sense of euphoria.

Brandon glances at me quickly before smiling, too, and punches the gas again. I wrap my hands around the chest strap of my seatbelt, trying to focus on the track as we fly down it. The bleachers on the sidelines blur together as we pass, almost like we're traveling through time and space. It's the most exhilarating experience I've ever had.

And I've done cocaine, so that's saying something.

I can't stop laughing, and I don't — not until I lose track of how many laps we've done and Brandon slows us to a stop at the starting line again.

"That was incredible!" I scream, even though I don't have to anymore. My ears are ringing, everything still muted. I tear my helmet off and shake my hair out, smiling wide at Brandon as he removes his, too.

"Have fun?"

"Are you *kidding*?! Let's go again!"

He laughs, removing his sunglasses to wipe them clean with his shirt. Then he lifts his chocolate eyes to mine. "Wanna drive?"

It was hard to get me off the track after that.

We spent the entire afternoon and well into the evening taking turns driving, competing on who could get to one-hundred the fastest or who had the fastest zero-to-sixty or lap time. I couldn't believe he trusted me enough to let me drive his car, especially at such high speeds, but he didn't seem to be even the slightest bit worried.

When my stomach was growling loud enough for him to hear it, I begrudgingly said goodbye to Rodalfo and his crew, and we grabbed a quick bite at a café nearby before heading back to campus.

We shared casual conversation over dinner, mostly about my pole dancing since he'd been curious since I'd mentioned it. I left out all the drama, of course, but it was nice to talk to someone about one of my passions. It made me realize how much I missed it, and now I find myself wanting to look up local classes again, even if just for weekend workouts.

But the drive back to campus was quiet, leaving my brain room to run over the long list of thoughts I've been avoiding all day — like why the CEO of a successful event agency wanted to take his intern on a date, or what this means, or what we do next. Was it even really a date? Did he really just donate to charity as a nice gesture? And if it was something more… does he expect something now? It doesn't make sense, why a powerful, sexy-as-hell man like him would risk his reputation and more to get me in bed.

And that's all it could possibly be, right?

I'm a full ten years younger than he is. Other than my body, I'm not sure what else I could offer him that another, older, more mature woman couldn't.

I shake the thoughts from my head as Brandon pulls around to the back of the sorority house, finding a parking spot under a large tree covered in Spanish moss before cutting the engine. When the silence envelopes us, the nerves that had disappeared on the race track are back again, and I sit on my hands to keep from wringing them together.

"Thank you for joining me today," he says, voice low and steady as he eyes me from the driver seat.

"Thanks for letting me drive," I reply with a laugh. "It was fun."

I swallow as his eyes rake over me, all the way down to where my hands are tucked under my thighs before they find mine again. "I make you nervous."

Blowing out a breath, I shake my head. "You confuse me."

"How so?"

My stomach turns, hands forming fists between the seat and my skin. "The auction, not talking to me for over a month, the lead event planner position… and now today? I just…" My voice fades as I glance at him through my lashes. "What are we doing, Mr. Church?"

He inhales a stiff breath at his last name rolling off my lips, lips that his eyes are on now. "I don't know what I was thinking sending Mykayla to the auction. I came to my senses that weekend and decided ignoring you was best for both of us."

"What changed?"

His Adam's apple bobs hard in his throat as he leans in closer, hand reaching forward until his fingertips brush my jaw. I freeze at the touch, his skin like a shock to my entire system, zipping a hot line of wire straight down between my clenched thighs.

"I discovered you're impossible to ignore."

His lips find mine in a frenzy, hot and wet and demanding as I struggle to catch my breath. But my hands are already fisting in his hair, pulling him closer. I moan into his kiss, crawling over the middle console to straddle him as his hands wrap around my ribs. When I roll my hips, friction sparking between us, we both groan and Brandon sucks my lip between his teeth, biting hard enough to draw blood.

Kissing him is intoxicating, like the strongest shot of tequila injected straight into a blood vein.

My head spins with every touch of his skin on mine, blurring right and wrong together, no and yes as one. But when his hands yank at my body suit, unclasping the buttons that fasten it below my shorts and pulling the fabric free, I clasp my own over his wrists to stop him.

I break our kiss, our foreheads still pressed together, heavy breaths escaping our parted lips and fogging up the windows as his hands grip the freshly exposed skin of my hips.

"I'm sorry," I murmur, reaching blindly over the console for my purse and flinging his door open before crawling out of his lap. My body aches at the loss of his touch as soon as I'm free of him, but I focus on placing one foot in front of the other, blocking out everything else. He doesn't chase me and I don't look back, my heart pounding mercilessly in my ears as I race inside the house.

I push through the back kitchen door, shutting it quickly and pressing my back against it before sliding down to the ground. Pinching my eyes shut, I shake my head, still caught up in the feel of him while my brain battles to remind me why what I just did was a very, very bad move.

But he kissed me first.

I sigh, burying my face in my hands.

*What the fuck am I doing?*

# *Bear*

"SOUNDS LIKE MY LITTLE BROTHER," I say to Mac's mom with a laugh, adjusting the phone between my opposite shoulder and ear as I lay out the rest of my costume on my bed. She just finished telling me how he had two girls fighting over who he'd take to homecoming, so he told them whoever could kiss better would be the lucky lady on his arm.

Little bastard got two, steaming hot kisses from girls trying to prove something, and then invited them both to go, anyway.

And they agreed.

"He's something," she agrees with a chuckle of her own.

"Thank you again, Mrs. Harrison, for taking Clayton in and treating him like your own. I don't…" I pause, trying to find the words. "I'm not sure I'll ever be able to tell you what it means to me. To us."

"He's a good kid," she says easily. "Easy to love, and easy to care for. We wouldn't want him anywhere else but with us."

I smile, chest tightening, and distantly I wonder if my mom ever thinks about him — about any of us. I wonder where she is. The only reason I even know she's alive at all is because her and Carleton check in on his kids from time to time, long enough to send money or ask for it — depending on which side of the gambling ring they're on that day.

"What about you?" Mac's mom asks. "How is school?"

I rummage through my bathroom drawer for my suite mate's tanning oil, tossing it on the bed. "It's school. Classes are tough this semester, but luckily our fraternity is on probation, so I have more time to study."

She clucks her tongue. "I'm sure you're still finding ways to get in trouble."

"Dressing up as David Hasselhoff circa 1989 as we speak."

"Oh, God." She snorts. "Do I even want to know?"

"Skyler and I are dressing up as the *Baywatch* cast for a Halloween boat party today."

"That sounds like so much fun!" She sighs. "I'm really happy you have Skyler. And what she did for Clayton... I know he'll never forget it. She's a great friend, Clinton."

I frown, tossing my black Omega Chi sunglasses on the bed with the rest of my costume. "What do you mean?"

"Oh, my…she didn't tell you?" She sighs again, murmuring softly. "Humble on top of everything else."

"Tell me what?"

There's a pause, and for some reason my blood pressure ticks up a notch, like I'm about to hear something I don't want to, my body preparing me for bad news before my brain even thinks it's necessary.

"Clayton was in a rough place before your visit. My husband and I… well, we help him all that we can, and of course, you send him money every chance you get. And you worked the whole summer. But football is expensive, and he was going to have to make some tough decisions."

"He didn't tell me any of this," I shoot back. "Does he need money? I can… I'll get a job. I'll sell some stuff."

"You don't have to," she says quickly. "Skyler cut him a check, Clinton. She told him to chase his dreams and enjoy his high school years because she didn't get the chance to."

She keeps talking, telling me how much it was for, how they're holding the money and only giving him what he needs when he needs it. She tells me how Clayton is also looking for a job after football season ends, but I can't hear any of it over the ringing in my ears.

Skyler gave my little brother money, without telling me, without *asking* me if it was okay.

"Like I said," Mrs. Harrison says, snapping my attention back to her. "She's a great friend."

"Yeah," I clip. "I have to go. Please, tell Clayton to call me tomorrow."

"I will..." she says hesitantly, and before she can ask any questions, I end the call, gripping the phone hard in my fist.

I debate throwing it, but focus my rage on the person responsible instead of an inanimate object.

Everything is a blur as I walk to the Kappa Kappa Beta house, nostrils flaring the entire way. A small, quiet part of me tells me I'm probably overreacting, but the larger, screaming part reminds me that what Skyler did isn't okay. Maybe she had good intentions and just wanted to help, but Clayton is *my* brother, and my responsibility. I can take care of him without her help, and she knew I'd be upset by her helping, which is exactly why she didn't tell me.

I pound on the front door when I reach the house, working my clenched fists together as I wait for someone to answer. A girl I don't recognize, likely a new member, opens the door with wide eyes.

"Skyler. Now."

"Oh, I think she's getting ready for the Halloween party. Could you maybe—"

"NOW!" I roar, and she yelps, skittering off with the door open behind her.

A few other sisters pass concerned looks my way as they walk by, but eventually Skyler emerges, half-dressed in her *Baywatch* gear. She has her red one-piece on and half a face of makeup, her hair in a clip like she'd only begun to work on it.

Her brows pinch together when she sees me and she steps onto the porch with me, pulling the door closed behind her. "Bear? What's going on?"

"You gave Clayton three-thousand dollars?"

The words spit from my mouth like venom, and Skyler's face drains of color.

"Bear… listen, I just wanted to—"

"Help? Well, you should have fucking came to me first. He's my fucking brother and I can take care of him."

"I know you can. I never said you couldn't."

"Well, that's what you fucking implied by going behind my back like that."

She winces. "Come on, you know it wasn't like that."

"Wasn't it?" I challenge. "God, Skyler, you're so fucking selfish you can't even see it when you're in the wrong. There's a reason you didn't tell me, and it's because you *knew* I'd be pissed. And now that you're caught, all you can do is defend yourself. An apology wasn't even on your radar, was it?"

Skyler swallows, her eyes brimming with unshed tears.

"You call yourself my best friend, but best friends don't do this to each other." I shake my head, looking at the girl I thought I knew for what feels like the first time. "You should have come to me."

"I'm sorry," she quivers, but I just hold my hands up to stop her.

"It's too late for that now. Have fun at the party."

Without another look in her direction, I storm off the porch, feeling more alone than ever before.

# Erin

I AM WAY TOO SOBER to be balancing a huge wreath of fake fruit on my head.

The costumes Jess came up with for us turned out to be perfect, each of us able to pick out swim suits that complement our figures along with colors that look best on us. My tan is contrasted next to my bright yellow one-piece with a deep v-neck that goes all the way down to just between my hips, showing a little cleavage and my flat stomach. The arches of the fabric on the legs are high, too, giving my thighs and butt some action.

Although most people have no idea what we were going for and keep calling us "the Fanta girls," we look hot, and that's what matters most at a college Halloween party.

Well, usually.

I don't really care to draw attention to my body anymore, not when the desire to have someone touch it died right along with a part of me the night of formal last semester. I haven't gone a day without remembering that night, without reliving it — not since it happened. I wonder if there will ever be a day that I won't remember.

Shaking the thought from my head, I reach for my Bubba Keg from Spring Break last semester, taking a long pull from the straw as I kick back in my small beach chair. It's just water, but no one has to know that. I've done a pretty good job of evading shots up until this point, claiming I have to keep my head on straight and not party too hard with elections coming up soon. No one has pressed me.

The day is just as perfect as our costumes, the sun peeking in and out between fluffy white clouds as a breeze rolls onto the sandbar from the water. Hundreds of students litter the sand, some soaking up the sun while others play drinking games. All the Alpha Sigma boats are anchored down around the sandbar, swaying over the waves, loud music coming from each and every one of them. Half of the party is on the boats, the other half spilling out into the water and up onto the sandbar. Everyone is dressed up, having found ways to creatively turn classic Halloween costumes into beach wear, and even though it's just past two in the afternoon, most of the attendees are already smashed. The event turned out amazing, and I know Adam must be proud.

I want to be a president like that.

"The *Vamps and Tramps* boat is handing out Jell-O shots!" Jess screams excitedly, catching her breath from where she's jogged over from the other side of the sandbar. She reaches down for her own Bubba Keg in the chair next to me, draining it. "Come on. They're delicious."

She grabs my hand but I laugh, pulling back from her grasp. "Pass. Trying not to get completely tanked, remember?"

Jess pouts. "You don't even seem buzzed."

"Oh, I am," I lie, squinting my eyes before pushing my sunglasses up onto my head. "Drunk eyes. About to take a nap in this chair."

She laughs. "I'll probably do the same soon. Your tan is looking amazing, by the way."

Smiling, I put my sunglasses back on and nod toward where Ashlei and Skyler are playing a game of flip cup in the middle of the sandbar. "You should grab the other Fanta girls, though. Skyler can use all the shots she can stomach after what happened with Bear."

"Ugh, what the fuck was that, anyway? Skyler won't say a word about it."

"No idea," I answer. "But she's sad, so we should try to distract her with booze."

"My specialty," Jess says, wiggling her butt a little as she skips away. "You should at least come hang out on the boat!" she calls back behind her.

"Be there in a sec!"

I watch her run off, grabbing Ashlei and Skyler from their table on the way to the boat she'd pointed out. With a sigh, I reach for my phone, pulling up Kip's name before I know what I'm doing.

**- Hey, stranger, long time no talk. -**

I stare at the text, finger hovering over the send button. I'm not sure why it's him I want to text, or why he's the person I want to comfort me, or why I even need comforting at all. We haven't talked in almost four years, and I'm *fine*. Classes are going great, I recruited the best KKB class our school has seen, and I have a plan to get revenge on Landon.

But still I feel so… empty.

Numb.

I'm not myself, and I know I'm not the only one who's noticed it. And since I've pushed Clinton away and all the girls have their own drama to deal with, I've successfully isolated myself — especially after ditching out on my birthday.

And maybe this is for the best. Maybe, like my mom taught me, there's power in not leaning on anyone, in not exposing my weak spots.

No one knows what happened last semester other than Clinton, and I think he finally understands that I'm not going to talk about it. And I *do* feel marginally better each day… or at least, it's easier to pretend I do. Maybe this is my skin thickening, my scar healing even more, that shiny pink skin stretching and tightening to form a hard shell.

Every time I've given in before, I've been taught a lesson on why I shouldn't. Drinking and partying leads to bad decisions, which leads to horrific consequences. I don't want to experience them anymore.

And if that means being a loner, then so be it.

I have the presidency to focus on, anyway. In a little over a month my sisters will vote on who will take my Big's place, and if I have anything to do with it, there will be a clear choice.

Me.

So, instead of joining Jess, Ashlei and Skyler on the boat, I lean up to adjust the back of my chair and flip over onto my stomach to even out my tan.

# Adam

OF COURSE, SHE DID.

That's the theme of the night, because even though I should be focusing on how kick ass the Alpha Sigma Halloween boat party turned out, I can't focus on anything or any*one* but Cassie.

Of course, she showed up to the boat dock with Grayson, and of course, they took the boat I *wasn't* on to get out to the sandbar. Of course, she wore a tight, incredibly sexy, white, two-piece swim suit, one that crosses over her chest in just the right way to remind me how hot that body of hers is, the one she usually hides under modest dresses and blouses. Of course, she dressed up as Cleopatra, complete with a golden headband that makes her green eyes even more distracting than usual. Of course, she stayed on the opposite end of the sandbar, cozying up with Grayson in a beach chair and tossing her head back like he was the funniest man in the whole goddamn world.

Of course, she did.

I've been trying to ignore her, trying to enjoy myself, but it's been largely unsuccessful. Play a game of beer pong, search out Cassie in the crowd. Judge the costume contest, watch Cassie dance with Grayson on the *Mummies and Mimosas* boat. Do a keg stand, hear Cassie's laugh from across the sandbar as she slides off one of the boat slides into the ocean.

It's maddening, especially since the last time I talked to her I made a complete and total ass of myself.

And the strangest thing is that all day, all I want is for her to come talk to me.

Until the exact moment she does.

"Hey, you," she says, wading out into the water to where I'm standing. The sun is starting to set, so all eyes are on the shoreline in the distance, watching as bright oranges and pinks streak the sky.

I swallow, tucking one hand into the pocket of my board shorts, the other holding my red plastic cup of beer. "Well, if it isn't Queen Cleopatra. Nice headdress." I tap the gold piece hanging over the bridge of her nose with my finger and she giggles.

"Thanks. And you're…" She pauses, eying my open collared, relaxed fit, white shirt tucked into my dark blue board shorts. A simple, red cloth belt separates the two, and a sword is fastened to my hip. "A rookie pirate?"

I laugh. "Prince Eric, but thanks for crushing my spirits."

"Prince Eric," she deadpans, and I shrug, offering her a sheepish smile. "A little late for that, don't you think?"

The weight of those words slam into my chest like a boulder, and I lift my cup to my lips instead of answering her, eyes back on the sunset. She dressed up as the Little Mermaid last year, and instead of dressing up as Prince Eric then, I'd chosen Danny Zuko from *Grease* to match Skyler.

"Having fun?" I ask after a moment.

"*So* much fun," she says, crossing her arms lightly over her middle and facing the sunset, too. "You really are making a name for Alpha Sigma, Adam. You should be proud."

I don't know why it hurts when she says those words, when she says anything, really. It's like hearing any semblance of love from her kills me, like it'd almost be easier if she just hated me.

"I am, of some things, at least. Not so much about that phone call I made." I peek at her in my peripheral.

"We all drunk dial sometimes," she answers easily, eyes still on the shoreline.

Grayson comes splashing through the water and picks Cassie up from behind, spinning her around as she kicks and squeals. "There's my queen!"

"Put me down, you animal," she teases.

When he drops her feet back into the water, she pecks him on the lips, and I tear my eyes away, thankful I have my sunglasses to hide behind.

"Hey, Brooks," Grayson says, as if he just saw me standing there. He's dressed as Mark Anthony, Cleopatra's one true love, and suddenly I feel a little foolish in my own costume. "Great party. Seriously. And, hey, no hard feelings about the dodgeball game. You guys won fair and square." He holds out his hand toward me. "Truce?"

I grit my teeth, wanting more than anything to smack his hand away and tell him to eat a dick, but I grab his hand and shake it firmly instead. "Yeah, man, and thanks."

He turns back to Cassie. "The first boat is about to head back to shore," he says, twisting a strand of her hair between two fingers. "I was thinking maybe we should be on it… take this party back to my place." He runs those same two fingers across her collarbone and over her shoulder, trailing them all the way down her arm before tucking them into the band of her swimsuit bottoms.

Chugging the rest of my beer, I keep my eyes on the sun, now starting to dip beneath the clouds just above the horizon. Every muscle in my entire body is tense, so much so that I'm sure I'll wake up sore in the morning.

"Yeah," she answers breathily, and my cup cracks in my grip. "Just give me a minute. I'll meet you by our beach chairs?"

I feel Grayson's stare drilling into the side of my head, but ignore it, pretending like I'm not listening to their conversation. "Okay. But hurry, they're loading people up now."

"I'll be right there," she promises, kissing him once more before he's wading back up to the sandbar.

I don't know how long we stand there, silent, her eyes on me and mine focused in the distance. In my mind it's both forever and just a split second, so I'm not sure which it really is before I completely lose all common sense and rationality.

"You're going to sleep with him."

It's not a question. I don't want her to answer, but she does, anyway.

"He's my boyfriend, Adam…"

I grit my teeth so hard a sharp pain rips through my jaw and I crush the empty cup in my hand, the broken edges of the plastic digging into my palm.

"Don't," I say, finally turning to face her. "Don't leave with him, Cassie."

Her bottom lip is pinned between her teeth and I use every ounce of willpower I have left to keep from pulling her into me and sucking that lip between mine, instead. She feels like mine, even when she's not. And I don't know how to make that go away. Or, if I even want to.

"How can you ask that of me?"

I push a heavy breath through my nose, pinching the bridge of it with a shake of my head. "I don't know. I guess the real answer is that I can't, not really, but I am anyway."

"I think I love him," she whispers, watching where she's wringing her hands together before looking up at me through dark lashes.

I scrub a hand over my face, feeling so out of control I want to scream. It's like being trapped in a slow-motion car crash with a broken seatbelt.

"I don't know what to say to that."

She scoffs, dropping her hand to her thigh with a slap. "Unbelievable." She shakes her head. "You don't have to say a damn thing to that, Adam, because it doesn't matter what you think about it. It's how I feel. And, yes, I'm leaving with him tonight. That's where your need to know ends."

"He doesn't deserve you," I spit, desperate, latching onto anything I think will make her stay, knowing nothing will.

"And you do?" she asks on a laugh. Stepping closer, she lowers her voice. "This isn't your decision to make, Adam. You don't own me."

I press my lips into a hard line, and when she turns for the shore I involuntarily reach for her, just late enough to not even brush her skin before she's too far gone. I watch her leave, watch her walk all the way up to the shore, to Grayson, who wraps her in his arms with a long kiss. His stare lands on me afterward, making sure I saw, and then he tucks her under his arm and steers her toward the boat loading up to leave.

And just before she steps on, Cassie looks back at me, and what I find in her eyes almost knocks me to my knees. Because it's not love, or apology — but pity, and I feel it all the way to my core.

She knows it as well as I do.

It's *her* who owns me.

There are only five yachts left on the sandbar by the time midnight hits, and the captains we hired to drive tell us we have one hour left before they need to take us in. Not that I need another hour to get tanked, because I landed there roughly twenty minutes after Cassie was gone.

A little beer sloshes out of my cup and into the water below as I take a drink, elbows resting on the rail at the back of the *Gin and Jack-O-Lantern* yacht. I watch the shore with heavy eyes, knowing she's there somewhere, in bed with another man. I don't want to torture myself, don't want to be pathetic, but I'm powerless to change the way I feel — at least for the night.

So, I let it happen, let the longing fill me from the inside out, suffocating to the point of barely breathing.

Who needs air anyway, right?

"You're looking very Hamlet for someone who just hosted the best party of the year."

Skyler slides up next to me, stealing my beer from my hand and lifting it to her lips. My hand is still molded to the shape of the cup even though it's gone now, and I hold it out over the rail, the shore lights blurring a bit as I turn to face her.

"Hi, stranger."

She smiles. "Hi, yourself."

Skyler and I broke up on civil terms last semester, even going so far as to fuck one last time before we called it quits. Still, we've barely spoken since, not even sharing more than a few "likes" on social media over the summer and no more than two words since school started back.

I can't explain why, but breath comes a little easier with her beside me.

"You're not a Fanta girl like the rest of your crew," I observe, eyeing the red Spandex one-piece painted on her body.

*"Baywatch,"* she answers on a sigh. "Bear was supposed to be my David Hasselhoff, but he's not talking to me as of twelve hours ago, so…"

"What happened?"

She scrunches her nose. "I don't really want to talk about it, honestly. If that's okay."

I nod, stealing my beer back and taking a pull. For a while we just stand there together, listening to the water lap against the back of the boat. The party seems to have died down a little, but there's a small bonfire in the middle of the sandbar, and everyone who's still conscious is gathered around it. Everyone but me and Skyler, anyway.

"So, how have you been?" she asks, breaking the silence. "I see you're kicking ass at president, just like we all knew you would."

I give her a crooked smile, eyes still on the shore. "It's keeping me busy just like I thought it would, but I'm happy," I lie.

Skyler nods. "I get that. I'm pretty much in an exclusive relationship with poker."

"Is he at least good in bed?"

She snorts. "I wish. How about you, you find any time to date or at least have a little fun between throwing all your awesome parties and philanthropy events?"

"I barely find time to shower, let alone date."

Skyler laughs.

"Besides, I doubt there's a single girl out there who would be okay to show up at odd hours of the night, fuck, and then leave. Not without feeling used or demanding a cuddle session, first."

"No time to cuddle either, Brooks?" she teases.

I smile, taking another drink from my cup before passing it to her. "Savage, I know."

"Why can't that be a thing, though?" she asks on a sigh. "Why is there this big stigma against casual sex. At the end of the day, we're animals. And we have needs. Is it so bad to find a release in someone without taking them to dinner first or making them breakfast after?"

"Right? Like what's wrong with catching a nice orgasm and then catching some Zs?"

Skyler tosses her head back on a laugh, and I chuckle, too, distracted from thoughts of Cassie, at least temporarily.

"I miss you," she says, still smiling as her hair blows behind her in the soft breeze.

I nudge her. "Miss you, too."

Skyler is still watching me, and when I turn to meet her gaze, my eyes drop to where her tongue is wetting her lips.

A rush of memories floods through me all at once — Skyler spread out in my sheets, my hand between her thighs, her nails raking down my back. I flick my gaze back to hers and find hooded eyes, watching me, waiting.

The next thing I know we're stumbling inside the yacht, fumbling our way down the stairs into the bottom cabin, a tangle of arms and mouths and hands. I slam her against the door in the bottom cabin as soon as the door is shut and locked behind us.

"Just tonight, no one needs to know," she says, sliding the straps of her one-piece off her shoulders and peeling it down to the floor. She kisses me hard as soon as she's naked, hiking one leg up over my thigh.

I run my hand down between her spread legs, brushing her wet center just enough to earn a soft moan from her lips. "Just tonight. No breakfast."

She laughs into my mouth, spinning until I'm the one pressed against the door. "I hate eggs, anyway." And with that, she drops to her knees, pulling at the strings on my board shorts as I make quick work of the buttons on my shirt, tossing it somewhere into the dark. I don't even know where we are or what kind of room it is. It's pitch black, no windows, just the two of us feeling and touching and tasting.

Every breath is amplified as I kick out of my shorts once she drops them to my ankles, and before I can even prepare for it, her mouth is wrapped around my cock.

"Oh, fuck," I groan as she rolls her tongue over the crown before sliding her lips down to my base. I've never met a girl who gives better head than Skyler Thorne, and I'm immediately reminded of that fact as one hand grabs my balls and she pulls me all the way to the back of her throat.

I'm thankful for the alcohol coating my system, because otherwise I likely would have come right then.

Fisting my hands in her hair, I let her take the lead, head hitting the door behind me with a *thunk* as my drunken senses are overwhelmed with the way her mouth feels. When she starts using her hand in sync with her mouth, it's too much. I reach for her arms blindly, pulling her up until our lips are sealed together again.

Even though it's been months since I've touched her, she still feels familiar — a little like home, a little like my favorite vacation spot. I reach down for the backs of her thighs and lift, letting her wrap herself around me as I stumble forward into the darkness for something to fuck her on. There's a clamor of dishes when we hit a counter, and it's then I realize we're in a small kitchen.

Perfect.

Skyler giggles and kisses down my neck as I feel my way along the countertop. Finding a flat-top stove completely clear, I slide her up onto it, leaning her back and thrusting two fingers deep inside her wet pussy as soon as my lips take hers.

She cries out, hooking one leg over my shoulder to give me better access as I pull my fingers out and slide them back in. Her nails grab at my neck, my back, pulling me closer, wanting more, and I'm all too eager to deliver. I push my fingers in deeper, sucking her lip between my teeth and wiggling my fingertips deep inside, hitting the spot that used to always send her tumbling.

"Oh, God, yes," she pants, breaking our kiss and whispering her pleas into my ear. "Deeper, yes."

I growl, thrusting deeper, and she clenches around me, biting my shoulder to muffle her moans as she comes on my fingers.

It's such a powerful feeling, making someone else fall apart, and I revel in it, pulling her to stand before spinning her around and bending her over the stovetop. I slap her ass, more than ready to fuck her, and it's only when I line up at her wet entrance that I realize I don't have a condom.

"Fuck," I curse, dropping my head to her back. "I, uh… I wasn't exactly prepared for you tonight."

Skyler laughs, spinning to face me again before kissing me hard. "I could say the same. Nice to know you still remember what buttons to push."

She runs her tongue along my bottom lip before reaching down between us to wrap her hand around my shaft. She pumps long and slow, gripping me firmly in her small hands as I thrust into her.

And then she drops to her knees again.

But in that exact moment, my mind decides to be a dick again, because I can't help but wonder if Cassie is on her knees right now, too.

I try to shake her from my thoughts, try to clear them, but it's useless once she's in that space again.

Skyler keeps working me, dropping her mouth to my tip and swirling her tongue around and around. And I know it's Skyler down there, but I can't help but feel in the darkness like it could be Cassie. Imagining it's her hands on my shaft meeting her perfect little mouth, that it's her moan vibrating over my cock as she takes me deep in her throat — it's all it takes to push me to the edge.

I grunt out my release, fighting the urge to call out Cassie's name as I come in Skyler's mouth. But she's all I see. She's all I feel. She's all I want.

When I'm finished, Skyler uses my arms to climb her way back to standing, swallowing like a champ and giggling as I come down from my high. "I have no idea where any of our clothes are."

I laugh at that, feeling through the darkness for my board shorts. When I find them, I dig in the pockets for the water-proof Ziploc bag my phone is in and click on the flashlight, helping Skyler locate her bathing suit.

We get dressed quickly, both of us still smiling, but before I can open the door to lead us back upstairs Skyler pushes me back against the fridge, shoving her tongue in my mouth. She kisses me like a punctuation mark, like she needs to do it just in case I get any ideas. And when she pulls back, the light from my phone illuminates her just enough for me to catch the wink she throws.

"See you around, Brooks."

She bites her lip, shaking her head as she slips out the door and lets it close behind her.

And I just turn the flashlight off, letting the darkness consume me.

# Ashlei

"YOU KILLED THAT!" Mykayla whisper yells at me as the last few of our colleagues leave the boardroom. Two of them, Kimberly and Sam, watch me with narrowed eyes as they mumble to each other, and Mykayla follows my gaze to them. "Don't let them get to you. Jealousy is a virus, babe, and those two are sick as hell."

She laughs at her own joke, adjusting her breasts in the tight dress she's wearing before collecting her papers and binder from the table.

"But seriously, that was awesome. No wonder they made you lead event planner. If you're not careful, you might leave here with a job before you're ready for one," she says.

I rub my temples with my pointer and middle fingers, still feeling hungover even though the Alpha Sigma Halloween party was six days ago. "Thank you, Mykayla. Although if I did get offered a job, something tells me I wouldn't have any friends here."

"You'd have me," she reminds me cheerily.

When the table is clear, we turn out the lights in the boardroom and make our way back to the intern cubes, Mykayla chatting the entire way about the Halloween bar crawl she did over the weekend. I'm listening attentively until we round the corner by the break room and Brandon is walking our direction.

My breath catches at the sight of him, all suited up like I'm used to, but now that I've seen him outside of work, I can't help but long to see his arms in a casual white t-shirt.

Mykayla keeps talking, her voice muted to me now as my eyes stick like sap to Brandon. But he keeps his on the papers in his hands, shuffling through them as he passes right by us without so much as a glance up, and my heart sinks right along with my hope.

He hasn't said a word to me since our... whatever that was, and that was the weekend before Halloween. He still sent the email about me being the lead event planner on the *Bare•ly* project the following Monday when we came in, but not a word was said to me otherwise. Not that I can blame him much after I left him with a massive case of blue balls in the back of my sorority house.

But what was I supposed to do?

I panicked. I needed to think straight, to make sense of it all, and I'd even decided that I would tell him we couldn't do this. It was risky — for both of us.

It looked like I wouldn't have to tell him that, because he'd decided for us. But I wasn't so sure I liked the decision, now.

*Being a girl sucks.*

"Want to grab a drink after work?" Mykayla asks when we reach her reception desk, just before my cube. "It's Happy Hour down at The Lift."

I shake my head, pointing to the stack of binders in my arms. "I've got a hot date with a catalog of chair and linen choices."

She laughs. "Make sure you wear your sexiest bra for that."

"Already got it on." I wink, heading for my desk as Mykayla waves me away with a grin.

The rest of the afternoon passes quickly, which seems to be a pattern now that I've secured the lead event planner position. It's just past five when I wrap up the last email I needed to send and I power down my Mac with a yawn, packing up my oversized handbag before slinging it over my shoulder.

Mykayla is still at her desk when I pass by, and I call out a goodnight to her before rounding the corner toward the elevators. But before I can push the button, she stops me.

"I'm so glad I didn't miss you on your way out," she says, calling me over to her desk. "You're going to flip your shit when I tell you what just happened."

I force a smile, a little too tired to hear office gossip, but I adjust my bag on my shoulder and ask anyway. "What's that?"

"Okay, so, there's a huge event agency award conference in Atlanta every Thanksgiving. It's mostly for agencies in the southeast region, and I'm sure you can imagine, we clean up in pretty much every category. Mr. Church always attends, they usually have him give a keynote speech, and basically he just spends the holiday rubbing elbows with other big wigs in the event industry and bringing back any trends he thinks we should jump on. Anyway," she says, shaking her head with a wave of her hands. "That doesn't really matter. What *does* matter is that he usually goes alone, but this year he requested a plus one."

She looks at me expectantly, her bottom lip pinned between her teeth as she bounces in her chair. When I just offer a raised eyebrow, she leans forward over her desk.

"He requested *you*."

My heart stops, kicking back to life a few seconds later as I stare blankly back at Mykayla. "He did?"

She nods excitedly. "Mm-hmm. But I need an answer from you on whether or not you want to go. Like… well, pretty much like now. He's going to offer it to someone else if you decline. Which you should totally *not* do, if that was even an option in your mind. This has never happened before. It's a big opportunity."

I'm suddenly too aware of my posture, and I have the distinct feeling someone is watching me. When my eyes trail down the row of cubes to Brandon's office, he's watching me from the door, his dark eyes piercing a laser line straight to me. Mykayla goes over the dates and details, clicking through the information on her computer, but I keep my eyes on his.

"So, what do you think? Do you want to go or should I ask the next in line?"

I tear my eyes from Brandon's, swallowing past the wad of sandpaper in my throat. "Well, I guess I'd be stupid to say no."

She bounces again, a squeak escaping her mouth as she softly claps her little hands together. "I'm so excited for you! I'll tell him you've accepted. I hope you'll take a break from your hot date tonight to have a celebratory drink, because this is huge."

I try to smile, but it falls too quickly as I glance toward his office again. I try to make sense of the request, or of the look he's giving me now, but it's all I can do to hold tight to Mykayla's desk and not let my weak knees crash to the floor. The way he's watching me, I'm not sure if I should be excited or scared. His gaze is dark, hungry, and I feel it through my skin, my veins, all the way down to my bones.

I thank Mykayla, turning for the elevators again. When I look back at Brandon, he holds my gaze with his own before shutting his office door, leaving me to stare at the sleek metal door just as the elevator dings its arrival.

A few days later, I shove an abnormally large bite of salad in my mouth just as Jess blows through the kitchen door with a growl.

"Boys are the root of all evil, Lei," she says, tossing her phone onto the kitchen island. It slides across and hits my bowl with a *tink*, which causes her to pause and eye the contents. "Ew. Is that your dinner? Because if so, it personally offends me."

I laugh around my mouthful, swallowing before reaching for my water bottle. "Listen, I eat so horrifically at my internship all week that all I want when I get home is something without carbs and grease."

"You're not human."

"Tell me why boys are stupid today," I say, shoveling another mound of kale into my mouth and effectively changing the subject.

"Ugh," she huffs. "Jarrett had to postpone my trip to see him, so I'm not going up to New York for Thanksgiving anymore." She tries to hold her anger, but it slips, leaving a sadness in its place that makes me pause mid-bite and drop my fork back into my bowl. Jess is a pretty tough girl, especially when it comes to handling guys, so to see her with glossy hazel eyes and a wrinkle between her eyebrows makes my chest ache.

"Oh, Jess, I'm so sorry." I reach for her wrist, squeezing it once. "What happened?"

She shrugs, eyes on her hands as she picks at her deep red nail polish. "Work. What always happens?"

Nodding, I take another bite, trying to find the right words to soothe her. I know how important work can be to someone who has a drive and passion, someone who wants to succeed, but at the same time I can't imagine coming second to that. It takes someone who is really understanding and patient, someone who is secure in who they are and what they have with their significant other.

"Are you okay?" I finally ask.

As if those words snap her back into the kitchen with me, Jess lets out a long, loud breath, shaking her head. "Yeah, I am. I really am. I get it, and I know he didn't want to have to cancel. I'm just making the most of the situation," she adds, popping her hands on the counter before forcing a smile my way. "Which is why I was looking for you. Tell your parents you're not coming home for break. We're having a Friendsgiving."

I choke a little. "A what?"

"Friendsgiving! Oh, come on, like you haven't seen every episode of *Friends.*" She waves me off. "Anyway, I already tracked down the rest of the crew and they're all in. Erin, Skyler, Cassie. I even let her invite Grayson and convinced Bear to put aside his differences with Skyler, whatever the hell is going on there." We both exchange a look then. "Adam might come, too."

I clear my throat, which is suddenly dry. "Jess, I'm so sorry but… I can't come."

"Your parents will understand, dude. Just tell them the situation. They love me!"

"I know they do," I agree, playing with the soggy remains of my salad before pushing it away from me. "But it's not them. It's my internship."

She blinks.

"I got invited to go to a conference over the holiday, and it's a pretty big deal. Usually just our CEO goes, but he invited me along with him. I think…" I swallow. "I think I'm really making an impression on him."

*That's one way to put it.*

"Well, shit." Jess plops down on the bar stool next to me, dropping her head into her hands. "I can't even be mad at you for that."

I chuckle. "Sorry."

She sighs, sitting up again and turning to me with a smile. "It's okay. Really. That's awesome, Lei, and I'm really proud of you. I knew you were going to knock their socks off."

With that she grabs for her phone, checking the screen before huffing again and flipping it over to face down on the counter.

"Waiting for a text from Jarrett?"

She nods. "I love him so much. It scares the shit out of me because I legitimately feel crazy."

"Want me to play some Beyoncé so you can twerk it out to *Crazy in Love* and get it out of your system?"

"Shut up," she says on a laugh, but then she leans her head on my shoulder and I rest mine against hers, petting her hair. "Just tell me everything is going to be okay."

"Everything's going to be okay," I assure her, and maybe myself a little, too. Because in just a few short weeks, I'll be on a plane to Atlanta with my hot CEO. The same CEO who had his tongue in my mouth and his hands under my shirt two weeks ago.

I stare at my salad, suddenly craving something with a lot more anxiety-calming power.

"How do you feel about walking to Froggy's for a triple scoop cone?"

Jess hops down off her stool, tucking her phone into her back pocket as she points in my direction. "*Now* you're speaking my language."

And with that, we link arms and head out the back door, both of us hoping like hell that ice cream is the answer to all our problems.

Episode 5

# Ashlei

"HAVE A GOOD THANKSGIVING," Hannah, one of the other interns, says to me as she hooks her messenger bag on her shoulder. "Can't wait to hear about the trip!"

I smile, my stomach doing a backflip at the mention of the trip with Brandon. It's the last Friday in the office before the holiday, though we don't leave for Atlanta until Tuesday. The rest of the office has the entire week off until the Monday after the holiday.

"Thanks, Hannah. Enjoy your holiday, too."

When she's gone, Kimberly pushes her chair in under her desk and turns to me with a tight smile. "Yeah, can't wait to hear about the trip. You must be *so* excited."

She narrows her eyes, but it doesn't take her resting bitch face for me to know how she feels about me. She hasn't been the least bit shy in telling everyone exactly why she thinks I got invited on the trip, along with the lead event planner position. But the gossip she's spreading about me "sleeping my way to the top" doesn't faze me. My dad prepared me for this over the summer — the way others would react to someone who was driven to succeed. And being that I'm a woman, being successful usually means I'll either be painted as a slut or a bitch, depending on my leadership style.

Still, I can't help but feel a little uneasy as Brandon comes up behind me, placing a hand on my shoulder, Kimberly's eyes glued to the spot where he's touching my bare skin. Because the truth is that while I may not be sleeping with him on a mission, I am attracted to him. And we did cross a line.

One that seems completely nonexistent now.

"Can I speak with you before you leave, Miss Daniels?" Brandon asks, voice commanding attention as always.

Kimberly purses her lips, cocking one eyebrow at me like she has me all figured out before snatching her blazer off the back of her chair and swinging it over her arm. "Happy Thanksgiving, Mr. Church," she says as she passes, and I close my eyes tight before turning to face him.

"Yes, Mr. Church?" I ask, looking up at him from my chair.

The corner of his mouth twitches a bit at the sound of his name as he casually puts his hands in the pockets of his slacks. "I just wanted to make sure you have the itinerary and everything else you need for our trip on Tuesday."

I hold up the folder Mykayla left with me earlier. "All set. I have a dress for the award ceremony and business attire for the conference. I also printed out a few copies of your speech, just in case we need it to review or anything." His eyes widen just slightly at that. "I haven't read it," I assure him.

Brandon relaxes a bit, nodding. "Okay, then. Be at the hangar at four sharp on Tuesday afternoon. They'll have light snacks and refreshments on the jet but we'll have dinner once we've landed in Atlanta."

I swallow, still a little freaked out that I'll be riding in his private jet. "Sounds good. I won't be late."

Brandon just watches me then, his eyes flicking down to where my legs are crossed, exposed in the pencil skirt I'm wearing, before he lazily pulls his gaze back up to my own. "Looking forward to it."

My skin burns from where his eyes just roamed and I squirm in my chair, uncrossing my legs just to cross them the other way. He smirks, like he knows exactly what he's doing to me, before finally turning for the elevators.

"Don't stay all night," he throws back behind him. "I've already got you working on a holiday week. At least take the full weekend off."

I relax just a hair, smiling. "I'm out of here in ten. Promise."

He pushes the down arrow for the elevators, tossing me a wink before the doors slide open and he steps on, leaving me and a few girls in Corporate Relations as the last ones in the office.

The tension between us since our date at the auto racing track has been like an electric wire pulled taut, threatening to break and spark a fire at the slightest contact. Every look he's cast in my direction during meetings, his gaze always hard and steady, seems to pull it tighter and tighter, the coils stretched to their limits.

Something tells me when those doors close on that private jet, leaving just the two of us alone again, we won't have a chance in hell of keeping it from snapping.

A few hours later, Jess tries unsuccessfully to catch a kernel of popcorn in her mouth after launching it up in the air. It hits her nose and bounces to the floor next to Skyler's freshly painted toenails and Jess eyes it for a moment before shrugging and digging into the bowl again.

"I'm so glad we decided to do this," Skyler says, blowing on her turquoise nails. We're all sprawled out in the floor space between the two beds in her and Jess's room, mountains of pillows and blankets surrounding us along with three bottles of wine we smuggled in and an ungodly amount of junk food. "It feels like it's been forever since we had a girls' night."

"It has been," Erin agrees. "I mean between me preparing for the election, you racking up money to pay the entry fee for that poker tournament, Ashlei spending all her time at her internship and Jess loading up her plate with extra classes since she switched her major, none of us have had a free Friday since the semester started."

"I just wish Cassie was here, too," I say, still clicking through the movies on the small TV in the corner near Skyler's bed.

"I know. Poor thing, midterms have her so stressed out. She's been at the Greek library every night for the past two weeks and her last midterm isn't until *Wednesday*," Skyler says.

"The day before Thanksgiving? What a dick professor!" Jess shakes her head. "Shouldn't even be allowed. I'm already done with mine."

"Is that why you've been in a better mood?" I ask, settling on *Pretty Woman* and pushing the play button on the remote. "Or did you and a certain tattooed hottie make up?"

She sighs, tucking her knees up to her chest and shoving another handful of popcorn in her mouth. "It's not his fault he got put on another project so soon. Well," she clarifies, swallowing. "I guess *technically* it is, because he's so damn good at his job. But I know he wouldn't have cancelled unless he absolutely had to. It's hard right now," she admits. "But I love him and I know he loves me, so I'm just trying to focus on that."

"Good girl," Erin says.

Jess claps her hands together. "Plus, Friendsgiving! It's going to be so much fun. Erin, you're still getting the turkey, right?"

"Picking it up that morning from the place my mom ordered from. She said they're the best in town."

"Maybe Bear will actually talk to me then," Skyler says on a sigh. "You know, being that the holiday spirit will be flowing and all."

Erin and Jess both frown, all of us eyeing each other as Skyler keeps her gaze on her nails.

"Do you want to talk about it?" I try, knowing it's probably useless. She hasn't told any of us the details of why Clinton is suddenly acting like she is dead to him, which likely means it's something personal, something only the two of them need to know.

She shakes her head. "Not tonight. I'd rather talk about happy stuff, like this awesome trip you're taking for your internship. Jess, feed me popcorn, my nails are still wet," she adds and Jess laughs, obliging as everyone's attention turns to me.

"It's not a big deal, really. It's just this award banquet thing and Mr. Church will be giving a keynote speech. There's a conference, too, but nothing special."

"Lies," Jess says, popping another popcorn puff into Skyler's mouth. "Stop selling yourself short. You said this is the first time he's ever invited anyone else to attend with him, and you're an *intern*, Lei."

"Oh, my God," Skyler says around a mouthful. "Is he the smoking hot guy who dropped ten thousand bucks on you at the Alpha Sigma concert auction? I saw him pick you up a few weeks ago."

"You didn't tell me he bid on you." Jess narrows her eyes.

"He was just doing it for the charity, guys. He's a philanthropic man."

Skyler laughs. "Mmm-hmm. Is he a God-fearing man, too? Because Lord, take me to church." She fans herself while Erin cracks up.

"You're shameless, Skyler."

Jess ignores Erin's comment, typing away on her phone. "Oh, my God, I just Googled him. Holy shit, Lei! Why didn't you tell me how fucking hot this guy is?!"

Erin and Skyler gather around her phone while I bury my face in my hands. "Because I'm trying my hardest *not* to notice how bangable my CEO is."

"Yeah," Erin scoffs. "Good luck with that."

They all giggle at my misfortune and I just shake my head, eventually giving in and laughing, too. "I'm screwed, huh?"

"Yup," they all agree in sync, Jess tossing popcorn at me while we all laugh even harder. It's like coming home to a warm fire and hot chocolate after walking through the snow, having a girls' night with my three best friends. I'm reminded that no matter what happens to any of us, we always have each other, and that's a pretty amazing thing.

We go through three movies, three bottles of wine, and at least three-thousand calories in salty snacks and chocolate by the time the night is over. Erin is the first to pass out, followed closely by Jess and Skyler, the three of them sleeping with pillows propped up against legs and shoulders in a sort of cuddle pit on the floor. Empty snack wrappers litter the space around them, only the soft glow from the television illuminating their peaceful faces.

I smile, pulling out my phone and snapping a picture of them before uploading it to social media with the caption, "Love my girls. #GNI." Then, I adjust my pillow against Erin's back and curl up, too.

# Cassie

I'VE NEVER CLIMBED a mountain, or run a marathon, or jumped out of a plane just hoping a parachute would open and help me float down safely to the ground. I've never seen the breathtaking islands of Greece or the first snow on the mountains in Colorado, and I've never backpacked across Europe discovering new sights with every turn.

But I have been touched and loved by Grayson Anderson.

I imagine it's the same feeling — the rush of adrenaline, the high not even the best drug could provide, the sense of impossibility, like there's no way this moment is actually happening, that this is actually real. It's a combination of discovery and familiarity, of passion and vulnerability, and I haven't been able to get enough of it since the night we left the Halloween party.

Now, the Sunday before Thanksgiving, Grayson and I are still in bed even though it's almost noon. It's a cool and rainy day, the dark clouds casting a soft gray light across his entire room, but we've been too wrapped up in the covers and each other to care what the weather is like outside. Grayson has already brought me to ecstasy twice in the last twelve hours — once last night and once this morning—but here he is again, face between my thighs and legs hooked over his shoulders as he tries for number three.

I moan as he slips one finger just barely inside me, sweeping his tongue hot and flat over my clit at the same time. It's so sensitive after all the action it's had lately that just him blowing on it makes my entire body tingle. He works his finger slowly, knowing I'm tender, and takes his time building my pleasure. It's almost like I'm in a dream, a weird state of feeling everything and feeling nothing at all, my eyes low and lazy, heart stuck somewhere between a gallop and a flat line.

"Please," I whisper, tugging on his hair to pull him back up my body. He plants kisses across my skin the entire way — on my hips, my ribs, my breast, my neck, until he eventually settles between my legs, capturing my mouth with his.

"Please what?"

I dig my heels into his backside, aching to have him inside me again.

His grin is devilish as he kisses me harder, the tip of him running the line of me, the tease nearly killing me. "I want you to come again."

Everything goes hazy at those words, like a zap to all my senses, effectively muting them before sparking them all back to life at once. "I don't know if I can."

"You can," he answers quickly, and then slowly, with every centimeter stretching me wider around him, he slips all the way inside me. "You will."

The way he feels inside me without a barrier between us overwhelms me every time. My eyes flutter shut, back arching up off the bed as he withdraws slowly and opens me wider the second time he pushes inside. We'd used a condom the first few times, but since we're both clean and are exclusive to each other, we'd decided we wanted to have the full feeling of just the two of us.

And, God, what a feeling it is.

Grayson groans when he finally stretches me to fit all of him all the way inside, dropping his face into my neck and sucking the skin there. "Fuck, you feel so amazing, Cassie."

He works me slow and steady, so different from the way he took me mercilessly last night. It's as if he's matching the slow tempo of the rain pattering on his windowsill. In and out, a kiss and a touch, a sigh and a moan, a boy and a girl.

When he gently rolls until I'm sitting on top, thighs straddled on each side of him, his hands find my waist as he helps me ride, guiding me to match the rhythm he had before. I lean forward over him, elbows braced on either side of his head as I kiss him, wondering if he feels the way I do in this moment. Pure bliss.

When he starts rocking into me deeper, friction catching me in the perfect spot, I feel my orgasm mounting. But it feels just out of reach, like my body is too exhausted to extend a hand out even one inch farther to capture it.

"I'm so close," I breathe into his mouth, kissing him again as he flexes his hips.

Grayson speeds up, just a little, just enough to turn embers to fire. As it catches, billowing through me like an explosion, I gasp against his kisses, whimpering, pleading — for what, I'm not sure. And when the fire has run its course, I collapse, heavy on Grayson's chest as he kisses me softer, slowing his pace.

I rest for a moment before pushing up off his chest to sit straight up, riding him slow again, ready to bring him with me. He's already close, I can tell by the way his face twists up, his eyes closing as his hands grip my hips tighter. When they work their way up to grab both of my breasts, he curses, bucking into me with more force, and then he comes, my name a breath of a whisper on his lips.

Best. Sunday. Ever.

We both groan as I roll over, breaking our connection and spreading out in the sheets next to him as I try to catch my breath. Grayson just reaches his pinky out to graze mine, our eyes on the ceiling, hearts still racing.

"Be right back," I say, kissing his cheek before hopping up and limping to his bathroom. I'm so sore, so I take my time, relieving myself first before running a warm wash cloth along where I ache the most.

When I make my way back into the bedroom, Grayson still hasn't moved. He beckons me over to the bed and I crawl back under the sheets, letting him pull me under his arm with my head resting on his chest.

"I wish I could stay in bed with you all day," I say wistfully, watching the rain wash down the window through his sheer curtains.

He kisses my hair, running his fingers gently through it. "I do, too. I'm not even a little bit ready to play at this coffee bar tonight. It's probably going to be slow with the rain, anyway."

"At least you don't have to study," I grumble.

He laughs, pulling me in for one more kiss before I stand, searching for my clothes. I find my cotton boy shorts first by the foot of the bed and tug them on.

"Are you going to the Greek library again?" he asks, chin propped on his hand, shamelessly watching me as I pull my lacy bralette over my head and adjust it into place.

"Yeah," I answer with a sigh. "I practically live there now. Adam is meeting me there in a few hours, though, so at least I'll have some company."

I pull my Kappa Kappa Beta tank top over my head, and when my eyes find Grayson's again, his smile is completely gone, his body tense.

"You're hanging out with Adam tonight?"

"*Studying* with Adam," I correct him. "Not exactly my version of hanging out or having any fun whatsoever."

Grayson is quiet a moment as I search for my jeans.

"I don't like it," he says finally.

I sigh, finally spotting my jeans draped over his desk chair. I swipe them off and tug them on one leg at a time. "He's my friend, Grayson. And we're just studying. I thought you guys were cool now?" I'd watched them shake hands the night of the Halloween party, and though I knew they'd never be best friends, I hoped they could at least be cordial.

"I can study with you," he tries.

"You're busy tonight. And literally every night until my final."

"Well, isn't studying more of a solo sport anyway? Maybe you should just hang out in your room."

"Grayson," I deadpan.

"Well!" He huffs, throwing the sheets off him and yanking on his boxer briefs before running a hand through his hair, frustrated. "Try seeing this from my point of view, Cassie. How would you feel if there was a girl I knew before I met you whom I spent time with? *Alone*. Without you. A girl who you *knew* had more than friendly feelings for me."

"Adam doesn't—"

"Cassie." He stops me, face flat as he challenges me to finish my sentence.

Sighing, I sink down onto the bed next to him, pulling my hair into a braid over my right shoulder. "It's just… I care about him, too, Grayson. He's one of my best friends, and I'm sorry if that hurts to hear but it's true. He's been there for me through a lot of tough times and…" I shrug, not sure what else to say. "I don't want to upset you, but I don't want to lose my friendship with him, either."

Grayson's jaw tenses, but he pulls me to face him, taking both my hands in his. "I'm not asking you to not be friends with him, okay? I just… what if, at least for a while, you see him when we're all together? It would make me feel a lot more comfortable. Please," he pleads, eyes earnest. "You're going to see him at Jess' Friendsgiving thing when we're all there. Can you study with one of your sisters? I know it seems silly to you, but it matters to me."

Those last words squeeze my heart. I try to put myself in his shoes, imagine how it would feel if he had an Adam, and I had to know they were alone together in an empty library. I know I'd be uncomfortable, too, even if he assured me they were just friends.

Jealousy is an untamable beast.

"Okay," I concede. "I'll cancel with Adam and tell him I decided to study off campus."

"Thank you," Grayson says, smile back as he brings my hands to his lips and kisses them. "Now go study, future Dr. McBee."

He pops me on the ass as I stand and I swat at his hand with a laugh, grabbing my backpack off his desk. But when I'm outside, balancing an umbrella in one hand as I type out a text to Adam with the other, I can't help the sick feeling that washes over me. It feels a little like abandoning Adam, like making a choice I never intended to make between two important people in my life.

Of course Adam writes back right away, completely understanding, even cracking a joke at my expense. Because that's who Adam is — kind, forgiving, always there, even when I maybe don't deserve him to be.

Grayson said he only wants me to see Adam in group settings for now, just until he's comfortable. But will that day ever really come? And if it doesn't, do I have a right to be upset?

Can I have a strong relationship with my boyfriend without sacrificing my friendship with Adam?

I don't have the answer.

And something tells me I wouldn't like it if I did.

*Jess*

MY EYES ARE WINGED, lips painted a deep red, and hair curled to perfection as I jump into bed. Normally I wouldn't go all out for a night in, but Jarrett and I have a video chat date set to start in less than five minutes, and I want to make him want me so bad he's booking a plane ticket.

Okay, so I know that's not possible right now, but if I can at the very least make him say, "*Damn,*" I'll be happy.

I'm dressed in nothing but a lacy thong as I dive under the sheets, thankful Skyler has another poker tournament keeping her busy and out of our room for the evening. I pull my top sheet up over my chest, leaving just the sweetest view of cleavage in the camera line before dialing Jarrett's number.

My face fills the screen as it waits for him to connect and I touch up my hair again, running my fingers over the curls. But when the phone rings for almost a full minute before disconnecting completely without an answer, I frown.

*He said eight o'clock, right?*

I check our text messages and the time on my phone again, just to be sure.

Sighing, I lay my phone on my lap and wait, convincing myself he's probably just getting out of the shower or something. But when ten minutes goes by without a call back, I try again.

No answer.

When it's half past eight and there's not even a text from him, my excitement fades into disappointment and uncertainty.

**- Hey, we still on for tonight? -**

I send the text, heart flipping in my chest when I immediately see the three bouncing dots that tell me he's texting back.

**- One sec. -**

I smile, flipping on my camera to check my lipstick and fluff my hair again, but when his name finally fills my screen along with a picture of us from his last visit, it's a regular phone call, not a video one.

"Hey, babe," he says immediately when I answer, though I can barely hear him over the loud music and laughter behind him. "I'm stepping outside, just give me a second." My heart sinks, the background noise clearing when he's outside, replaced by the soft, almost muted sound of traffic. "Sorry about that. How are you?"

"I'm fine. Aren't we video chatting tonight?"

Jarrett sighs into the phone. "I'm so sorry, Jess. I completely forgot. Today was absolute hell at the office. We're in crunch time for this project and they had assigned Matt to help me and Jenny, but he's been sick for a week now, so it's just the two of us again and we're beat. We ended up stopping for a drink after work."

All the warmth drains from my face, slipping slowly down my neck. "Oh."

"It's just a drink, Jess," he assures me. "We're both under a lot of pressure right now and needed to take a break before we both lose our damn minds."

I swallow despite the knot in my throat, nodding even though he can't see me.

He sighs. "You're pissed, aren't you?"

At that I close both of my eyes tight, two twin tears rolling down opposite cheeks. "Just tell me the truth, Jarrett. Are you and Jenny... are you messing around with her?"

"What?!" Jarrett huffs. "No. And I told you this last time you accused me of it. I've had a shit day at work and I needed a beer. So did she. So, now we're taking *one* fucking hour to decompress and I don't understand why I can't do that without you throwing a childish fit over it!"

His words only slice me deeper, more tears pouring hot down my face as I wipe at my nose. "I miss you!" I scream back. "Is that my crime? That I miss you and I'm sad when you blow off our date to have a drink at a bar with another woman? How would you feel if you were me?"

"I'd be understanding," he snaps back. "And I'd tell you I'm sorry to hear you had a bad day, and I'd ask you to call me later when you get home."

"Bullshit," I whisper, sniffing and batting at the tears on my face. "That's bullshit and you know it."

"All I *know* right now is that I'm tired of having the same argument. Nothing I say is going to make you believe me."

"Actions speak a lot louder than words."

He barks out a laugh. "Wow. I can't believe we're having this conversation."

I shake my head, heart breaking with every cold word that leaves his lips. "We're not anymore." And with that, I hang up the phone, dropping my face into my pillow and letting my tears consume me.

Every breath burns my lungs, like the air is left toxic from our fight. I know he's working hard, and I understand that need to relieve the stress, but it doesn't change the fact that he forgot about me — about our date — and that hurts more than anything.

*He didn't even apologize*, I think, which makes the tears come harder.

I should be on a plane tonight, a plane that would take me to him, into his arms, the place where I feel safe and comforted and okay. But instead, I'm crying alone in my bed, wondering why we're even doing this to each other anymore. Maybe he'd be happier without me breathing down his back, needing his constant reassurance. Maybe I'd be happier without him breaking promises, without feeling like a nuisance more than a girlfriend.

Just the thought of living without him makes me curl into myself tighter, shaking my head as a new wave of tears rush down my face, soaking my pillow. I've never loved anyone the way I love Jarrett, and I know I wouldn't be happier without him. I'd be miserable.

But does he feel the same?

# Ashlei

MR. CHURCH MUST be hungry.

That's all I can think as I cross my legs even tighter, fighting against the heat building between them. It's hard enough not to squirm sitting in a board meeting with Brandon at the head of the table, but with just a small table separating us in a private jet it's damn near impossible.

I'd shown up at the hangar on time, just as promised, and we'd quickly loaded up into the jet, the personnel taking care of our bags and offering us a glass of champagne as we stepped inside. I'd found it hard not to gasp when I boarded, seeing the beautiful leather interior, complete with three sets of comfortable, reclining chairs with tables between them, and one long couch. The leather was a cross of beige and black, cut with thickly sewn stitching that reminded me of Brandon's car interior. There were dark brown and maroon suede pillows on the couch and one small one in each chair, pulling all the aesthetics together, making it scream business and comfort all at once.

Brandon had taken a seat at the back set of chairs, the one across from the couch, and I'd followed suit, sitting across the small table from him. He'd been quiet as the flight crew explained our route and how long it would take, offering us more refreshments, and he'd remained silent until just after takeoff. Once we were in the air, he'd started small talk — literally talking about the weather in Atlanta and asking how my midterms went — before he fell back into a quiet state.

Except this time, his eyes weren't on the newspaper.

They were on me.

And *that* is when I decided that he must be hungry, and that our first stop when we land will most certainly be a restaurant. Because the way he looked at me, the way he's *still* looking at me, is like he's a starved man and I'm a surf n' turf buffet of the highest quality.

I glance at the small screen behind Brandon's head, one with a map of our route and a little white airplane to show us where we are. It also details how fast we're going and our approximate arrival time, which isn't too long, being that the trip from Miami to Atlanta is a quick one in a jet. I try to keep my focus on that little screen, but I feel him in my peripheral, boring a hole into my skin with his gaze.

"I have a proposal for you, Miss Daniels."

*Are we back to last names now?*

I snap my attention to him, swallowing hard as he steeples his fingers over his lap, his eyes dark and intense.

"And what's that, Mr. Church?"

He smirks. "For the past month, the two of us have been acting like what happened between us didn't happen. Which is professional, and certainly the right thing to do."

I search his face for signs of sarcasm, but find none. So, I just nod in agreement. "Yes."

"Yes," he echoes me. Pausing, he watches me for a moment before leaning forward over the small table between us, his hands disappearing underneath it. "However, I'm in quite a predicament, Miss Daniels. Because it seems that you have awakened a rather persistent itch, one that I don't see going away until I give in and scratch it."

Warmth crawls up my neck, burning my cheeks as I reach for my champagne glass on the table, draining the last sip of it. Every nerve of my body is at full attention, hanging on his words, waiting for what he'll say next.

"Now, I could live with this itch," he says, catching my eyes with his before trailing them down over my chest. "But, judging by the way you're clenching your thighs together under this table…" He leans forward a little more, and then I feel the warmth of his finger — just one — as it brushes the inside of my knee so slightly I'm almost sure I'm imagining it. "And the way your cheeks flush when I touch you, something tells me you've got an itch to scratch, too."

It takes everything in me, including a tight grip on the armrests of my chair and a tight closing of my eyes, not to moan when the one finger on the inside of my knee turns into a flat, hot palm, sliding just an inch up, just enough to brush the hem of my skirt.

"So, what's your proposal, Mr. Church?" The words leave my lips in something like a whisper and a groan, my eyelids cracking open again as I find his gaze.

"Until this jet touches down in Miami again, you're mine," he nearly growls the words, running his tongue along his bottom lip as he eyes mine. "And I'm yours. No boundaries, no rules, no thought of consequences. Just two people scratching an itch and keeping a little secret." He shrugs. "And when we land back in reality, it's hands off again. Responsible. Professional."

My breaths are silent, almost nonexistent as I watch him, debating. "And you think we'll be able to do that," I challenge, uncrossing my legs to spread them just an inch. His nose flares at the bold act, his hand skating up a centimeter more. "You think you'll be able to fuck me this week and let me go on Sunday night? That you'll be able to see me in the office every day, knowing you'll never touch me again?"

I run my fingers through my hair and trail the tips of them down over my neck, my collarbone, running them along the neckline of my blouse with my lip pinned between my teeth.

Brandon inhales a stiff breath, eyes on fire. "I think I'd rather know that torture than continue living in this one."

My brain is in overdrive, ticking through the possibilities and the consequences if we were caught, but the overwhelming thought pushing everything else down is that the likelihood of us getting caught is slim to none. As long as we keep our hands to ourselves when we're in public, and we go back to normal when we're in the office again, no one would need to know.

And, *God*, how I want to taste him again, to touch him again, to know what he feels like inside me.

*Fuck it.*

"No one finds out. And when we land again, I'm off limits. No looking at me across the boardroom like you want to fuck me on the table while everyone watches."

"You have my word," he says, smirking. "So, do we have a deal?"

He doesn't move his hand any higher, doesn't lick his lips or raise an eyebrow — he simply waits.

"We have a deal."

The last word doesn't even leave my lips before Brandon clears our glasses and his newspaper off the table in one sweep of his arm, sending them crashing to the floor before flipping the table between us up to hook on the wall. He drops to his knees in front of me, and then his hands are in my hair, and his mouth is on mine, tongue sweeping in to claim me like I was never anyone else's, like I'll never be anyone else's again.

I'm still catching my breath against his kisses when his hands trail their way down, following the curves of my body until both palms are pressed on the inside of my knees. He pushes them apart, earning a gasp from me as he slides his hands up my inner thighs, pushing my skirt up with them.

"This is really stupid of us," I pant as he kisses his way down my neck, hands still climbing. "You know that, right?"

"Completely idiotic," he agrees, then he fists the bunched up fabric of my skirt and yanks until my ass is hanging off the edge of the seat.

With slow precision, he unfastens each button on my blouse, tugging it from where it was tucked into my skirt and leaving it open, exposing my simple nude bra. Brandon pulls the cups down until my breasts spill out of the top, pulling both of my nipples between his fingers and thumbs as I arch into his touch with a moan.

"You are so fucking sexy," he growls, and then his hands drop to my thighs as he reaches up under my skirt for my panties, ripping them down my legs until they fall around my ankles. I can't even step out of them before his face is buried between my thighs.

A string of curse words leave my lips on a breath as he runs his tongue along the length of me, swirling my clit at the top before diving between my lips like I'm his last meal. My heart is racing like his NSX, running laps as my breaths struggle to keep up, my hands grasping for anything to hold onto — the arms of the chair, the sleeves of his dress shirt, the last shred of my morals. But I can't catch my grip, not on any of it, so I let go, let him pull me down, two sinners in the clouds just waiting for the fall into hell.

Brandon is an expert with his tongue, sucking and teasing my clit until my legs are quivering on either side of his face. But when he runs two warm fingertips up my inner thigh, coating them in my wetness before sliding them inside, I learn he's an expert with his hands, too.

"Come here," he husks, wiggling his fingers deep inside me as his free hand pulls me in to kiss him. His mouth is hot on mine, his kisses hard and demanding as he pushes me closer and closer to release. Every part of me is held captive — his hand locked behind my neck, holding my mouth to his, his fingers inside me, his eyes devouring what little of me is left.

And I let him take me, let him tease me and ruin me and claim me until it's too much.

"Enough."

I press my hands hard into his chest, pushing him off me, his fingers taking my breath with them as he slips out and lands with his back against his chair. He eyes me with a wild gaze, licking his lips as I crawl out of my seat and across the floor, propping myself on my knees in front of him as I rip at his belt, desperate to have him as naked as I am.

He helps me, lifting his hips when I finish with the zipper and kicking off his dress shoes, allowing me to pull his pants down and off, flinging them to the side before I spread my legs over his thighs to straddle him. Just the length of him pressed against my center makes my breath catch. I haven't been with a man since Spring Break, since everything with Bo and me went up in flames. The thought of her shocks my system, coming out of nowhere, and I quickly shove her to the back of my mind again, fingers frantically working the buttons of Brandon's dress shirt as he fumbles in the pockets of his discarded pants for a condom.

"Up," he commands when he finds one, ripping the package open with his teeth.

I lift my hips, pressing my lips to his as I pull his dress shirt open, running my hands along the length of his hard chest, his defined abdomen, my nails digging into his flesh.

His hands disappear between us for just a fraction of a second, strapping the condom on before they find my waist, gripping hard, and he lines up the crown of him with the wet opening of me.

And for a moment, everything stops, time suspended between us, our breaths slowing before stopping altogether. My arms wrapped around his neck and his hands framing my face, foreheads pressed together, Brandon searches my eyes with his own, asking permission again.

Slowly, with my mouth finding his again, I slide down, the hard length of him stretching me open centimeter by aching centimeter.

I wince against the pain, laced with overwhelming pleasure, my body in shock at the feel of being reopened after so many months. I dig my nails into his back even more, working as slow as I can to fit him all the way inside.

"Goddamn, Ashlei," he groans, brows bent together and hands gripping my waist like that's the only control he has to stop himself from slamming into me. When I finally sink all the way down, the base of me touching the base of him, we both let out a long, almost pained breath.

The first time I tried cocaine, I remember feeling shock and understanding all at once — the rush of blood, the lightheadedness, the intense awareness, the awakening. Still, I hadn't found it difficult to walk away from. But with Brandon's arms wrapping all the way around me, his hands curling on my shoulders, head buried in my chest as he flexes his hips into me, stealing my breath again, I realize distantly that *this* is a real high. This is the high addicts are born from. Walking away from this, from him, won't be simple. Part of me wonders if it will even be possible at all.

Like a light switch, I turn off my thoughts of the future, surrendering to the now as I ride Brandon steadily, my orgasm mounting with every brush of my clit against him, with every deep thrust of him inside me. When his hands find my ass and squeeze, pulling me harder against him as he sucks the sensitive skin around my nipple, my breath catches and I hold it there, reaching blindly for my climax.

"Say my name when you come," he growls, sucking my nipple hard before moving up to kiss the skin under my ear. "I want to hear it."

"Oh, fuck, Mr.—"

"No." He cuts my words short, stopping his movements altogether. "Wrong name."

I writhe in his lap, the sensation that had been rising fading off as I try desperately to hold onto it. I rock against him, crying out, nails digging into his arms. "Please," I beg. "I'm so close."

He answers my plea, thrusting hard and deep, and sparks fly behind my pinched eyelids, flames licking my skin from the inside out as I come apart. "Oh, God, Brandon. Fuck. Don't stop."

He groans at his name, pumping harder, and as I ride out my climax, he finds his. The groans escaping his lips are enough to ignite my orgasm for another round, both of us gripping onto each other, pushing and pulling and scratching and digging until we're both spent, collapsing into each other in a heap of shallow breaths.

When it's over, the high receding, my body sore and aching in all the right places, Brandon holds me in his lap. He kisses the skin on my shoulder, soothing his fingertips over my back as I rest. When I peek up at the screen behind him, I see we only have a half an hour before the jet will land in Atlanta.

"We should get dressed," I whisper.

Brandon pulls back, searching my eyes with his own. "Is that really what you're thinking right now?"

"Well, we land soon," I point out, feeling a little self-conscious. "Why, what are you thinking?"

He pauses, eyes flicking to the ceiling as he thinks. "I'm hungry."

A laugh rips from my throat and Brandon chuckles, too, pulling me into him for one last kiss.

*I knew it.*

# Cassie

"MAYBE WE SHOULD just start," Skyler suggests, her wary eyes on Jess as she waits for her to blow. We've all been waiting, the tension like a cloud of gnats hovering around us at the Friendsgiving table. "I'm sure she'll be here soon. We can at least eat the sides while they're hot."

Erin was supposed to be here already — with the missing turkey — and with both her and Ashlei missing in action coupled with the fact that Jess is only throwing this because her boyfriend cancelled her trip to see him, it's not exactly a joyous occasion. I'm thankful Grayson is here with me, at least.

Clinton scoffs, crossing his arms with a hard roll of his eyes. "Oh, right, because you always know what's best, don't you, Sky?"

Skyler's face crumples and my heart aches seeing my Big like that. She's always so strong, so sure, but Clinton is her best friend. Their fight is taking a toll on her and we all know it.

"Bear, please. I apologized. Can we just… can't we have a nice meal?"

Everyone watches Clinton carefully, like a bomb with three seconds left on the timer and a red wire about to be cut.

After a moment, he picks up his fork, but before I can even let out a sigh of relief he grits his teeth and drops it back to the table again.

"How the fuck are we supposed to have Thanksgiving without a goddamn turkey," he growls as he stands, and without another look at any of us, he blows out the back door.

My eyes find Skyler's and I reach for her wrist, squeezing it gently.

"He's not mad about the turkey," she explains on a sigh. "He's just worried about his little brother and…"

"It's fine, Big," I say, smiling sympathetically. "I agree, we should just eat."

"Yeah, who says you can't make a meal out of green bean casserole?" Adam chimes in. "Challenge accepted."

My eyes find his then, silently thanking him. He just winks, reaching forward for the mashed potatoes and piling them on his plate to get things started. But when he tries to pass the dish to Skyler, she's still staring at the door Clinton just left through.

With a shake of her head, she drops her napkin onto her empty plate and pushes back from the table. "I'm sorry, I just need to check on him. I'll be back."

Jess watches her leave with murderous eyes, and when the door swings shut again and it's just the four of us — Jess, Adam, Grayson, and myself — the swarm of gnats buzzes even louder than before.

Adam swallows, offering the dish across the table to me, instead, as Jess drops her head into her hands, kneading her temples.

I take the dish from Adam, our fingers brushing just slightly. I can't stop the flush that colors my cheeks. We haven't had a chance to talk face to face since Halloween, not after Grayson asked me to cancel our study date, and I feel Adam's eyes burning into me from across the table. There have always been way more questions in those eyes of his than I've ever had answers for.

Jess's phone buzzes on the table and I say a silent prayer that it's Erin with news on the turkey, trying to keep spirits up until she can get here. But before I can even serve myself a scoop of mashed potatoes, Grayson's chair scrapes against the floor as he stands.

"Oh, for Christ's sake, what now?!" Jess huffs.

I pause with the bowl in my hands, looking up at Grayson as he glares at Adam across the table.

"I can't do this anymore, Cassie," he says, and my heart sinks as I follow his gaze to Adam and back again. "You have to choose. Him," he snarls, thrusting a hand toward Adam. "Or me."

"Andddd, that's my cue." Jess stands, throwing her napkin down and waving her hands. "You guys can have your pissing match. I'm going to get a cheeseburger."

But I can't even ask her to stay, or tell her I'm sorry, or do anything other than stare blankly up at Grayson, wondering what the hell is going on.

"Grayson—"

"No," he clips, jaw set. "No, I'm serious. I can't just fucking sit here while he drools over you from across the table."

"Maybe I should leave," Adam tries, placing his hands on the table to stand.

"Sit the fuck down," Grayson growls at him, turning to me next. "This is getting settled. Tonight. I thought I could deal with you guys being friends, but his lack of respect for our relationship isn't going to make that possible. I don't want you around him, Cassie," he says, the sentence like a punctuation. He's like an alien in this moment, a foreigner I don't recognize.

"Please," I whisper, reaching for his hand, but he jerks it away.

"Don't want her around me?" Adam sneers, chair flying behind him as he stands to match

Grayson's stance. "I was her friend before she even knew you *existed*."

Grayson scoffs. "Friend, my ass."

"Guys, please." My voice is so small compared to theirs, like a bird chirp competing with a train horn.

"Sounds like someone's threatened," Adam shoots back. "Don't worry, Grayson. Can't steal a girl who doesn't want to be stolen. You should be fine, since you spend so much time with her and really make her a priority in your life."

"Not helping, Adam!" I shout as Grayson beats his fists on the table.

"Enough!" he growls, turning to me with wild eyes. "Do you love me?"

My voice cracks, throat thick with an unswallowable knot. "Of course."

"I'm about to walk out that door." He thrusts his finger toward the back door, the one Skyler and Clinton both blew out of earlier. "And if you love me like you say you do, you'll come with me."

He glares at Adam once more before doing exactly as he said he would. He doesn't look back, doesn't wait for me to come, just plows through the door, letting in the last sliver of fading sunlight before it shuts again, leaving Adam and me alone.

I don't know how much time passes, how many times my heart beats and breaks before I look up from my hands at him. Seconds stretch into years, years reduced to just seconds as I watch one of my best friends try not to fall apart. The skin is stretched tight over his jaw, his eyes hard on the door, fists clenched at his side.

"Adam," I whisper, throat raw.

"Just go."

My eyes flood with tears, Adam's face blurring as my heart splits in two, one jagged half breaking away from the other. "Please," I beg. "Look at me."

"What?" he snaps, tearing his eyes from the door to find mine. His chest is heaving, nose flaring. "You love him, right? So, go."

I choke on a sob, tears spilling down my cheeks like boiling hot water, and I feel every scar they leave behind. "I don't want it to be this way."

"Well, it is." His voice breaks but he clenches his jaw against it. "Go, Cassie."

I cry harder, shaking my head.

"Go!"

Ripping myself from the chair, I try to ignore the pain in his voice as I turn my back on him, following Grayson out the back door. Something crashes to the floor behind me just before the door shuts, but I don't look back. My arms crossed tight over my middle, I close my eyes, shuddering on a breath that burns with unfair reality more than it heals with oxygen.

I spot Grayson across the street, seated on a bench outside the Communications building. He breathes a sigh of relief when he sees me, standing, knowing then that I loved him enough to do as he asked. But with every step toward him, I hate myself more.

How long did I really expect it to last? How long could I expect Grayson to understand, knowing the way Adam feels… the way I feel?

It's not unfair, what Grayson's asking. It's not unfair of him to feel the way he feels. But I still hate it all the same.

Because Adam was right — I didn't lie. I do love Grayson.

But my heart still splits in two, because the words I didn't say before I let him believe I chose another man over him will forever haunt me.

*I do love him, but I love you, too.*

*Jess*

BY THE TIME I MAKE it to Ralph's and see how completely dead it is inside, the fire I had in my belly when I stormed out of the KKB house is all but ash. Suddenly it doesn't seem like a brilliant idea to push Jarrett's buttons, and seeing as how there are only three other small groups of people in the bar other than myself, there aren't exactly a lot of options for pawns in my game.

There's a small group of girls, all giggling and playing pool, having their version of a Friendsgiving, I assume. I recognize Landon, the guy Erin had a fling with last year, in the corner with some of his buddies. He's off limits since he was with Erin, but even more so, the guy gives me the creeps. Other than that, I don't see anyone standing out.

Maybe it's because none of the guys, no matter how hot they are, hold a candle to Jarrett.

Sighing, I order a vodka tonic and drop my phone onto the bar top in front of me, dropping my head into my hands with my eyes still on it, willing it to ring.

Jarrett hasn't talked to me since our fight on Monday.

304

He has a right to be pissed, and I'm fully prepared to apologize, but I also won't deny that I'm a little disappointed *he* hasn't apologized yet, either. And now, a little after seven on Thanksgiving, he's still yet to call me. Or answer my call.

The bartender is a slight little thing that I assume to be my age, probably staying around campus just because someone has to serve the poor suckers like me who stumble in here on a holiday weekend. She pops my drink down in front of me and then kicks back against the register at the other end of the bar, texting away on her phone with a giant grin. She looks like she's texting someone she cares about, someone who cares about her. I know that goofy grin.

I used to wear it.

Twirling the ice in my glass with the plastic stirrer, I keep my eyes on my phone, pushing the home button every now and then just to make sure I didn't somehow miss a text. I'm so focused on my pathetic pity party that I don't even notice the guy who sits down next to me until he speaks.

"You know, I've tried that method," he says, breaking my daze. I glance over at him, eyes widening at the bright, boy-next-door smile I find there.

"Excuse me?"

He nods toward my phone on the bar. "The whole *stare at it until it does something* method. I've tried it. Usually leads to sucking down booze like water and drunk texting someone I know I shouldn't."

For the first time tonight, a tiny smile breaks on my face, and I don't even hide it as I take the time to check this guy out. The first thing I notice is his smile — I have never been so attracted to someone's teeth before. They're bright white and perfectly straight, like a dentist commercial, and one little dimple pops on his left cheek when that smile reaches its full wattage. All his features are dark — the jet-black mop of hair on his head, the deep brown of his eyes, the glorious tan skin stretched out over the amazing muscles on his arms, the perfect-length stubble on his jaw. This guy is the definition of tall, dark, and handsome — and suddenly, my game face is back on.

"Maybe I want to send drunk texts."

He laughs. "No, you don't. No one wakes up the morning after sending five unanswered texts in a row happy about it."

This time it's him who lets his eyes wander, and though it feels nice to be devoured by his eyes, it doesn't change the fact that he isn't Jarrett. Every guy just seems so... *blah*, compared to Jarrett. He's ruined me.

"I'm Jess," I say when his eyes finally reach mine again.

"Greg. You're in Kappa Kappa Beta, right?" He motions for the bartender, holding up his empty beer bottle before turning to face me again.

"I am. Are you Greek?"

"Omega Chi Beta."

"Oh, shit, the probation boys," I tease. "I have a really good friend in your fraternity — Bear. Although, he's kind of pissing me off currently."

Greg rolls his eyes. "He's been pissing pretty much everyone off since the beginning of the semester. I think he's just taking the probation thing hard. He's helped us a lot, though. There were still a lot of brothers being stupid after the meeting with nationals — me included — but he reminded us what's at stake. Still," he adds, tipping his new beer toward the bartender before taking a long pull. "His attitude is a lot to handle."

"I think he and Skyler got into some kind of fight, but neither one of them is saying why."

"Doesn't surprise me. Those two are pretty tight, even if they aren't getting along right now." His lips find his bottle again, eyes still on me. "Anyway, enough about them. Tell me about you. Any particular reason you're in Ralph's on Thanksgiving instead of home with family?"

"Ugh," I stick the plastic stirrer in my drink like a dagger, fishing out an ice cube before popping it in my mouth. "That's a long story. You should probably answer that question first."

"My parents took a cruise for the holiday," he answers easily. "So, I stayed here to party with a few brothers. But if I had to guess by the way you're watching your phone, your reason involves a guy, doesn't it?"

I chew my ice cube. "Maybe."

"Boyfriend?"

I pause mid-crunch, swirling the cold remains of the cube with my tongue as I debate how to answer. I could easily lie, play the game I was set on playing when I walked in the door, but suddenly it all feels stupid. So, I just answer with a nod.

"Ah, figures," he says, a defeated smile on his face as he peels the label off his beer bottle. "Doesn't make sense for a girl who looks like you to be single."

"You're sweet." I watch him for a moment, waiting for him to make some excuse to walk away. "Guess now that you know I have a boyfriend, in your mind I've practically sprouted three heads and a dick now, huh?"

He chokes on a laugh, that damn dimple making an appearance again. "Not at all. I was actually going to ask if you would still be okay with a little company tonight. You can talk to me about him, if you want," he offers with a shrug. "Or, I can talk your ear off with turtle facts."

This time it's me who nearly chokes. "I'm sorry?"

"Biology major," he answers. "I'm doing a marine mammal and sea turtle rescue internship next summer, so I've been studying, upping my turtle game."

I laugh, finally feeling marginally better and oddly thankful that Greg wandered into Ralph's tonight. "Okay, you have my attention. Hit me with a turtle fact."

And, so he does. For the rest of the night, we make easy conversation, first with his hilarious but fascinating knowledge of sea turtles and eventually we end up talking about our families, our majors, our love for pizza, our favorite songs and movies. I lose count of how many drinks we both have as well as how many laughs we share. All I know is that it feels good to sit in a bar with an attractive boy who can't stop staring at me but is respectful enough not to make any moves since I have a boyfriend. It's refreshing, and maybe some attention was all I needed, after all.

A loud commotion breaks the spell Greg has me under somewhere around midnight. We eye each other cautiously before abandoning our drinks at the bar and rushing outside. Landon is cursing and screaming, his buddies all gathered around him trying to calm him down. When Greg and I step around the first row of cars in the parking lot, we see why.

"Oh, my God." I cover my mouth, trying to hide my smile and fight down the laugh I feel coming on.

"WHOEVER DID THIS IS DEAD, DO YOU HEAR ME?!" Landon screams, grabbing his friend's beer bottle and hurling it across the parking lot. It hits the brick wall of Ralph's and shatters, splinters of glass raining down on the sidewalk like a parade in his honor. "DEAD."

"I wish I would have grabbed my phone off the bar," I say to Greg, eyes wandering over Landon's car. "I so need a picture of this."

"Something tells me you'll see one on social media in about two minutes," he says, nodding to the group of girls who were playing pool earlier. They all have their phones out, giggling and snapping pictures before Landon sees them and roars for them to put their phones away. I can't blame him for being mad, but even more than that, I want to know the genius behind the prank.

His entire car is covered in dildos.

And not just any kind of dildo — tiny, micro-penis dildos, all Saran Wrapped to his hood, his doors, the roof, the windows. It's impossible to even get inside the car without breaking through the cellophane first, and thus breaking loose at least a hundred tiny, rubber dicks. The tires are shredded, the windshield busted, and nearly all the paint has been keyed up. And to top it all off? There's a message, loud and clear, written in bright red paint on the hood.

**Now the outside matches the inside. Go fuck yourself.**

I'm still laughing when the police show up and Greg and I dip back inside Ralph's, finding our place back at the bar and slipping easily back into the conversation we were holding before. The night is turning out to be much better than it started.

"We should take a picture," he says about an hour after the dildo commotion, smacking his palms on the bar. "To commemorate one of the best Thanksgivings I've had in a long time."

I chuckle. "A Turkey Day selfie, huh?"

"Absolutely." He pulls his phone out of his pocket, flipping the camera to face us before reaching down and grabbing the edge of my barstool. He pulls me closer to him, hand finding the small of my back as he holds the phone up. "Say turtle."

I laugh, and he snaps the picture with my hand on his chest, my eyes staring up at him, mid-laugh. His smile is wide and lazy, both of us clearly a little intoxicated, but as we both look the picture over, I can't help but think we look cute together.

"Are you allowed to be here?" he asks.

"What do you mean?"

"I was going to post it," he says, nodding toward the picture. My barstool is still touching his, our bodies brushing. "Can I tag you?"

It's funny, how the exact thing I was going to do — the mission I had been on — ended up happening even after I'd dropped the notion. I had my goal set on coming in here and finding some poor sap to use to make Jarrett jealous, but I'd gotten so caught up just having fun with Greg, I'd dropped the initial thought.

Frowning, I realize I haven't checked my phone in a while, and I turn, grabbing it off the bar and clicking the home screen.

No missed texts.

No missed calls.

My heart sinking, I drop the phone back to the bar with a sigh, turning back to Greg with what I'm sure is a pathetic smile. "You know what? Tag me."

"You sure?" he asks, eyeing my phone before finding my gaze again.

"Positive."

He watches me a moment more, his eyes flicking to my lips, but he swallows and tears his gaze away and back to his phone. I watch him type out a caption, draining the last of my vodka tonic as the loading bar fills on his phone, and then the screen re-loads and he grins.

"Posted."

# Ashlei

"EVERYONE ALWAYS asks me, 'Why *Okay, Cool*?'" Brandon starts, kicking off his keynote speech in front of a ballroom of at least a thousand people, all eyes fixed on him. "And it's my favorite story to tell."

I'm seated just a few tables from the stage, my heel grazing the dance floor that stretches out in front of the stage, separating me from the tables on the other side of it. Looking up at Brandon in his deep red suit with golden accents, tie and pocket handkerchief popping as bright accents, he looks absolutely regal. But as handsome as he looks on that stage, I know the man *beneath* the suit now.

I know the abs that stretch from his rib cage down to the deep V, cut at an angle that leads me right to eight inches of heaven. I know the striking compass tattoo that hugs his left tricep, the imprint his teeth leave on his lip when he bites it hard enough, and the sounds he makes when he's on the brink of ecstasy.

The last few days with Brandon have been pure bliss — from sneaking long, hot, passionate kisses in dark corners and hidden hallways during the conference to not even leaving our hotel room on

Thanksgiving, we've both been making the most of our "no rules" weekend. I'm deliciously sore and satisfied, yet never truly sated, always wanting more of him. Even now, as I try to focus on his speech, I can't wait to get him back to the room for our last night together before reality hits.

"It's no secret that growing up in foster care isn't fun," he continues, and a heavier weight settles over the room at his words. "It's hard growing up not feeling valued, or important, or like you belong anywhere in the world. It's even harder when you're surrounded by opportunities to maybe find a sort of family, but you know those opportunities are bad — and likely to land you in jail."

My heart aches as I watch Brandon strip his soul bare in front of an entire crowd of people. I promised him I wouldn't read his speech before he gave it tonight, and I kept my word. Now, I'm hanging on to everything he's saying, wanting to know him more, even though I know I shouldn't.

"I won't lie, I don't know how much longer I would have been able to stay out of trouble had it not been for a young entrepreneur who found me by the grace of God and kept a steady head on my shoulder. His name was Darnell Cohen, and he owned a small but reputable catering company in the town I grew up in." He clears his throat. "He was twenty-five when he offered me my first job. I was only fourteen.

"Darnell didn't have to take a chance on a kid with dirty shoes and a bad attitude, but he did. He gave me somewhere to be after school, a way to make money, and more than that, a brotherhood. He was my big brother in every sense of the word. And the more years I worked under him, the more I realized that he was exactly the kind of man I wanted to be — intelligent, humble, kind, and giving."

I smile at that, because in my mind, Brandon is all of those things to a T.

"'Okay, cool,' was Darnell's answer to everything," Brandon continues with a smile. "When I had a new idea for the business? 'Okay, cool. Let's do it.' When I was late for an event? 'Okay, cool. Don't let it happen again.' When something went wrong and everyone else stressed out? 'Okay, cool. Let me think for a second, I can fix this.' Even when the most beautiful woman I'd ever seen gave me her number to give to him... 'Okay, cool. I'll call her later.'"

The room laughs a little at that, and I cover my smile with my hand, completely enraptured with Brandon's speech.

But when the laughter dies down, his eyes soften, and he smooths his hands over the podium. "And when I came to him on my eighteenth birthday, not able to stay even one more day in my foster home, and asked him for a place to stay… he didn't even hesitate." Brandon lifts his eyes to the audience again. "'Okay, cool. Let's get you into college.'"

I swallow, my throat thick with emotion, my hands aching to reach out to him.

"And, he did," Brandon continues. "He helped me get into college, and helped me realize that just because I'd come from nothing didn't mean I had nothing to become." He pauses. "Darnell was thirty-two when he was murdered."

The entire room inhales a breath, none of us letting go of it as we watch Brandon on stage.

"He was just in the wrong gas station at the wrong time, trying to save the life of a young cashier. And, he did…by sacrificing his own."

Silence.

"So," he continues after a moment, sniffing. "*Okay, Cool* is just one of the many ways I honor Darnell with my life, trying to hold onto his memory for as long as I can and show the world who he was, and who he helped me become."

Brandon continues on to talk about chasing dreams despite obstacles, and rising above the circumstances life hands you, and eventually finishes with his final words of advice for event industry entrepreneurs like himself. It's a moving speech, one that earns him a standing ovation at the end, and his eyes are on me as he smiles and exits the stage to the sound of the string quartet band starting up again.

I'm still standing when he finally reaches our table again, which isn't until after he's stopped by nearly every person he passes, all wanting to shake his hand and tell him how wonderful his speech was. He blows out a long breath when he makes it to his seat, dropping his notecards onto the table and kissing my cheek before we both sit.

"At the risk of repeating what everyone else just said, your speech was... beautiful, Brandon."

He reaches for his drink — a Manhattan — and takes a quick sip. "Thank you. But I'm glad it's over," he adds with a laugh. "Now I can finally enjoy myself."

"You were nervous?" I ask, surprised.

"Always. Speaking in front of a large crowd is not my idea of a good time."

I laugh, placing the delicate white linen napkin over my lap just as the first course of dinner is served. "Well, I would have never guessed. You looked casual and comfortable up there." I pause. "Did you picture everyone in their underwear?"

"Just you," he fires back with a wink.

Brandon is the center of attention all through dinner, the three other couples seated with us asking him question after question that lead to story after story. By the time dessert is finished and our drinks are refilled, I can tell he's ready for a break, so I take a longer sip from my champagne glass and stand.

"Dance with me?" I ask.

His eyes fire up with a mix of relief and hunger, and he wipes the corners of his mouth with his napkin before laying it gently beside his plate. "It would be my honor. Excuse me," he says to the rest of the table, and they all lift their glasses or offer us polite smiles and nods as I take his arm.

"Thank you," he says when we take our places on the dance floor, one of his large hands finding the bare skin at the small of my back as he takes my hand in the other. "I'm going to need a solid week of introverting when we get back to South Florida."

I smile as we start to dance, not even surprised that he moves so smoothly with me in his arms. The man is astounding. "I'll need a week of recovery, myself," I tease.

Brandon's eyes spark, a devilish grin spreading on his face. "I won't apologize for that." His eyes sweep over me, landing on mine just as he twirls me out and pulls me back into his arms. "You look absolutely stunning tonight, by the way."

"This old thing?" I tease, gesturing to the floor-length gold dress I'd picked out for the evening. The high neckline is conservative, my simple earrings and natural makeup complementing the look, but the back of the dress is virtually non-existent, the fabric sweeping wide and low before meeting in a V just above my tailbone. The dress hugs my curves all the way down to the middle of my thigh before sweeping out just slightly, a low slit revealing my left leg and heel when I walk.

"I've been imagining all the ways I can strip you out of it," Brandon admits.

"Even while on stage?"

"*Especially* while on stage."

I laugh, spinning under his arm again before wrapping my arm back around his shoulders. "Our last night," I remind him, eyes searching his for a sign of… well, anything — sadness, excitement, regret, fear, hope.

He swallows. "We'll have to make it count."

"Back to reality tomorrow."

He nods as the band finishes the song, still holding me in his arms when the last note plays. "Indeed."

The room claps politely, the band smiling in thanks before striking up the next melody, but time is frozen where Brandon holds me in the middle of the dance floor. The way his hand grips the skin on my lower back — just slightly, enough to send a wave of chills over my arms — has me anxious to get back to the room.

If we really only have one more night together, I don't want to waste a single second more of it here.

"I'm suddenly very tired," I breathe, my eyes flashing over his lips.

Brandon grins. "Then let's get you to bed, Miss Daniels."

That night, Brandon touches me slower, longer, with more intent and purpose than before. It's as if he's memorizing the way every inch of my body feels beneath his, the way my breaths enter and exit my lungs, the way my lips move over the moans and whispers of his name.

And I memorize him, too — wondering how I'll ever let him go once our jet lands back in South Florida.

We knew the game we were playing was dangerous before we even dealt the cards, and now here we are, nearing the end, both of us winners and losers in equal measure. It's time to pack up.

Time to go home. Time to keep our promises, leaving our brief time together in the past, in a memory, never to be relived.

But with Brandon's lips on my skin, his hands on my waist, his breaths in my ear — I can't help but feel like this game is *far* from over.

# Episode 6

# Ashlei

I KNEW AFTER THANKSGIVING, the rest of the semester would fly by. There were only a few weeks left, after all, and now here I am, packing up the last of my belongings in the little cube I've called home all semester.

The Monday after the holiday had started off with a bang, the entire team full on mashed potatoes and drive to make the *Bare•ly* event successful. We'd all joined forces and thrown our all into it, and two weeks later, we'd rocked that event like I knew we would all along. It was chic, elegant, modern and classy — everything our clients had asked for. And for the first time, I'd been in charge of an event from beginning to end, handling the crises as they came and putting out fires left and right, all while never dropping the illusion that everything was going exactly as planned. It was a perfect launch party, and Mrs. Delure had assured me I had a high recommendation letter coming from her whenever I graduated and set out looking for my first job.

"I knew you'd be the last intern out of here," Mykayla says, propping her hip against the wall of my cube as she watches me pack up. "But then again, I knew you'd be different from the other interns the moment I met you."

I toss my sticky notepads into the box, the contents now threatening to spill over the top, and pause to face her. "Aw, Mykayla. I'm going to miss you."

"Same here, girly. But," she clarifies, stepping into my cube with outstretched arms. "I'm serious about you coming to Happy Hour with us every now and then. Your sorority sisters can share."

I laugh, hugging her tight. "Absolutely. You have my number. I'm there anytime."

She sighs, squeezing me once before letting me go. "I'm going to finish up some emails and then we can walk out together, if you're finished?" she asks, eyes on my now very empty desk.

Picking up the last highlighter and tossing it into a vacant corner of the box, I nod. "Yep. I guess this is it…" I swallow, glancing at the office down the hall with the door still open. "I just need to say my goodbyes to Mr. Church and I'll be ready."

Saying his name out loud makes my stomach lurch, though Mykayla is oblivious, taking my box from the desk. "I'll hold this for you. Poor Mr. Church, hope you don't make him cry. He's already going to be here working all weekend long. Add that to the fact that his favorite intern is leaving?" She smiles, nudging me. "You were everyone's favorite, truthfully."

"Oh, stop." I laugh. "Why is he working all weekend?"

She shrugs. "I dunno, last minute event or something. He mentioned it in passing and I told him to let me know if he needed anything, but you know him. He'll work his weekend alone in quiet, suffering, and leave the rest of us alone."

"Yeah…" My eyes find his office again, his face hidden but hands visible as they type away on his keyboard. "Sounds like him."

"Anyway, let me go send these emails and you go say goodbye. See you in a sec!" And with that, she trots off.

When she's gone, I blow out a long, shaky breath, flattening my palms over the skirt of the same dress I wore on day one. Flashes of Brandon in the elevator, of our first exchange, mingle with the intimate way I came to know him over Thanksgiving break as I walk slowly down the hall toward his office. It's after five on a Friday, leaving only a handful of associates in the office. Usually he's gone by now, but something tells me he was waiting for me to come say goodbye.

True to our word, we haven't crossed any lines since the jet touched down back in Miami that

Sunday after the holiday. He's kept his gaze neutral in meetings, just like I asked, and with so much of my focus being on the *Bare•ly* event, I only really had time to pine over him in the privacy of mine and Erin's room at the sorority house.

But I'm not immune to him. My breath still hitches when our hands brush, my heart still skips when he calls my name at an event or in the office, and my body still aches with need for him every night when I lie down in my empty bed.

I wonder if he aches for me, too.

He seems so unfazed by me now, like he truly did itch his scratch and has no want or need for me anymore other than to be a good intern. His gaze never lingers over mine longer than it should, he never winks when no one is looking, he never texts me late at night with wistful thoughts. He has kept his word, and I never thought that would hurt as much as it has.

"Mr. Church?" I rap my knuckles on the doorframe to his office, causing him to pause mid-type and look at me. Just that glance alone nearly has me doubling over. "Sorry to bother you, I'm just… I'm about to head out, and I wanted to say goodbye."

His expression is blank, completely void of emotion. He watches me for a moment before standing, fastening the button at the bottom of his suit jacket and stepping around his desk. "It's been a pleasure having you on the team, Miss Daniels," he says, extending his hand for mine. "If you ever need a reference — or anything at all — don't hesitate to give us a call."

My heart sinks, pulling my smile with it as I let him take my hand. He shakes it firmly, like he would anyone else, and I try not to let it show just how badly that hurts. "The pleasure has been mine. I can't thank you enough for the opportunity."

His jaw ticks, like he's biting back the words he can't say — the words I long to hear. I try to hold onto his hand longer, try to feel connected to him for as long as I can, but he pulls back after our handshake, sliding his hands into the pockets of his slacks with his eyes still on me.

"Bye, then," I say, excusing myself. When I'm just past the door, he calls out my name.

"Miss Daniels?"

I turn, finding just a hint of longing in his dark eyes, like he's fighting with every ounce of power he has to keep his hands in his pockets and off of me. It was the look I asked him not to give me, the one I missed, the one I wasn't sure still existed.

"Keep in touch, okay?"

Smiling, I nod, holding his gaze for as long as he'll let me before finally turning for good. I walk slowly down the hallway, hoping he's watching, and when I reach Mykayla's desk, she's already waiting and holding my box for me.

"Ready?"

On an exhale, I nod, looking around the office with an ache in my chest. "Ready."

As we wait for the elevators, I feel his eyes on me, but I wait until Mykayla steps in and it's my turn to let him know it. My eyes find his down the hall, and without any words exchanged, I finally feel it.

*He's going to miss me, too.*

He smiles, offering me a slight wave, and I smile in return before stepping onto the elevator, all the while wondering if that's the last time I'll ever see Mr. Church.

*Skyler*

"UGH, THIS SUCKS," I say to my empty room, scrolling through the list of classes still available for spring semester. After filling my schedule with a whole array of classes this semester, I still haven't found anything I'm passionate about — nothing I would want to make a career of, at least — and so here I am, on a Friday night, throwing darts at a spinning wheel again and hoping something sticks.

This semester has been hard.

Classes have been weird, none of them meshing together which, surprisingly, made studying even more difficult than usual. Poker has been consuming my life, especially since I officially decided to enter the big tournament next May. I haven't paid my entry fee yet, but I did give an exclusive interview to one of my favorite poker blogs. Now the poker world is buzzing about my entry, and it's crunch time.

Clinton *still* isn't talking to me, ignoring all my apology texts and voicemails. And, in the strangest turn of events, I haven't had a boy to occupy my time, other than the now two drunken times I've found myself hooking up with Adam. If it wasn't for him being cool with a no-strings drunk hookup situation, I likely would have gone mad from No D Disease by now.

Sighing, I pull the trigger and sign up for my last class — Writing for Television. And with my course load full, I snap my laptop shut, head collapsing on top of it once it's closed with my hair splayed all around me. My phone buzzes from the corner of my desk and I reach for it blindly, peeking through my hair at the name on the screen.

And then I sit up straight, eyes widening.

Sliding the message open from the home screen, Clinton's contact opens, showing me all the unanswered texts I've sent since Halloween. But now, right under the last one, is a text from him.

**- Can you come over? -**

I don't even bother running a brush through my hair or changing out of the leggings and tank top I have on before I'm running down the stairs and out the door. I'm about halfway down Greek Row when I realize I *also* didn't stop to put a bra on, but I don't turn back, because all that matters in this moment is that Clinton texted me, and he wants to talk to me, and that's all I care about.

My mind is running wild with all the things I'll say when I get to his room — how sorry I am, how I never meant to upset him, how I'll make Clayton do some kind of work for the money if that will help, or let Clinton pay me back if he wants. But I don't get a chance to say any of it, because when I burst through the Omega Chi Beta doors, the entire house is full of brothers.

And all of them are staring at me.

Josh, Clinton's Little, steps forward first, eyeing my outfit with appreciation and a wink that makes me roll my eyes before the first word leaves his mouth.

"Skyler, Bear called on all of us to help him, because apparently he's been a real fucking idiot and not a very good best friend lately," he starts, and it's then that I realize every brother in the room is holding a notecard in their hands. "He didn't want to just apologize, he wanted you to know how special you are to him. So, he wrote down something for every day that you guys haven't talked."

He holds up the notecard in his hand with a goofy smile and my hands fly to my mouth, eyes glossing. I am *not* a cryer, but damnit if the tears don't gather, anyway.

"You are, by far, the best poker player this country has ever seen, and I can't wait to see you take the title in May," Josh reads, and then another brother steps forward, reading from his card next.

"No one cuddles better than you do." The guys all laugh as he steps back, and then another card is read. And another. And another.

"There's no one I'd rather split a twelve-pack with."

"I would go to war for you if you asked."

"Your laugh is the best sound in the world, and the only thing that makes me feel better on a shitty day."

"There isn't a girl on campus who looks better in cut-off shorts and a sorority jersey."

A slew of whistles rings out at that and I laugh, blushing.

The list goes on and on, some of the cards making me smile, some making me laugh, and others making it really difficult not to cry. And after every brother standing in the living room and on the stairs lining to the upstairs has read their card, Clinton steps out from the back hallway, walking straight up to me.

"No matter how many cards I write, I could never truly tell you what you mean to me, Skyler," he says, apologies in his eyes before he even says them. "You are my family — no, you're *more* than family. You're my best friend, and I'm so sorry I let you think for even one second that you don't mean everything in the world to me, because you do. I am so, so sorry for being a giant dick. Will you please let me make it up to you by taking you to Semi-formal and being the best date you could ever ask for?"

I sniff, nodding with tears blurring my vision before launching at him. He catches me easily, wrapping me in the fiercest Bear Hug yet.

"You owe me *so* many burritos for this."

All the guys laugh again, clapping and cheering, and Clinton high fives them and thanks a few as he tucks me under his arm, leading me back to his bedroom. I can still hear the guys laughing and joking with each other, reading the cards with girly voices as Clinton shuts the door behind us.

"Seriously, Skyler. I am so sorry."

"No, no," I shake my head, wrapping my small arms around him again and resting my head in the dip of his chest. "*I'm* sorry. I should have asked you before I did what I did. At the very least, I should have told you. It was selfish and stupid and—"

"It wasn't selfish," he says, cutting me off. "It was sweet and kind, and something I would have done for your family in the reverse. I just… I was upset, he's my brother and I want to be the one to help him, to protect him. I needed a little bit of time to see past my pride, Skyler. And I'm sorry I took so long."

He squeezes me tight, and when he pulls back, I grab his large hand and drag him to his bed, climbing in first and sighing with relief when he slides in behind me and wraps me in his arms again.

"I've missed you so much, Bear. Everything has been so hard without you." My voice sounds small, weak.

"I know," he says, kissing my hair. "I'm so sorry. Tell me everything. How many hearts have you broken since Halloween?"

I laugh. "Zero. Poker has been my only serious relationship this semester."

"Well, who knows. Maybe next semester, some guy will sweep you off your feet and you'll have a date in Vegas."

Rolling my eyes, I twist in his arms and snuggle into his chest, his chin fitting on top of my head like we're the last two puzzle pieces. And for the rest of the night, he catches me up on his life — including how his brother is doing in Pittsburgh — and I tell him my fears about the tournament, and how hard it will be to earn the last bit of the entry money.

Suddenly, everything is right in the world again.

I have no idea what next semester holds, or the rest of my life, for that matter. Maybe I'll figure out my major, maybe I'll win the poker tournament, or maybe I'll still be a confused girl with a best friend who will support me no matter what happens.

And that's more than okay with me.

*Jess*

WHEN I GET A TEXT from Skyler saying she's staying at Clinton's for the night, I breathe a sigh of relief, typing out a text to her that Jarrett and I are finally going to video chat in less than an hour. She wishes me luck and then I plug my phone into the charger, letting it get juiced as I do my makeup in the bathroom.

The last time we were supposed to video chat, I had been so excited.

Now, all I am is sick.

I ended up texting Jarrett the day after Thanksgiving, apologizing for everything and telling him I would give him his space, and to just call me when he was caught up on the project and a little less stressed out. I told him we could see each other over Christmas break, and that I understood, and that we would be okay. I thought it was the right thing to do — the mature thing to do — but when all he wrote back was a simple *thanks*, I wondered if it was already too late, if he would ever forgive me.

Ever since he went back to New York after coming to visit, everything with us has been so rocky. Between the communication breakdown and the long distance, my heart is raw and aching. He can't hold me to make me feel better, and I can't kiss him with my apologies. We can't just jump in his truck and drive to the beach, splitting a joint and having sex until the sun rises. Everything about our relationship is different, and I'm not sure who we are in this new space.

As shitty as it is, Greg has been a huge help keeping my mind off Jarrett the last couple of weeks. He's listened to me talk about Jarrett, offering advice when he had it and just a shoulder to lean on when he had nothing to say. He's funny, and kind, and I appreciate his company. And maybe a small part of me realizes that I just enjoy the fact that a man cares about me, and is attracted to me, and is giving me attention.

Something else inside me, something deep in the trenches of thoughts I like to leave *un*thought, tells me this phone call is either going to make or break me and Jarrett. And as much as I have a whole string of apologies ready to go, I also have questions, and concerns, and things *I* want to talk about. I understand his side of things, how he needs me to be able to trust him and understand how demanding his job is, but relationships are about compromise — and I need love and support, too.

I feel so unlike myself, so vulnerable and defeated. The girls have started to notice, too — wondering where my spunk has gone, and I know I won't get back to myself until I face whatever is about to happen with Jarrett.

When my makeup is flawless and my hair is straightened, I slip on a pair of sleep shorts and a tank top, propping my laptop up on my desk to wait for his call. And when his picture and name fill the screen at exactly ten o'clock, I take a deep breath and answer.

The screen is fuzzy at first, and when it clears, Jarrett is sitting at his small kitchen table, giving me a view of practically his entire studio apartment. The city lights burn through the window behind him, mixing with the low light of his apartment to cast him in a soft glow. Finally seeing his face, his lips, his eyes — it hurts as much as it heals.

"Hi," I breathe, a weary smile finding my lips.

"Hi."

I watch him for a moment, wishing so badly he was here. I just want to touch him, to hold him, to have him hold me. "I wish I could jump through this screen right now."

His eyes are sad, defeated, and he only nods in response.

It's strange, how someone you love can seem so foreign in moments like these, moments when everything hangs in the balance.

Steeling myself, I sit up a little straighter and start my long list of apologies. "Listen, I am so sorry I went off on you for missing our date. That was an immature reaction and a little dramatic and I wish I could take it back. I know you had a long day and I know you can't help what projects you get put on or whom with. I want to be more supportive, but… I need you to understand my side of things, too. I need—"

"It's over."

I pause, mouth still hanging open, the words I'd planned to say next frozen in my throat. I close my mouth, open it again, nose flaring and eyes watering as I try to convince myself I didn't just hear the man I love tell me he doesn't want to be with me anymore.

"Wh-what?"

"It's over, Jess. We, this," he motions to the screen and back to himself. "I can't… I won't do this anymore."

Shock rips through me, my head shaking of its own accord. I knew this phone call wouldn't be pretty, I knew he was upset, I knew there were things to be said and to be decided but still, even if I pretended to prepare for the worst, I didn't actually think it would happen.

How can Jarrett break up with me? After all we've been through, after all he's said, after all we've promised?

"Jarrett, we can work through this. I said I'm sorry, I… I'll try harder. I'll do better. It's just a silly fight, it isn't—"

"I saw the picture." His eyes bore holes through mine from thousands of miles away, the heart he always keeps sheltered now bloody and marred on his sleeve for me to see. "I don't play these games. I put up with you parading other guys in front of me last year, trying to make me jealous, playing me like I'm just another guy to you but I thought we were past that."

Panic rises in my throat like bile. "He's just a friend, Jarrett. I met him that night, we just talked. I swear, that's all."

"But you went into that bar on a mission, didn't you? A mission to find a poor sap to twirl around your finger and make me jealous. You thought it'd make me call you. You thought it'd make me, what? Worship you?"

I shake my head frantically, tears rushing my eyes and billowing down my cheeks before I can stop them. "I didn't… Yes, I wanted your attention, but I didn't do anything with him. I promise. And he posted the picture, not me."

"But he tagged you," Jarrett points out. "Which I'm sure you asked him to do."

"Please," I beg, reaching out to touch the screen. "Just let me come see you. Let's talk about this in person. You don't mean this, you don't—"

"YOU HAD ME, JESS!" he yells, his face twisting as I choke on a sob. "You had me, and now you don't. It shouldn't be like this, I shouldn't have to choose between you and my career, or worry about how you'll react to me *working* with another female. It's just like the surf lessons last year. Nothing I say to you and nothing I do will ever convince you that I am yours, and I have continually paid the price. Do you know how sick I've been, wondering what you did with that guy to get back at me?"

"I didn't," I try, but my voice breaks.

"I love you. And you said you loved me, too." He shakes his head, jaw tight. "This isn't how you treat someone you love."

"I'm sorry," I choke, letting the tears run. "I'm so sorry."

"Me, too," he says, finally lifting his eyes to mine. He searches them, looking for the girl he knew, the girl he fell in love with. When he shakes his head, I know he's come up empty handed. "I have to go."

"Jarrett, please."

But the screen just goes dark like the rest of my world.

I've read about these sensory deprivation tanks, where you lie in a tub of water filled with Epson salt to make you float in a soundproof pod with no light. You just float there, completely weightless, emerging on the other side of the experience almost as if in a trance. Some claim it has healing effects, others claim hallucination.

That's the closest comparison I can make to how I feel right now, lying on my bedroom floor, in the exact same place I fell last night after Jarrett ended our call. I only know it's morning because light started breaking through the curtains at some point, though I have no idea how long ago that was. Everything is numb. Everything is on fire. My eyes sting and burn, my brain replaying every word he said, every word he didn't. But somewhere in the numb of the night, I came to a conclusion.

I don't want to fall apart.

I earned my nickname, J-Love, because when I was younger I said I loved pretty much any guy who gave me his attention. And though what I had with Jarrett was much realer than that, in the end, I can't help but feel like I lost a little part of myself with him, too. I don't want to let the end of our relationship be the end of me.

I know I'll need to break, and cry, and I know in the deepest part of my being that there is no getting over Jarrett. Not really. He will always own a part of my heart, and losing him will forever be one of my biggest regrets. But I want to grieve in silence, alone.

Jess Vonnegut is a bad ass. She is a vixen, a fighter, a man-eater, a tough bitch. She doesn't stop the party for any drama, and she doesn't stop her life for any boy.

Swiping at my face as if it isn't already dry, I crawl to the desk and pull my phone down, sinking against the drawers as I type out a text to Greg.

**- Take a break from studying turtle facts tonight and go to Semi-formal with me. -**

I drop the phone to the floor beside me, kneading my temples, my head throbbing between my fingers. When my phone buzzes, I unlock it quickly, smiling as much as I physically can in this moment at his response.

**- I'll bring the vodka. -**

And I'm not sure how much longer I lie there before eventually peeling myself off the floor, along with what's left of my dignity, holding onto it as tight as I can. Soon, the girls are all getting ready, music blasting, makeup and hair product everywhere. I tell them about Jarrett with a straight face, my tears all spilled last night, and they console me. Ashlei asks if I want to skip Semi. Skyler wants me to talk about it. But I decline both offers, telling them I already invited Greg, and I'm fine.

It's a lie, and they know it, but they don't press me on it.

At least for tonight, I'm going to be okay. I'm going to dance and sing, laugh and party, and pretend like everything will be okay. I'll fake it until I make it — make it back home, that is. And then, I'll have three weeks of winter break to get over it.

That's that.

When the limos are pulling up outside, I pull up Jarrett's name and type out one last text before blocking his number and tucking my phone in my clutch, ripping the Band-Aid off, ready to scab and heal.

**- I will always love you. -**

# Bear

"CHUG! CHUG! CHUG!"

I hear my brothers chanting as Skyler and I race to see who finishes our beer first, which is ridiculous, really, because she's a tiny little peanut compared to me. It's kind of comical watching her throw down when she's dressed to the nines, beer dripping down her chin and landing on the large gold necklace she's paired with her burgundy dress. In the end, I finish first, wiping my mouth with the back of my wrist and joining in with my brothers chanting as she finishes.

She's just as smiley as she would have been had she won, holding up her empty glass in victory as her sisters cheer. Then she grabs my hand, pulling me back out onto the dance floor.

Everything is back to normal now that I finally manned up and apologized to Skyler. She deserved it way earlier than it happened, but thankfully she'd still accepted. Once I talked to my baby brother and heard the whole story from him, I knew I was being an ass — hell, I knew it before then — but it helped me clear my mind enough to realize I was in the wrong.

So, I booked a flight home in a little over a week for winter break to stay at Mac's place and help Clayton find a job, or at least some way to earn some extra cash. I also made it clear that next time he was worried about money, I wanted him to come to me — even if he felt like I was busy or he didn't want to bother me. Then, I got my brothers together and made a plan to apologize to Skyler.

The semester hasn't exactly been the best for me, with Omega Chi being on probation and the fight with Skyler, but I finally feel like everything is falling back into place. We still get to recruit new members in the spring, which means we'll all be busy when we get back to campus. Add in the facts that I get to spend a few weeks with my brother and Skyler and I are good again, and I'm finding plenty to be thankful for.

Skyler starts the cabbage patch when the DJ spins a disco track and I follow suit, pointing one finger up into the air before crossing it over my hip to point down and back up again. Jess and Ashlei join us, along with Greg and a few of my other brothers, and we make a dance circle, taking turns doing ridiculous dance moves in the middle to a crowd of cheers.

When a slow song comes on, most of the floor clears, making way for couples. Jess and Greg stay on the floor while Ashlei, Skyler, and I make our way back to our table.

"I'm going to run to the restroom," Skyler says, pointing over her shoulder. "Grab us fresh beers and meet back here?"

"On it."

She skips off with Ashlei's arm linked in hers and I head toward the bar at the far end of the ballroom.

Semi-formal is always a little more casual than Formal held in the spring, but everyone still dresses up, and the setting is always some sort of fancy hotel or venue with a ballroom. This one also has a garden, one that connects to the back end of the ballroom where one of the bars is, and when I glance out the door as I wait in line and spot Erin sitting alone on one of the benches, I frown.

Abandoning my spot in line, I dip through the glass double doors, the heat of the night hitting me as soon as they close behind me. It may be December, but it's still South Florida, and there's a thin sheen of sweat gathering on the back of Erin's slender neck as she stares down at her lap, rolling something over and over in her hands.

It's just the two of us outside — probably because ties and tight dresses already make you sweat enough without adding humidity to them

— so I take the open seat next to her on the detailed metal bench.

For a moment I let my eyes roam the garden, taking in the low-hanging trees and wide array of bright flowers. There are a few bird baths, too — the water gently running from each of them serving as the only soundtrack as I try to think of what to say to her. Erin and I haven't spoken since the night of her birthday, and she made it pretty clear that she didn't want my help… or maybe even my friendship. But I can't just walk away from her, not when she's hurting — even if she denies that she is.

"My mom used to have a garden," I say finally, my voice soft and low. "When I was younger. Maybe like five or six or so? Before the drugs became more important to her than anything else."

Erin pauses rolling whatever it is she's holding and clasps her hands over it tight, listening.

"I would help her sometimes. She didn't grow flowers as much as like vegetables and stuff. I remember we had fresh tomatoes in our dinners almost every night — in a salad, on a sandwich, mashed up into chili — whatever." I shake my head. "The garden just turned into a dried-up mess of weeds after she got into drugs, though."

"I'm sorry," Erin whispers.

"It's okay. I really don't think about her much, honestly. But something about this garden struck that memory, I guess."

Erin nods and I finally look down at her, taking in the soft shape of her face, the rosy tint of her cheeks, the long slender slope of her nose. She's always had such a classy and regal look about her, which fits perfectly with the all-black pantsuit she's wearing tonight. It's cut deep in the front, right between her chest, but tastefully so, and the back is open, too. Something tells me she decided to wear pants instead of a dress for a reason, a statement of sorts, even if she's the only one she's making it for.

"You look gorgeous tonight, Erin," I say, still watching her.

"Thank you."

I pause, waiting to see if she'll talk, but when she doesn't, I try for humor. "What? Not going to compliment me on my dope threads?" I pull at the cuffs of the gray, black and white plaid jacket I paired with an all-black dress shirt and forest green dress slacks, popping my collar with a grin.

Erin eyes me, a soft smile cracking at the edges of her lips. "It's a wonder what wearing something other than basketball shorts can do."

"I think there was a compliment in there somewhere."

She smiles a little more but it drops from her face too quickly, reminding me that she's still a sad girl sitting alone on a bench at her Semi-formal.

"What's on your mind?" I ask, nudging her gently.

Erin shakes her head, fists closed tight around the object of her hand. "Did you hear about Landon's car?"

My fists clench just at the mention of his name. "Yeah. Fucker deserved it."

"I did it," she says quickly, lifting her eyes to look at mine for just a split second before focusing on her hands again. "I thought it would make me feel better, to get some sort of revenge." She shrugs. "But it just made me feel worse. Because there's absolutely nothing I could ever do to him that would be as horrible as what he did to me."

It's like a fiery arrow is shot straight into my chest at her words and I reach my hand out, grazing her lower back just enough to let her know I'm here. "You could press charges."

She scoffs. "Don't, Bear."

I know her stance on it already — that she feels like it doesn't matter what she says or does, he'll get away with it. She was drunk, they'll say she was "asking for it." And even if they did give him jail time or anything else, it wouldn't make her feel better, and then she'd just be the poor girl who was raped. These are all things she's told me multiple times since that night, but I hate hearing them, hate that she believes them… hate that in many ways, she's right. Our justice system doesn't seek much justice for rape victims, not the way it should.

Erin laughs a little. "And then, to add insult to injury, I was walking by the Student Union earlier and this perky little sophomore on the Orientation Team stops me, telling me that they're fighting back against sexual assault on campus. And she hands me this," she says, opening her hand and holding up a small, teal and orange whistle — PSU's school colors. "'It's a *rape whistle,'* she said." Erin laughs again. "Like this will save anyone. Like this will make it stop."

Suddenly, Erin pops the whistle in her mouth and starts blowing it, loud shrieks piercing the otherwise quiet night around us. She blows it over and over again, her eyes welling with tears, face red when I finally take her in my arms and hold her tight to my chest.

She keeps blowing it, and to drive her point home further, no one inside the ballroom even looks our way. She might as well be whispering.

Finally, the whistle falls from her mouth and she catches it in her hands, choking on a sob as she leans into my chest.

"It's okay," I whisper, running my hand over her hair as I hold her tighter. "I'm so sorry, Erin."

She lets me hold her for a short minute before she's shoving me off, wiping at her face like she's stupid for crying. "Whatever. I was just making a point. Even if I would have had this," she spits, holding up the whistle again. "This stupid *thing*, I would have maybe been able to blow it twice before it would have been ripped from my mouth. And that's *if* I could even manage to get it out of my clutch. And, even if I did, no one would have heard me."

"I was too late," I say, fists clenching at my side again. "I should have known something was off. I should have found you earlier."

"How would you have known?" she challenges, looking at me again. "The door was shut. The music in the ballroom was loud. There's nothing you could have done." She hiccups, wiping at her face again. "There's nothing anyone could have done, other than Landon and his friends." Her face twists. "I don't even know their names."

I reach for her again but she pulls away, standing.

"You need to talk to someone, Erin."

"I'm fine."

"Clearly," I deadpan. "You're going to break if you don't get this off your chest and start working through it."

She laughs, eyes brimming over again. "I'm already fucking broken."

"You're not broken, but you are losing yourself."

"Yeah?" she asks, patronizing me. "Well, maybe I'll like the new girl I find. Maybe she'll be stronger and not take any shit."

"Or maybe she'll be a cold shell of the amazing girl I used to know. And dead inside," I counter.

Erin's eyes catch mine then, her face as smooth as stone. "Better to be dead inside than live with this pain anymore."

My heart is too broken to say another word before she turns, tucking the whistle into her clutch and walking back inside the ballroom.

# Cassie

MY STRAPLESS DRESS is a giant pain in my ass.

I tug it up by the sides again, for what feels like the fiftieth time, as I wait for Ashlei to finish touching up her lipstick. It's a beautiful dress — navy blue with gold sequins and studs swirled in a floral design over the sweetheart neckline down to my waist, where the navy tulle flares off and ends right above my knees. But I purchased it before Thanksgiving, and I've lost too much weight since then for it to fit properly.

Not that I'm *trying* to lose weight, but apparently it's a side effect of losing someone you care about.

Ever since Thanksgiving, everything has felt off. Grayson and I *seem* fine by all accounts — we're having great sex, spending more time together, making plans for the future — but it's like I'm only living with half of myself turned on, like the other half is stuck in a dark coma. I can't study to save my life, which is not conducive to the final exams I have coming up. I can't eat, I can barely sleep. Because the truth of the matter is I made a choice that day, on Thanksgiving — one that I didn't want to make. And now I'm facing the cold, hard truth of it all.

I don't want to live without Adam in my life.

But I have to in order to keep Grayson.

Adam hasn't spoken to me since that day — hasn't even tried to. He understood, he knew I didn't want to do it but that I had to. Still, everything has been so empty without him. Even tonight, not seeing him staring holes into the back of my head from across the dance floor bothers me. Is that selfish? Probably, but I want him here.

I'm not allowed to want that, but I do.

"Is it just me, or does Semi kind of suck this year?" Ashlei asks on a sigh, popping her violet lips together before dropping her lipstick back in her clutch.

"It's not just you."

She turns to me, head tilted to the side. "Well, I'm stag, so I know a little of the reason why it sucks for me. Why does it suck for you?"

*Where to begin?*

I smile, waving her off. "We've just had better venues, that's all. And I'm so tired from all the studying I've been doing lately."

"Ugh," Ashlei agrees, linking her arm through mine to head back out to the ballroom. "You really have been hitting the books. Remind me again why you chose biology for a major?"

"Damn aspirations to be a doctor."

"Oh, yeah." She giggles. "That."

We make it back out to the dance floor just in time to hear the music shift to a slower rhythm, once again causing a mass exodus from the dance floor. Clinton ends up keeping Skyler out there this time, and everyone is laughing at the two of them doing some sort of fake waltz to a slow Usher song.

I search for Grayson, wanting nothing more than to just be held by him as we sway back and forth on the dance floor. I feel so weird lately, and being close to him is one of the only things that helps. It reminds me why I made the choice I did, why I sacrificed someone who means something to me. Grayson is the first boy I've ever truly loved, and who loves me, too. It's powerful and addictive, like the best kind of drug, and all I want tonight is to drown in him.

"Hey, have you seen Grayson?" I ask Jess and her date, Greg. It's still a little weird seeing her with someone other than Jarrett, but she's smiling and seems happy, so I'm thankful he's here.

"Oh! Him and his friend — Malik? — went outside to the garden to sneak a few drinks from their flasks, I think," Jess answers, letting Greg pull her up from her seat at the table and onto the dance floor.

"Thanks!"

I walk as fast as I can in my high heels toward the entrance to the garden at the back of the ballroom, pushing through the double doors to find an empty bench. I frown, letting the doors close behind me as I look for Grayson. The garden is small, but the winding path leads back a ways, so I follow it, guessing he and Malik are probably hiding out somewhere.

When the stiff stench of marijuana hits my nose, I know I've found *someone*, but I'm a little surprised when I spot Grayson through the tall bushes near the back corner taking a joint from Malik's hand and holding it to his lips.

The sight of it stops me still in my tracks, my heart thundering in my ears. It's not that I necessarily have anything against smoking, but I never knew Grayson was into it. He never told me. And in this moment, it feels a lot like something he should have told me.

It feels a lot like something he's hiding.

My feet are still glued to the garden path when Grayson passes the joint back to Malik, his voice strange as he tries to hold in the smoke and talk at the same time. "I mean, don't get me wrong. It's not like I see her being a forever sort of thing." He blows out a cloud of smoke, checking over his shoulder at the opening in the path. "She's just college, and I get that. But at least now he's out of my way."

"I'm surprised you were cool about it for as long as you were," Malik says. "That kid has it bad for her. She's lying if she says she doesn't see it."

Grayson shakes his head, dipping into his jacket for his flask. "I don't know. Cassie is just kind of naïve like that. I'm not sure she really sees it, but I do. Which is why I put my foot down and put an end to it."

My throat closes at the mention of my name, heart still racing. I shouldn't be eavesdropping, but now I can't stop.

"Atta boy," Malik says, handing the joint back to Grayson as a puff of smoke leaves his lips. "Speaking of complications, is that groupie finally leaving you alone?"

"Ugh, I wish. That girl cannot take a hint. If only she was as bright as that neon pink hair of hers."

Malik chuckles. "Hey, at least she gives good head. You going to miss that?"

My stomach lurches as Grayson grins, taking a hit from the joint and passing it back. "Nah. Surprisingly, Cassie is pretty hot in bed."

"Now that she's actually fucking you, that is. Think she'll ever find out about the groupie?"

"No way. She knows I love her. Alexis was just a stress relief until Cassie was ready. Had to get it from somewhere, you know?" he jokes, and Malik grins with approval. "Once Cassie let me hit, I stopped texting Alexis altogether."

"Wow, what a great boyfriend," I spit, rounding the bushes until Malik can see me. His eyes widen and Grayson turns, all the color draining from his face when he sees me, too. "To give up your hook ups with a groupie once you got in my pants. So charming."

My voice is just as shaky as my hands and I hate it, rolling them into fists as I try to stand tall, trying to control the racing of my heart long enough to put Grayson in his place. I ran from the last guy who fucked me over, letting him make a fool of me.

Not this time.

"Cassie, I don't know what you heard but—"

"Don't touch me," I seethe, cutting Grayson off mid-sentence as his hands reach out for me. "You'll never touch me again. I hope she was worth it."

"Come on—"

"No!" I shake my head, eyes bouncing between Grayson's like I've never seen him before in my life, like he's a stranger who somehow has the power to break my heart. "No, I'm not listening to another word. And you asked me to give up my friendship with Adam because — what — *your* conscience wouldn't let you sleep at night?"

Grayson swallows, joint still burning in his hand as he pleads with his eyes for me to see him, to want him, to listen to him — but I do none of the above.

"Is she why you were late to the Alpha Sigma concert?" I shake my head, the need to cry burning at the back of my throat and eyes but I refuse to give in. "Is she why you cancelled our date that night?"

He swallows, lips in a flat line and face ashen, which is all the answer I need.

I choke, almost breaking down before shaking it off. "I knew you were a performer," I say, holding my chin up. "But had I known you were playing me like your fucking guitar, I would have stopped buying tickets to the shows a long time ago."

"Cassie, just please—"

"Go fuck yourself, Grayson."

I turn without another look in his direction, not stopping when he calls my name or sprints after me. I snatch my clutch off the table, fighting back tears as Ashlei and Jess swarm me, asking what's wrong. Skyler is there next, pushing Grayson away as he tries to break through the crowd to get to me.

"I just want to leave," I choke out, trying so hard not to cry I can't breathe from holding the tears in.

"Let's go." Skyler grabs my hand, telling Clinton to call us a cab and meet on the curb outside. She holds me in her arms as we walk, not asking any questions, knowing I can't talk in that moment.

It's not when we make it outside that I let myself cry. It's not in the cab ride home, or in Skyler's arms as she hugs me tight at the house. No, it's not until well after midnight, when I've finished telling her what happened and walked numbly up to my room, stripping out of my dress and removing my makeup before slipping into my sheets that I finally break down.

Because my sheets smell like him.

It's like those sheets are covered in betrayal and lies and every breath is me suffocating in them, fighting for oxygen that doesn't exist. I let the tears fall, choking on the toxic air and hugging my arms tight around my middle, as if they can somehow squeeze out the pain racking through me.

I loved him.

No, that's a lie, because it implies past tense. I *love* him — here and now, writhing in sheets that smell like him and replaying the words he said that broke my heart — I still love him. It's the worst feeling, to love someone who has hurt you. But love isn't a pencil mark. It can't be erased so easily.

I wonder if I'll ever be able to erase it at all.

It's with that aching thought that I cry myself into the worst sleep of my life.

# Ashlei

AFTER CASSIE, SKYLER, and Clinton leave, I'm basically alone with Jess and her date.

Erin is here, too, but she's pre-occupied, running around taking care of girls who are too drunk and getting in those last few good impressions before we vote for president. I know she's going to get it — hell, we all do — but it doesn't stop her from taking on the role of KKB Mom tonight.

And then there's me.

Feeling amazing in a beige fit and flare dress that hugs my neck and dips down low in the back, with just a few strings tying it together, and rolling completely stag.

It wouldn't be so bad if my mind wasn't focused on the absolute last person it should be — the one person I can't have. I survived my internship, I only have two finals left and both of them should be easy as pie, I'm healthy and happier than I've been in a long time. By all accounts, I should be ecstatic tonight, but I can't stop thinking about Brandon.

"I think we're going to head out," Jess says, her hand around Greg's as they come back to the table from where they'd been dancing.

I frown, searching Jess' eyes for a sign of the breakdown I know is coming. She loved Jarrett, and she may be trying to put on the tough bitch act, but I see right through it. "Okay. Are you guys going to be alright?"

Jess smiles, but it's weak. "Yeah, we'll be fine. See you later at the house?"

I nod, eyes softening. Jess just shrugs when Greg turns, heading toward where the first bus is loading up to leave.

*I love you*, I mouth to her, and she smiles, offering a half-wave before following Greg.

For a moment I just sit at the table by myself, sipping on my fruity cocktail and watching everyone on the dance floor. I could leave on the first bus, too, I suppose, but what would I be leaving for? Erin is still here, which means I'd be going home from my Semi-formal *early* just to sit alone in my room.

And then it hits me.

"Why can't I be with him?"

I actually say the words out loud before I clamp my hand over my mouth, smiling under it at my ridiculousness, but my mind keeps rolling the thought over and over. My internship is over, he's not my boss anymore. Why *couldn't* we have a thing, even if just a casual hookup thing, now that I'm no longer his employee?

Checking the time on my phone, I jump up, motioning to Erin that I'm heading out before bolting for the doors. I bypass the bus and jump into the first taxi cab waiting, giving the address of the office to the driver as I adjust my makeup in my small compact mirror.

Mykayla said he's working late all weekend long, so I take the chance, saying a silent prayer that he's still there while my stomach somersaults with every passing mile.

I don't have keys to let me into the building anymore, but luckily the night guard recognizes me and lets me in, walking me to the elevator in casual conversation. When the doors finally shut and I'm on my way up to the thirty-second floor, I feel so nauseous I actually press a hand to my stomach, trying to soothe it along with my nerves.

*Please, be here. Please, be here.*

When the elevator dings and the doors open, I shoot out of them, turning right immediately and jetting down the hall toward his office. His light is the only one on, and when I drop my clutch on a desk as I pass, he leans back in his chair, peering down the hallway with knitted eyebrows.

Then his eyes go wide.

It's like the hallway is my runway, my heels carrying me down it like a force of nature — a hurricane heading straight for him. And just as fast as the surprise flits across his face, it's gone again, and he's standing, rounding his desk to meet me at the door with a hunger in his eyes so dark I shiver. He's in the doorway just a split second before I am and then I'm in his arms, mine wrapped around his neck, our mouths crashing together like the first bolt of lightning.

It's like the universe around us bubbles out before zapping back into focus, pulling both of us into its gravity with a sizzling snap of energy. I can't calm my breaths, panting louder and louder as Brandon's lips move from mine down my neck, over my exposed shoulder, his hands frantic as he tries to untie my dress in the back.

"I can't figure this thing out," he pants, kissing me again.

"Leave it on."

Dropping to my knees, I rip at his belt and the buttons on his slacks until they're loose, pulling his pants and boxer briefs down his legs in one swift motion. He doesn't even have time to kick out of them before my hands are wrapped around his hard length, pulling him to my lips.

Brandon groans as I swirl my tongue over his crown, flicking at the sensitive skin under it before dragging my tongue all the way down to his base with my eyes locked on his. He drops his head back with another moan, hips flexing into my hands. I'm high off the power he gives me, the power to make him lose control, the power to bring him to ecstasy with just my hands, my mouth, my body. It's addicting, and I don't want to let it go.

Moving my hands from his shaft to his ass, I pull him in deep, guiding his hands into my hair to take control. He's careful not to hurt me, working his hips slowly and pulling at my hair as I open my throat for him. When he hits the back and I gag, he curses, ripping me up from the floor and spinning me around until my palms are flat on his desk.

Chills race up my thighs as I wait, lips already swollen and heart galloping full speed. Just being in his proximity lights my skin on fire, the anticipation of him touching me almost as pleasurable as the actual act of it.

There's a faint rip of a condom wrapper behind me and then his feet hit the inside of my ankles, making me spread my legs wider. One hand comes down on my back, pushing me flat to the desk, and then that same hand drags slowly down my back to the skirt of my dress, flipping it up and over.

Brandon groans with appreciation, running his palm over the apple of my ass before smacking it with a force that has me biting my lip and stifling my own moan. He smacks it again and I gasp, arching off the desk until my back is pressed against his chest. With his lips tracing my neck, he slides one hand under my skirt, moving my lacy thong to the side enough to run a single finger along my wet slit.

"Goddamn, you're ready," he breathes.

"I've been thinking about you all night."

He grins against the skin at my neck, biting it with a growl. "Yeah? What have you been thinking about?"

I blindly reach behind me, feeling along his thigh until I hold his hard cock in my hand again. "This," I pant, stroking him against my ass. "And this," I add, arching back until just the tip of him grazes my entrance.

Brandon yanks back, dropping to his knees long enough to pull my thong to the floor before standing again, rolling the condom over himself. He takes one of my thighs in his hand, propping it up on the desk and pushing me forward until my chest is on the cool metal again. With one heel still planted on the ground and the other spread wide over the desk, he flips my skirt up, and then with one powerful thrust, he's all the way inside me.

I cry out as my hips hit the desk with the force, the sensation of being full combined with being in an open office overwhelming me. I suddenly realize anyone could walk in on us at any minute, but I don't give a single flying fuck. Let the whole world watch, for all I care. All I know in this moment is I want Brandon Church, and right now at least, he's mine.

Brandon smacks my ass before sliding inside again, his hands moving to the bend of my hips, holding on with a tight grip as he pounds me into the desk over and over again. My hands writhe on the edges of the desk, desperate for something to ground me as he lifts me higher and higher. I'm so worked up from not having him that I'm already close to coming, and he must sense it, because he pulls out long enough to flip me over, hiking my thighs up onto his forearms with my back on the desk before slamming into me again.

It feels so dirty and forbidden — him still in his dress shirt and me in my dress, the bottom of it hiked up enough to allow him access to my pussy and nothing more.

"This wasn't supposed to happen again," Brandon says, his voice a deep growl as he leans down over the desk. He captures my mouth with his, hips still rocking inside me, hitting me at a new depth with my hips angled up toward his like this.

I whimper, so overwhelmed by the feel of him that I don't have words. "Neither one of us are the type to follow rules."

He grins, kissing me again before lifting himself to standing again, still hitting me at the point of pressure I need the most. When I close my eyes, my climax just within reach, he runs his hand down over my breasts, my ribs, sliding it under my skirt to press his thumb to my clit.

I gasp at the added pressure, and when he starts circling it faster and faster, still pushing into me, it's the perfect combination to send me flying into the most powerful orgasm of my life.

Arching up off the desk, I reach for his neck, pulling his mouth to mine and panting into his kiss as I ride out my orgasm. Every nerve is on fire, my legs trembling where they're wrapped around him, and his hands fist in my hair as I finish. It's the sweetest release, the one only he can give me, and I savor it every inch of the float down.

"On your knees," he says when my breathing evens out, lifting me from the desk to stand. I do as he demands, dropping to my knees with my eyes locked on his as I take him in my mouth again. My pussy is still throbbing between my thighs and I clench them tight, already ready for another round.

His eyes close, head falling back as he guides my mouth over him. I work my hands in rhythm with my mouth, sucking and licking him closer and closer to climax. When his hips start moving slower, his hands fisted hard in my hair, I reach down and cup his balls, rolling them gently, and he lets out a guttural groan as he comes in my mouth.

"Jesus Christ," he moans, hands still in my hair as I swallow his release. When he's finished, I sit back on my heels, looking up at him and licking my lips clean.

He collapses on the floor next to me, leaning his back against the desk with a heaving chest. For a moment he just focuses on his breathing, his elbows resting on his knees, and I move to sit next to him. He pulls me under one arm, both of us silent for a while, but then he looks down at me, eyes dark and wild.

"Why did you come here?"

I wipe at the corner of his mouth where my lipstick stained it, erasing the violet smear with my thumb. "Because I wanted you. I wanted you so bad I couldn't stand it, and then I realized I'm not your intern anymore." I shrug. "I was in a cab before I could think any further than that."

The left corner of his mouth quirks up in a grin, his eyes roaming over me with appreciation. "You look thoroughly fucked."

I laugh, leaning up to kiss him. "That's because I am."

He keeps his mouth on mine, hand framing my face as he kisses me slowly, his tongue rolling over mine in a soft rhythm. When he pulls back, his brows are bent again, eyes searching mine. "I have to tell you something."

"Uh-oh."

He pulls me into his lap until I'm straddling him, brushing my nest of hair out of my face. "Your manager came to me this past week, before you left, saying she wants to extend your internship another semester."

I blink, a mixture of emotions kicking in. On the one hand, that's amazing — Mykayla said they've never invited an intern back for a second semester. But on the other hand, what does it mean that she suggested it, but I never heard of it until now?

"I told her I would think about it," he says. "And honestly, up until the very moment you walked out, I wasn't sure I could do it. I wasn't sure I could get a single ounce of work done if I had you around here for another five months."

My eyes drop to his chest. "I understand that."

"But you deserve to be here, Ashlei," he continues, knuckles lifting my chin until my eyes are on his again. "So, I'm going to offer you the internship. I don't want to let this... this lust between us get in the way of your career and your dreams."

"We can still be together," I try, but he's already shaking his head. "No one has to know. We can keep it a secret."

"And risk ruining the empire I've built and even more importantly, your reputation as a professional?" He runs his thumb along the edge of my jaw. "Ashlei, if someone found out about us, I would be judged, yes. People would probably call me a whole host of names, but at the end of the day, I would still be their boss, and they'd still respect me. But you?" His eyes soften. "Every opportunity you've had while you've been here, you've earned. But if anyone found out about us, it wouldn't matter how amazing you are at your job. All of that would be erased in everyone's mind and all they would see when they look at you is a girl who slept her way through her career. They would call you a slut and a whore and worse. And there would be nothing I could say or do to change their view of you."

"I don't care what people call me."

"But you do care if people respect you," he counters, and my chest deflates at the truth of it. "You're a hard worker, one of the most impressive interns we've ever had. Don't throw that away."

My eyes trace the stitching on his dress shirt again, fingers playing at the holes between the buttons. "So, what does this mean?"

He sighs, pulling me into him and pressing his lips against mine. "It means I'm going to call you on Monday and offer to extend your internship. And if you take it, then this... *we* can't happen again."

"What do you want me to say when you call?"

He thumbs my cheek, a soft smile on his lips. "I want you to do what you would if I was just the CEO at a company you interned at for a semester, calling to offer you an opportunity not handed out lightly. And nothing more." He motions between us. "This isn't a factor to consider, Ashlei. You can't let it be."

My heart breaks at his words, for selfish reasons I'm not even ashamed to admit. I want the internship, I want to keep moving forward in my career, but I want him, too.

And I hate that I can't have both.

"Now, come here," he whispers, pulling my lips to his again. With a gentle rock of his hips, I feel him harden between my legs. "If this is the last time I get to touch you, I'm far from finished."

# Erin

"TO OUR BRAND NEW cap-ee-tan and fearless leader, Erin 'Ex' Xanders," Jess says, lifting her margarita high in the air. "May you still remember how to party even in your role of responsibility."

"Here, here!" Skyler cheers, and the rest of the girls lift their glasses with a laugh as I do the same.

"Seriously, congratulations, Grand Big. I'm so proud of you." Cassie smiles, taking a sip of her drink before reaching for a chip.

"Thank you, guys. I couldn't have done this without you."

With elections and finals being over, it only made sense for all of us to get together one last time for margaritas and queso before going our separate ways for winter break. It's tradition, spending the last hours of each semester together, and just like every other time, we're all leaving PSU with a little more growth under our belts.

After having my complete meltdown with Clinton at Semi-formal, I finally feel like I've completely shut down, like I've blocked out that part of my life and looked into the future. Getting revenge didn't help me feel better, but I'm convinced that letting it all go and leaving it behind will. So, now that I'm president, I know I'll have plenty of other things to focus on.

Unlocking my phone as Skyler tells the girls about her poker tournament schedule for the break, I read over the unsent text I typed out to Clinton last night.

**- I'm sorry for how I acted, I know you're just trying to help. Please... let me handle this the way I need to. It's not your mess to clean up. -**

My thumb hovers over the send button and I finally push it, locking my phone as soon as the text is sent.

"How are you holding up, Jess?" Skyler asks, switching the focus of conversation off of her. "It looked like you had fun with Greg at the dance."

"I did," Jess answers quickly, stirring the ice in her nearly empty glass. "He's really nice. I'll be fine, it's not like I expected me and Jarrett to last forever."

We all exchange glances, landing back on Jess with a deadpan expression.

"What?!" She huffs. "I'm serious. It's fine, guys. Cassie has more of a right to be upset than me right now."

It's a shady attempt to change the subject again but it works, Skyler rubbing Cassie's back. "She's going to stay with me for a few days before heading home for break."

"You guys going up to your parents' place?" I ask Skyler.

She nods. "Yeah, we're leaving tomorrow afternoon."

Cassie looks like absolute hell, like she hasn't slept or eaten in weeks. Her face is pale, dark circles dulling her usually bright green eyes. "It just makes me sick to think about, you know?" she says softly. "He would be with her, touching her, and then lie in bed with me. It just feels so personal…"

All of us wince at her confession, reaching out to squeeze her arm or rub her back.

"He's an asshole, and he doesn't deserve you," Ashlei says. "He's just proof that some guys never stop playing games."

Cassie swallows. "It was never a game to me. I feel so stupid."

"Don't," I chime in. "Don't let a boy make you feel stupid. Ever."

Cassie nods, the table silent now. We take turns sipping from our glasses or eating chips, all of us thinking about our own games we've played over the years, and the battle wounds they've left behind.

A text from Clinton pings on my phone and I glance down, relieved that he responded.

**- Okay, Ex. Have a good winter break. Call me anytime. -**

**- I will, and you, too, Bear. XO. -**

"In other news," Ashlei says as I tuck my phone back in my purse. "*Okay, Cool* offered me an extension on my internship. I'll be going back again next semester!"

"What?!" Jess and I say in unison. "That's amazing!"

"Congrats, Lei. That's a big deal," Skyler chimes in.

"Thank you. I'm really excited," she says, tucking her hair behind her ear with a blush. "It's going to be hard, balancing everything again, but I think I can do it."

"I know you can," Jess says, hoisting up her glass again. "Looks like we need another toast!"

We all lift our glasses with a laugh, and Jess clears her throat.

"To this amazing group of bad-ass lady bosses conquering the world and taking absolute zero shit," she says, looking all of us in the eyes. "You bitches inspire me, and I love every single one of you."

"Cheers!"

As I clink my glass with theirs, I feel myself shedding the final layers of my old self, settling into the new Erin Xanders. And maybe that's what that scarred skin was — it was old skin, skin that needed to be shed to find my true self. I'm not scared anymore, and I'm not giving up on me, either. Maybe I just need to toughen up, to stop putting everyone else before me and start focusing on number one.

I will not be defined by what has happened to me, only by what I do to overcome it.

This is it — this is what I've been working for my entire college career. I'm going to be president of Kappa Kappa Beta, and as far as I'm concerned, my new story begins right now.

# Adam

I KNEW SHE WAS here before I even heard the knock.

It was a gentle rap of the knuckles on my window, nothing more, no demand or urgency in the sound. It was a soft, regretful notion, an apology, a plead for forgiveness. It struck me to the bone when I heard it, so much so that I'm still lying here in my bed, eyes on the ceiling, heart pounding hard in my chest as I work up the courage to go to my window.

I heard about what happened between her and Grayson the day after Semi-formal, and two things struck me at the same time — one, the need to run to her, to hold her, to make her okay again — and two, the outrageous and uncontrollable urge to break Grayson's jaw.

I'd wanted to give into both, but I'd stayed strong, doing neither. I knew Cassie well enough to know she wouldn't want me to run to her before she was ready to see me, and a small part of me wondered if she ever would again. She'd chosen Grayson over me, and although I wanted to believe she didn't have a choice, that she didn't want to, it still hurt. It still felt permanent.

And as much as I would have loved crushing my fist into Grayson's face, I knew that wouldn't have made Cassie happy, either. It would have only made things worse for her.

So, I've waited, my hope fading like a dying glow stick of light with each passing day. I leave to spend winter break at my aunt's house tomorrow, and I'd almost given up on Cassie.

But here she is.

Kicking my sheets off, I pad over to the window in just my boxer briefs, pulling the string on the blinds until I'm standing face to face with the only girl I've ever loved and hated simultaneously. I love everything about her, but hate the power she holds over me. The sweetest contradiction.

She's standing in a simple, white tank top and plaid sleep shorts, her hair tied up in a mess of curls on top of her head as her swollen eyes take me in. I reach down, heaving the window open, the light breeze of the night sweeping into my room as I stare at Cassie. She watches me, too, lip quivering as she shrugs and lets out a long sigh of a breath.

I just reach out with both hands, helping her climb inside just like I did almost exactly a year ago to the day.

And just like last time, she kicks off her Keds by the foot of my bed, climbing into it first and pulling the sheets up to her shoulders. I slide in behind her, hesitant at first until she reaches back for my arm, pulling it around her middle. With a relieved sigh, I pull her closer, fitting my body to hers and holding her tight.

"You were right."

The same three words she said to me last year, and they hurt just as bad this time around.

"I wish I wasn't."

I squeeze her a little tighter, fitting us a little more together, hoping she feels some sort of comfort from the fact that I'm here.

"I'm so sorry, Adam," she whispers, her voice breaking on my name.

Only the moon lights up my room, but it's enough for me to see the first tear slide down her cheek. I catch it with my thumb, wiping it away before pulling her even closer. "It's okay. I'm here."

"You always are." She squeezes her eyes closed. "I don't deserve it."

"You're always here for me, too," I remind her. "Even when I'm an asshole."

She twists in the sheets to face me, one hand pressed into my chest as she looks up at me. "I just left you there. I let him make me choose. I gave you up, and for what? To keep a relationship with a guy who was cheating on me for months." Two tears escape one right after the other, chasing each other down until they drop to my pillow. "I was miserable without you, Adam."

I swallow, my chest aching as my hand finds her hip, resting there. "I was, too."

"I'm not crying because of him," she says, waiting until my eyes are locked on hers again before continuing. "He hurt me, yes. But not as bad as I hurt myself by making a decision I didn't want to make, one that I didn't believe in. I'm just so sorry. Please, please forgive me, Adam."

"Shh," I whisper, pulling her into me and pressing a kiss into her hair. "It's over, we're okay. I'm here."

Cassie fists her hands in the sheets wrapped around us, digging her head into my chest. For a while I just hold her there, one hand pulling strands of hair from her hair tie as I run my fingers through it, the other rubbing soft, slow circles on her lower back.

"What now?" Cassie whispers into the darkness, her breath on the skin of my chest.

"We don't have to figure that out tonight."

She stiffens in my arms, her breathing nearly stopping altogether as she pushes away from me just enough to lift her head. I look down at her, too — our lips just centimeters apart as she searches my eyes with her own. I swallow, gripping her waist with one hand just as she closes the space between us, her lips finding mine on a sigh.

If time was a train, this is what it would feel like for it to slam on its brakes.

I've waited so long to touch her again, to hold her, to kiss her that it almost feels like a dream. It's as if my body isn't my body, my hands aren't my hands, my lips aren't my lips — like I'm watching it all from above. I wince as her mouth opens for me, my tongue sliding in to meet hers, and that's when the reality hits me.

She's here, she's in my bed — in my arms.

It's almost too much, too much history and pain and unexplainable pleasure rolled into one single moment. She melts in my arms as I deepen the kiss, one hand running the length of my abdomen before tucking into the band of my briefs.

I inhale a breath and hold it there, tongue still working hers as I flip us, sliding up between her thighs, her red hair spilling out of her hair tie and over my pillow. She moans when I kiss down her neck, sucking the skin just behind her ear as her nails dig into my back. Our breaths are so loud and heated, years of wanting pouring out without a filter now, my sheets the stage for the show long overdue. Cassie flexes her hips against me, the hot center of her meeting the bulge in my briefs, and I groan, pulling back.

Her eyes widen as I take a pause, squeezing my eyes shut, trying to think clearly.

"You don't… you don't want to…"

"Oh, I want to," I clarify quickly, cock aching at the thought of being inside her. But I lift my eyes to hers, running my thumb over her swollen bottom lip. "Trust me, I want to. But the first time I take you, I want it to be us — just us. No exes, no drama, no pain. I just… I know I'll never forget our first time, and I want to make it worth remembering."

Cassie swallows, nodding with tears misting her eyes as she pulls me down to kiss her again. She kisses me with all the unanswered questions we've shared, with all the *what ifs* and *what nows*.

"Don't let go tonight, okay?"

"I'm never letting go again," I answer, resting between her thighs again as I kiss her lips like I've never tasted them before, like tonight is all I have.

I slide one hand under the cotton of her tank top, groaning with appreciation when I feel she's not wearing a bra. My hands roam over every inch of her, palming her breasts before moving down to grip her waist again. Cassie arches off the bed, offering her neck to my mouth, nails digging into the flesh of my shoulders like she's holding on for dear life.

And for the rest of the night, we explore each other, kissing and touching with our clothes staying completely intact, even when it's nearly impossible to do. I take my time with her, showing her I'm in no rush, that I'm not going anywhere — and I hope she can say the same.

For the last year and a half, we've danced around each other, never fully giving in, always something or some*one* in the way. But now that I have her, now that there's nothing but scraps of cloth between us, I know there's no way I can ever let her go. I meant what I said about not figuring anything out tonight, but in my heart, I know as well as she does that this is it — this is our time.

Cassie McBee is finally mine, and I have always been hers.

With my heart in her hands, Cassie pulls me closer as the sun rises through my window, sealing that thought with the sweetest, most perfect kiss.

# Acknowledgements

I'm going to try to keep the acknowledgements for this season just like the episodes — short, sweet, and full of heart.

Before I jump into the peeps behind the book, I want to talk directly to you — the reader. *Palm South University* is my passion project, and if you're reading these acknowledgements, it means you've been with me through three whole seasons of it. I know the dedication and love that takes. You have waited between episodes, between seasons, falling in love with these characters right along with me and trusting me when I tell you I have more to tell. You've thrown these books at your friends, shared the sales and free promos, and without you, I couldn't write one of my favorite things to write. Thank you for taking a chance on PSU, and even more so, for staying along for the ride. I love you.

Now, for the ones who helped breathe PSU to life.

First and foremost, I have to give a huge shout out to my beta readers on this season. PSU is its own little beast, and without beta readers who know and love these characters as much as I do, it wouldn't be possible to keep the serial alive. So, thank you Kellee Fabre, Patricia Leibowitz (Trish Mintness), Ashlei Davison, Danielle Lagasse, Jess Vogel, Becca Mysoor, Katrina Tinnon, Natalie Williams, Mykayla Wilson, Haley Sue Brewer, and Sarah Green. You girls are absolutely incredible and your notes helped shape this season.

I also want to send some love to the girls who the KKB ladies are named after — Ashlei Davison, Erin Spencer, Cassie Graham, and Jess Vogel. Circle of Trust forever, babes. I love you.

To my tribe – Staci Hart and Brittainy C. Cherry — thank you for always pushing me to be the best that I can when it comes to my writing. I work on the hard days because of the inspiration the two of you constantly provide, and I'm so thankful to have you both to celebrate the small wins — like writing "the end."

I always have to thank my Momma and my best friend, Sasha, for being there between all the craziness of writing. Thank you both for grounding me and helping me work through my crazy emotions, whether tied to writing or not. I couldn't do this thing called life without you.

Kathryn Andrews — thank you for binge reading PSU in time to give me eyes on Season 3. I love your passion for my work almost as much as your passion for our friendship, and I am so lucky to have you in my corner.

Thank you to my editor and formatter, Elaine York, for putting that last shiny wax on this season and making it gorgeous, as always. You are amazing at working with me and my ridiculous timelines, and because of how quickly YOU work, I can be the spazz that I am and miss my own deadlines. That's more valuable than you know.

To Erin Spencer and Nina Ginstead, thank you for helping me spread the word about PSU and being the best promo peeps ever. I adore both of you more than I can say.

And lastly, thank you to my amazing readers in Kandiland (http://www.facebook.com/groups/kandischasers) and the Palm South University Discussion Group (https://www.facebook.com/groups/712042985606913/). You guys keep me going when I feel like I can't, and it's because of you that I get to do what I love for a living and live a dream I've dreamed for so long. I love you.

# More from Kandi Steiner

**The What He Doesn't Know Duet**
What He Doesn't Know
What He Always Knew

On the Way to You

A Love Letter to Whiskey

Weightless

Revelry

Black Number Four

**The Palm South University Series**
Rush (Palm South University 1)
Anchor (Palm South University 2)
Pledge (Palm South University 3)
Legacy (Palm South University 4)

**The Chaser Series**
Tag Chaser
Song Chaser
Straight, No Chaser
Tag Catcher

# About the Author

Kandi Steiner is a bestselling author and whiskey connoisseur living in Tampa, FL. Best known for writing "emotional rollercoaster" stories, she loves bringing flawed characters to life and writing about real, raw romance — in all its forms. No two Kandi Steiner books are the same, and if you're a lover of angsty, emotional, and inspirational reads, she's your gal.

An alumna of the University of Central Florida, Kandi graduated with a double major in Creative Writing and Advertising/PR with a minor in Women's Studies. She started writing back in the 4th grade after reading the first Harry Potter installment. In 6th grade, she wrote and edited her own newspaper and distributed to her classmates. Eventually, the principal caught on and the newspaper was quickly halted, though Kandi tried fighting for her "freedom of press." She took particular interest in writing romance after college, as she has always been a die hard hopeless romantic, and likes to highlight all the challenges of love as well as the triumphs.

When Kandi isn't writing, you can find her reading books of all kinds, talking with her extremely vocal cat, and spending time with her friends and family. She enjoys live music, traveling, anything heavy in carbs, beach days, movie marathons, craft beer and sweet wine — not necessarily in that order.

CONNECT WITH KANDI:
NEWSLETTER: bit.ly/NewsletterKS
FACEBOOK: facebook.com/kandisteiner
FACEBOOK READER GROUP (Kandiland): facebook.com/groups/
kandischasers
INSTAGRAM: Instagram.com/kandisteiner
TWITTER: twitter.com/kandisteiner
PINTEREST: pinterest.com/kandicoffman
WEBSITE: www.kandisteiner.com

Kandi Steiner may be coming to a city near you! Check out her "events" tab to see all the signings she's attending in the near future www.kandisteiner.com/events

Made in United States
Troutdale, OR
09/09/2023

12778723R00226